THE RETURN
TO ENGSTROM
HOUSE

Nasser Rabadi

Paperback ISBN: 978-1-954931-02-2

Hardcover ISBN: 978-1-954931-03-9

Also by Nasser Rabadi

THE RAVEN HILL BUTCHER slasher novel series

Book one: The Christmas Morning Massacre

Book two: Return to Camp Solgohachia

Book three: Noel Hell

Book four: The Curse of Raven Hill

Book five: The Final Chapter

Book six (reboot of Return to Camp Solgohachia): A New Beginning

Book seven (reboot of The Christmas Morning Massacre and Noel Hell): Winter Graves

Book eight: Santa's Space Station of Slaughter

Book nine: Santa Goes to Hell

Book ten: Into the Santa-Verse

The ENGSTROM HOUSE series

Book one: The Haunting of Engstrom House

Book two: Return to Engstrom House

Book three: The Curse of Engstrom House

NASSER RABADI

The LOVE KILLS series of dark romance thrillers
Book one: Scarlet
Book two: Lust
Book three: Desire

Contents

1

As RAIN SPILLED ACROSS Ashfall from a raven-black sky, the brooding house on the hill looked especially hideous, but it was good enough for two people with no other place to go. Their car was ruined from its collision with the tree.

Colleen couldn't breathe. Ambrose's hands grabbed hers and studied her. "Are you hurt?"

The words wouldn't form on her lips. She could only nod.

Ambrose came around to the other side of the car, forgetting his jacket that was in the back seat with their luggage, and opened Colleen's door. There were fragments of glass all over her body; she hadn't noticed them until Ambrose brushed it away—the crash was a haze and she was still processing the accident.

"*I'm so sorry.*" Ambrose hugged her. "I lost control."

"Are you okay?" Her lips moved slowly. After he receded from the hug, she turned a little to study him, despite the pain pulsing in her body when she moved.

"Yes. Let's get you inside."

Colleen was in too much pain to try and understand what he meant as he helped her out of her seat, but when she saw the strange house over Ambrose's shoulder, it clicked. Ambrose carried her up the hill. She shut her eyes. When she opened them, she and Ambrose were at the gate.

The gate yawned open, which was strange, because when she first glimpsed the house, she could have sworn that it was shut.

It's pretty, Colleen vaguely thought through warm pain flushing her body. She tried to stand under her own strength when they were past the gate, but she clung tight to Ambrose's arm. Something, Colleen thought, moved in one of the windows, but as she furtively searched, there was nothing there but darkness.

Ambrose turned the knob; it creaked under his touch. Together they stood motionless in the entrance. Colleen shivered as an icy draft of air passed over her drenched body. Immediately, Ambrose grabbed the poker and moved around half-burned logs that were in the fireplace.

"Do you see matches?"

"We need to explain," Colleen said. Her body ached as she spoke. "What?"

"We need to explain to the owners what happened to us."

"Look around. Nobody lives here."

"Ambrose I don't want to trespass. Let's find the owners."

Ambrose stepped with her through the sitting room. *"Anybody home?"* His loud voice spread through the house. *"Anybody?"* Then his eyes met Colleen's. "Nobody lives here."

"Let's make sure."

Exiting the living room, moonlight halted behind them, and instantly they were in pure darkness and total silence. Not even a gleam of lightning's unceasing blaze penetrated the sickly house; not a whisper of the storm reached them here. It was as if they had suddenly been stricken blind and deaf, and Colleen thought that for a moment she had been killed by a stroke of lightning as she had crossed the threshold. They traveled through the unknown. Vague outlines of doors could be seen if Colleen focused hard enough, and for one moment—maybe even less—she thought she had seen the outline of a face, but a closer look revealed nothing, and all she saw was thick blackness spreading through the ugly house. She missed the occasional luminosity of lightning that only reached into the living room. Colleen felt as if she'd fallen through dizzying darkness and end up in another world.

"Anybody home? My name is Ambrose, this is my wife Colleen. Our car is wrecked and we need a place to wait out this storm."

Silence from the decrepit house.

"Okay. I believe you." Colleen pulled on his hand.

Ambrose led her back through the threshold into the living room. Colleen pulled a white sheet from a couch and laid down.

"Are you comfortable?"

"Everything hurts. Especially my head."

Ambrose gave her a kiss then stepped away from her; her hand fell away slowly from his. He looked closely again at the fireplace and surrounding area, running his hands over the mantelshelf then wiping them off on his pants once they were stained with dust. Colleen wished Ambrose could find matches soon because the coldness was getting worse.

"Where I grew up, there were stories about an old dark house," Ambrose said. "Where bad things happened."

"Haven't we been through enough tonight?" Colleen shuddered. "Please, love, don't try and scare me."

"I heard about somebody who disappeared in an old house. Old houses such as this one, they used to have bunkers and places built in to hide. Suppose somebody found their way in, but couldn't find their way out."

"Honey, please, I don't want to hear about such things."

"I wish I were the one who was hurt from the crash instead of you," Ambrose said. "Hey, I'll be right back. I'm gonna take a quick look around. Maybe if I'm lucky I'll come across some matches in the kitchen or something."

"Don't take too long. Please."

Ambrose walked out. "I won't."

Suddenly her body was plagued with a feeling of bugs creeping under every inch of her skin. The laughter of children echoed from deep within the house. Colleen's eyes abruptly swelled with tears at the thought of her own daughter. The laughter ended, and the house was still. The house was so hushed that even the smallest movements would be heard.

Long minutes ticked by until Colleen heard the footsteps. Ambrose came back holding a box of matches. "They were in the kitchen."

Colleen's skin was crawling with shivers. As Ambrose lit the fireplace, she shut her eyes and tried to dream. Ambrose came to her side and held her hand and told her she'd be okay. Behind her closed eyes, she fell into darkness, drifting, dreaming, being carried away to the magical world of sleep.

Colleen's baby called her from its crib. The walls of the crib were raised high so that she could not see her baby, only hear her, and when she approached, she carefully peeked over the edge to find her daughter Amy drenched in mud, a leaf hanging between crooked black lips.

Amy screamed for her mother.

That was all her child could do; scream and try to move its stiff body, failing to shift at all. The poor child was in pain and she couldn't stand it. Colleen rushed to pick up her baby and cradle her, ignoring the mud.

"Hush little baby don't say a word, Mama's gonna buy you a mock-ingbird."

The child was cold all over, as if she had been made of ice instead of flesh. Colleen carried her baby through a long hallway and down creaking stairs until they were at the fireplace in her own home's living room, where she set her baby down after she knelt at the fire-place. One matchstick left in the box. Colleen struck it then dropped it in with the logs of wood. Flames erupted. Scorching warmth over-took the room.

Colleen wiped handfuls of mud from her baby. Flames licked closer. She rubbed her child again before the fire, returning warmth to her baby's body. The cries stopped. Minutes later Colleen felt Amy's pulse again—that beautiful pulse that was infrequent at first, then became a constant vibration. Amy's arms twitched then moved of her own will.

Shadows drew over Colleen's eyes, so that she was awakened with a sense that she was surrounded by souls; souls trapped in darkness, reaching for that one small light desperate to escape. So comfortable, so warm, so tired in a room full of life, she had not noticed that she was alone. It wasn't until she heard footfalls above her that she reached for Ambrose and knew he was gone.

Children laughed.

"Ambrose?"

There was a candle near the fireplace. Colleen lit it then crept out of the room. All her joints screamed with tight pains but she pushed through the torture. The first thing she saw after leaving the living room was a grand spiraling stairway, and a balcony on the floor above her. Where was Ambrose?

All the laughs and footfalls ceased; everything stopped completely dead.

The spiraling staircase curved so suddenly that anything could have lurked around its corner. Colleen ascended with a white-knuckled grip on the railing.

"Ambrose?"

Around the curve, nobody was hiding. She continued past the second floor to the third floor, where the sound of footsteps grew louder, and abrupt laughter was nearing her. The candle's flame tore through darkness like a razor cutting through flesh, and she continued toward the source of all the sounds, terrified at the hideous possibilities of what she might find.

She was chilled. Any warmth from the fire did not reach up here; coldness was all that accompanied her, and slithered like a serpent on her delicate skin. As carefully as she could, she went down one hall then another until, just past a window whose curtains were shut so that no glare from lightning could enter, she saw Ambrose.

Suddenly he stopped in place. He turned around to face her, holding a candle of his own. His eyes watched her distantly, as if they lacked a soul.

Ambrose walked up to her then held her hand with a furiously powerful grip. Her fingers tried to peel away from him, but she couldn't loosen her hand.

"What are you doing up here?"

"The children told me we could see her again."

"See who again?"

"Amy."

Strong laughter filled the normally silent hall.

"We are so close."

Colleen did not want to follow him, but his hand wasn't budging, and she had no choice but to either go with him or be dragged behind him. Laughter curled all around so that the children must have been standing right next to them, but as their lights illuminated the hall and cast amorphous shadows up and down, they saw that there were no children whatsoever.

As the whispers died, and they exited the new hall which unnerved Colleen—she had turned so many corners that she was sure she could never retrace her steps back to the front door—Ambrose halted. His hand slid abruptly over the knob of a door that looked like it should not exist; it was built into the *corner* of the wall, so that the door was bent.

Swiftly they were both inside, and Colleen pulled her hand away from Ambrose.

The room was suffused with a faint greenish light, the source of which Colleen could not determine, making everything directly visible, though nothing was sharply defined. The only objects within the blank stone walls of that room were human corpses. In number they were perhaps eight or ten—she did not count them. They were of different ages, or rather sizes, from infancy up, and of both sexes. All were prostrate on the floor except one, apparently a young woman, who sat up, her back supported by an angle of the wall. A baby was clasped in the arms of another and older woman. A half-grown lad lay face downward across the legs of a full-bearded man. One or two were nearly naked, and the hand of a young girl held the fragment of a gown which had torn open at the breast. The bodies were in various stages of decay, all greatly shrunken in face and figure. Some were but little more than skeletons.

Colleen stood stupefied with horror by this ghastly spectacle, standing by the open door. Ambrose fearlessly walked quickly to the center of the room, knelt beside one of the bodies for a closer examination and tenderly raised its blackened and shriveled head in his hands. Those dark eyes—eyes like a doll's eyes—blinked and watched her. Colleen felt herself falling, and in clutching the edge of the door for support, pushed it shut with a sharp click.

The door was of heavy riveted iron plates. Equidistant from one another and from the top and bottom, three strong bolts protruded from the beveled edge. When the knob had been turned, they were retracted flush with the edge; release it, and they shot out. It was a spring lock. On the inside there was no knob, nor any kind of projection—it was a smooth surface of iron. Ambrose was trapped.

Colleen remembered nothing after that; she woke up in a hospital in Ashfall, where she had been taken by strangers. For weeks she suffered from a nervous fever, attended with constant delirium. She had been found lying in the road several miles away from the sickly house she and Ambrose had trespassed into; but how she had escaped from it to get there, she did not know. On recovery, Colleen inquired the fate of Ambrose, but nobody knew.

Nobody believed a word of her story.

With all that afterwards occurred—the examination of the house, the failure to find any room corresponding to that which Colleen described, and all the accusations in the newspapers—she was still convinced that Ambrose was in the house.

2

DR. JAMES MCDOWELL, HAVING studied preternatural phenomena for his whole life, had a particular interest in the Engstrom House. It was an evil place, much more evil than any place he had studied before. And when he had gotten word of the disappearance of a man named Ambrose, and all the wicked things his wife Colleen had mentioned about the strange house in interviews, he decided to rent the Engstrom House.

As news of the man's disappearance spread, James did a deep dive into the history of the house. He came to the conclusion that it was cursed from its inception—but what caused a house to be evil from its origins, James wondered, so he decided to write the definitive book that would explain the disappearances and deaths that happened in the Engstrom House, or at least attempt to explain as many of them as possible.

Dr. McDowell had published four other books before: a personal journal about his experiences in two other 'haunted' houses he investigated titled *One Thousand Nights in Darkness;* a book about various other studies in the supernatural, including two research papers which were previously assignments from his college courses, which was titled *Ten Unsolvable Questions and a Delirium;* a book of selected interviews with his mentor, Dr. Holland, titled *Bizarre Worlds and Wonders: Selected Interviews of Dr. Holland;* and his most recent book, *What Walks Unseen,* about his own theories about unsolved cases he had worked on, and even further investigations and notes about solved cases. They all had good sales, and he was profitable enough that his publisher took on each of his subsequent books after *One Thousand Nights in Darkness* without formal proposal or query.

Dr. McDowell wrote frequently and wrote quickly, and had enough information lying around his office in uncollected piles—making a mental note to assign Margaret to sorting duties tomorrow—to publish an additional four books, but since royalties came frequently from the men in New York, and since his practice also yielded him great pay, he was never in any hurry to scrape together more chapters for another book, only publishing when a book felt absolutely ready and necessary.

James's payment for the three months' rent meant that the Engstrom House would be livable; its current owners, who requested to remain anonymous, and accepted the payments through a reputable third party company, immediately began work on the old mansion. It would have plumbing, electricity, central heating, and new mattresses and covers for the first time in a long time.

Meanwhile, until the house was up and running and he would be able to stay there, he needed assistants. There was his office assistant, Miss Margaret Lewis, who had volunteered for the trip before Dr. McDowell was able to secure the location, but they could not do it alone. She gathered for him a list of prospects, people who had been affected by the unnatural in very specific ways, then brought him a second list of people who claimed to have psychic abilities, who had claimed to contact the *other side.*

At the top of the first list, of course, was the woman he had been interested in since he heard her story—Colleen Tillman, whose husband had supposedly been trapped in a hidden room whose doorway could not be found. James wrote a letter to her immediately, requesting her assistance, and suggesting that he could in turn assist her with uncovering what really happened that night, and could help her find the truth. Letters were sent to five dozen individuals. With any luck, he'd have one or two others in the house with him and Margaret.

"All sent," Margaret said upon her return. She sat on his desk while he opened his wallet to reimburse her.

"That cost a pretty penny, are you sure you got enough in there? Hey, what's up, Doc? You look so upset."

Dr. McDowell handed her a couple bills. "Everything's fine, Margaret. Did you expect me to read all about these deaths and disappearances with a big smile on my face?"

"Guess not." Margaret hopped off the desk then straightened picture frames on the wall. "What should I do now?"

"Take the rest of the day off."

"You sure? There's still some filing I could get done, or calls I could make. Rosenberg left a message earlier to reschedule for next week, and you're free all day Thursday. Should I let him know?"

"Forget all of that stuff for now, go ahead and take the rest of the day off. Those things can wait."

Dr. McDowell drove home through a storm, wondering what those poor lost souls in the Engstrom House might have been doing all this time, what they might do for eternity. Were they in constant pain? Was there ever any relief? He shuddered. There was a chance, albeit small, that he might join them and the thought rose gooseflesh on his arms.

When he arrived safely at home, before he could leave his car, a sickly cold washed over him. His guts sank. Dr. McDowell had an awful feeling that something bad was going to happen. Suddenly he did not feel alone, and with his left hand frozen on the door, right hand hovering over his things, he decided to shut his eyes and say a prayer.

He prayed for safety for himself and for Margaret and for all those who were coming with them.

They were going to need it.

3

THE LETTER ARRIVED IN a plain white envelope along with a heavy brown box of books.

Dear Mrs. Tillman,

My name is Dr. James McDowell, investigator of the supernatural. Twice before I've studied situations similar to yours—Liddell House in Hollow Hill, and Curwen House in Cypress Grove—and written about them in my book, One Thousand Nights in Darkness.

Your experience is not the first trouble that the Engstrom House has seen. In its long history, many people have vanished or passed away. I believe that with your help, and with the assistance of a few others, we could more accurately investigate this mansion, and can conclude what happened to Ambrose.

I have arranged to rent Engstrom House for three months be-ginning exactly four weeks from now on the twenty-third of August. Should you wish to have further knowledge of my experiences, I have documented them in two other books: Ten Unsolvable Questions and a Delirium, *and* What Walks Unseen.

I know that this is not an easy time for you, but I think that I can help you, and that our findings together could benefit the world—if there is a barrier between life and death, between his life and past lives, then you have seen it broken, and we can decipher it. You may be one of the only two people—Ambrose being the other—that has seen realities intersect. If this is real, think of what else might be.

Now, you may have many questions, and I shall attempt to answer as many as possible here:

*I have taken it upon myself to use my own money to rent the Engstrom House; the current owners were happy to accept a low rate, since the house has remained unused anyways, and based on the royalties from my previous four books (*Bizarre Worlds and Wonders: Selected Interviews of Dr. Holland *being the biggest seller), I can safely assume that I will recoup anything spent on this adventure once my book about it is released. I will allow you to make any suggestions to any sections of my book regarding you and your experiences, and you will be compensated for all your contributions.*

I understand you may be reluctant to go back to an awful place like the Engstrom House, but I made sure to pay as much as possible to ensure that the house will be livable and comfortable. The house will be cleaned, and we will be provided with running water, electricity, and there will also be a cook who will serve three meals a day.

The Engstrom House's history is no secret, and I will not deny it, nor will I try to convince you to do anything other than what you want. I do plead with you, however, that you should *take this on, and I shall remind you that you will be compensated for all your help, I will reimburse you for any and all travel expenses.*

Also invited are five dozen other people who have each either experienced the supernatural before, or claim to have psychic abilities. I do not believe all of them will be joining us; in fact, I believe very few will even consider the idea. However, I am used to doing these investigations alone, or with the company of only one or two others assisting me.

I, obviously, cannot guarantee you any results, or that we will find Ambrose. I can only guarantee that I will do anything and everything in my ability to help you find your husband.

You are not obligated to stay at Engstrom House for any specific length of time. While I have rented it for three months, which is the length of time I have rented such houses for previously, the duration of our investigation most likely will not reach that timeframe.

I appreciate your time and consideration, Mrs. Tillman. My contact info is attached below.

Thank you.

Best wishes,

Dr. James McDowell.

4

THE LONGER COLLEEN THOUGHT about the offer to return to the horrible place where she lost her husband, the more she had to admit to herself that Ambrose might not be alive. If he were locked up in that room for so long without a way out…

Her skin grotesquely crawled with nervousness at the thought of being in that house again, that house where everything was absolutely evil and wrong. Her skin itched like she was in a barrel of spiders.

Colleen wanted to watch the Engstrom House burn; wanted to watch it devoured by cavernous flames against an eternally black sky.

Colleen took a deep breath and dialed the number that was left at the bottom of the letter. A woman answered.

"Office of Dr. James McDowell, this is Margaret Lewis speaking, how may I help you?"

"Hi, this is Colleen Tillman. Can I speak to Dr. McDowell please?"

"Just a sec." Margaret put her on hold. A minute later, the doctor answered: "Mrs. Tillman, it is a pleasure."

"I don't even know what I'm doing here. I shouldn't have called."

"Mrs. Tillman, as I said in my letter, you will be compensated and I will cover all expenses for your travel and your—"

"I know you'll cover expenses, I'm not worried about that. I shouldn't have called you, I guess I just wanted to talk to somebody about all this. Somebody who wouldn't think I was crazy." She paused for him to say something, but he didn't reply, so she went on: "It's been a long time. Ambrose, if he was in that house, he must be dead now. How many months could a person possibly survive locked up in a room all alone?"

"I'm sorry, Mrs. Tillman."

"I walked out of there with nothing, and you still have your book and life. Your life didn't get torn in half because of that house. Would I really get anything out of this besides giving you information for your next book?"

"If the book's holding you back, look, money is no issue, and I will gladly pay you as much as you want for your—"

"He's dead. It'll be a waste of time. What if everybody else was right, and I was wrong?"

"Were you? Were you wrong?"

"Maybe I was. I don't know."

"Mrs. Tillman, I think you really did see something. I believe you about the door, about all of it. And even if your husband... has passed, I strongly believe you owe it to him—and to yourself—to uncover the truth. With all the people who accused you, Mrs. Tillman, wouldn't you want to clear your name?"

"Please, just Colleen."

"Well, Colleen, if you happen to change your mind, then make sure you set out early. It's quite the drive from Piedmont. The twenty-third of August is when we meet, but I'll be there the twenty-second, and the house will be fully prepared by then. So if you'd like to be there early, you are more than welcome."

"Doctor, if I do this, it's not for you, it's for me. I need to clear my name. I want people to know what really happened."

Maybe, Colleen thought, Ambrose was not in the ideal condition for survival, but if time and space moved differently inside that room—or in the whole house, for that matter—then maybe, to Ambrose, only five seconds had passed this entire time since they were separated.

Already the voice in the back of her head was giving her sickening thoughts and sickening doubts—it was so much easier to believe nothing was going to happen, rather than believing that everything would turn out just fine.

5

EVEN AT A DISTANCE, the house was mocking her. Taunting her. It sickeningly looked down upon her from its hill.

Colleen set her bags down, shook the gate, but it didn't budge.

"Hello?" She paced up and down the fence, looking for people. *"Dr. McDowell? Doctor? Anyone here?"*

Colleen dragged her hand along the fence until she came back to her bags. Maybe she had been fooled—maybe nobody was in there; she had come all this way for nothing. Her fingers wrapped around two bars and she pulled again.

The fence rattled; it didn't give. Nervously, her grip loosened on the fence, and her hands fell to her sides. Had she been foolish to believe that there had been anyone waiting for her? It must've been all a big joke, to come here from Piedmont and expect everything to be paid for, expect anyone to help her. She had been fooled.

"Doctor?"

Let me in, Colleen thought.

As if she willed it into existence, an old woman with black hair pulled back into a bun opened the front door and was coming up to the fence. Equally dark bags were anchored under her eyes. She wore a blue apron, and her shoes looked as if they had been worn beyond all possible use. The woman smiled and it never wavered, as if she had been coming out from an amusement park instead of the most hideous place on earth.

The woman pulled out a large ring of keys from her apron pocket and unlocked the gate.

"Welcome, welcome. Are you one of Dr. McDowell's guests?"

"Yes ma'am."

The lady studied Colleen through the gate's bars as she unlocked it. "Oh waitaminute, *you're* the girl. Shame what has happened to a young woman like yourself. Come in, come in."

Passing through the threshold, there was no going back. Standing once again past the old house's gate felt so strange, as if existence as she knew it was bending under not only her touch, but the touch of everybody here. Things didn't feel quite right. Colleen had a premonition that everybody joining her and Dr. McDowell were doomed.

"I'm Mrs. Wilson, the chef. I wanted to make something of your choice, but the doctor wasn't sure what exactly you liked, so I have a few dishes planned—steaks tonight, for example—but you say the word and I'll make you whatever you might be in the mood—"

"Thank you so much, Mrs. Wilson."

The Engstrom House was vaguely different today; it looked clean, as if an army had scrubbed it down. She couldn't imagine being tasked with cleaning up a haunted house of all places; how many people from the cleaning crew had vanished?

Immediately Colleen was sick. The raging flames in the fireplace brought her back to that night; they were burning as if they had never stopped, as if they had been warming up the damn house since that night just for her, anticipating her return, waiting for her so that they could see her be tortured again. This house had already taken so much from her, but this time, she thought, she would win; she would make the Engstrom place burn.

At the moment she and Mrs. Wilson left the living room, sheer unreasoning terror possessed her. Colleen did not know what it was; she simply feared. Then, like a sudden recollection, she knew what it was; she was seeing *light* in these halls; they weren't stricken blind like she and Ambrose had been that night. Seeing the wicked house in such vivid detail made its extensive history that much more real; this had been an actual home, people had once lived in here. All those wicked things had happened here—they were all true, every last story.

"So where is—where is Dr. McDowell?"

"Oh, that Mr. McDowell he's always running late. He phoned roughly an hour ago I think it was, and he said he'd be here shortly. Plenty of others have already shown up already though. They're gathering for the doctor's inaugural meeting. Would you like me to show you the way?"

"Do I have a room?" Colleen was chilled by the thought of the never-ending rooms, and all the lives that had once filled them, and all the lives that had ended because of this house. "Where can I set down my bags?"

"I'm sure you have a room. It wouldn't be hard to find in this place."

Colleen opened the nearest door in the nearest hallway. The bedroom seemed as though it had been ripped out of time and brought to the current moment. Colleen stepped through the room as if stepping into a dream, running her fingertips across the vintage wood of the wide dresser, and admiring the painting on the wall near the open door that led to an adjacent bathroom. Her eyes swept across every detail; the room was gorgeous down to the way the sheets were folded at the end of the bed.

Colleen set her bags down in the length between her bed and the dresser. "Mrs. Wilson, you said some people were already here. Where are they?"

Silence.

The doorway was empty. Mrs. Wilson was gone.

Colleen left her things where they were and looked into the hall; she was in the very first room, and all the way down at the other end, where the passageway turned a sharp corner, voices echoed distantly. Afraid to be alone, Colleen followed the sound of fading conversation. Around the corner, in an identical hall, she was all alone again, and part of her mind was wondering if there had actually been anybody there at all.

Nervously walking through darkened hallways, a thin light spread from a slightly open door and cut draping shadows in half. Colleen tiptoed nearer to the door and peeked in. Heat radiated from the fireplace and reached her all the way at the door. The walls were tearing, revealing slats of plaster boards. A few wooden seats devoid of any people were set in front of the fireplace, and a metal table had been set up with cardboard boxes for some sort of presentation. At the left side was a bar where a man with glasses was taking shots of whiskey.

He grabbed a second shot glass and filled it. "This one's for you."

Despite the scorching flames, chills dragged over Colleen's skin as she stepped through the room. She leaned against the bar with the stranger.

"I'm gonna need it." Colleen downed the shot. Glasses poured her another one.

"Are you the girl?"

"I don't think I should have come here. I guess desperation makes you do dumb things."

Glasses poured himself another shot. "I've heard a lot about you."

"I hope they were good things," Colleen said. Then she blurted out: "Why did you come here?"

Glasses tapped his fingers on the countertop. "The pay, why else? Doc's an old friend, I knew the check would clear. Doc likes having me around, if it weren't for me he wouldn't figure out half those things he writes about in his books."

"What's your name?"

"Scott."

Two laughing girls entered the room. One with dark hair and one with big eyes. They went across the room to the front chairs and sat closest to the fireplace. Dark Hair was drinking tea while Big Eyes was putting a cassette into her tape recorder.

"I never thought we'd find our way back," Big Eyes said. Then, into her recorder, she said, *"My name is Jane Adams. I am recording the first day in the Engstrom House exploration."*

Dark Hair leaned closer to the tape recorder. "Right now we're anticipating the arrival of the world-renowned Dr. James McDowell."

"Yeah," Jane said, "I suppose he wants to make a grand entrance."

"Ladies," Scott said, "you haven't said hi to our newest guest."

Jane and Dark Hair looked back at Scott and Colleen. Before Colleen could get a word out, Scott asked, "Would you two like a drink?"

"Absolutely," Jane said.

"Sure," Dark Hair said. Then, joining them at the back of the room at the bar, Dark Hair said to Colleen, "I didn't think anybody else was showing up. We've all been here for quite a while. And can you believe there's been no sign of the doctor this whole day? His assistant is here, Margaret's her name, she's been telling us all about him and what this adventure might entail."

Jane spoke into her recorder, "The Engstrom House is home to Ashfall's most delicious whiskey."

At that moment a woman with long brown hair joined everybody. "God it's so easy to get turned around in a place like this. I told the doctor we should have written up little maps. This is *just* like him, keeping us all waiting. Guess it doesn't matter, he'll pay us regardless of his punctuality."

Immediately behind her, a blonde lady with a pixie cut came along. "How many people are going to show up before this so-called 'doctor' I've heard so much about? And where do you two get off ditching me?" Pixie Cut stared at Jane and Dark Hair. "This place gives me the *creeps.* This place would give a *mummy* the *creeps.*"

"Guess we were distracted," Dark Hair said. "We were playing Truth. Like Truth or Dare, but only with telling the truth."

Pixie Cut crossed her arms. "Guess it's about time they made a game out of telling the truth."

"What is your problem?" Jane put her hands on her hips. "We *said* sorry."

Pixie Cut rolled her eyes. "You know what? You—"

"Apologies for being late. How are you all doing this lovely evening?"

A pudgy face. Thick glasses. A cleanshaven man in his late forties or early fifties with a full head of hair. He was wearing a black shirt with a purple tie that he was adjusting. A briefcase in one hand, and a glass of water in the other.

Dr. McDowell was exchanging hellos with Pixie Cut, Dark Hair, and Jane, then he set his things down on the bar and shook Scott's hand. Colleen stood apart from the group, backing slowly toward the doorway. The chills in the room were stronger, and Colleen had a sense that everything was going to go wrong.

Then the doctor greeted her. "Mrs. Till—*Colleen,* it is a pleasure to meet you. I apologize again for being late, I know you must have been... eager to get the evening's investigation underway immediately."

"I only arrived a... a few minutes ago." Colleen couldn't shake the feeling that was clinging to her like ivy clings to a tree. It was tightening around her; choking her.

"*Doctor,*" Margaret interrupted when Dr. McDowell was about to say something else to Colleen, putting an arm around him and pulling him aside, "did you..."

Colleen couldn't hear the rest of what Margaret was saying because Margaret and the doctor went to the front of the room, away from everybody else, and Samantha approached Colleen, extending a shot glass to her.

"You left your shot."

Colleen grabbed it with a shaking hand. Goosepimples rose on her arms.

"Sorry I didn't say hi to you when Jane and I walked in, I honestly hadn't noticed you. Anyways, did we even get acquainted? I couldn't help but overhear who you were, Colleen. I read about you in the papers all those months ago. Believe me, I never suspected you for a second."

"Have you done anything like this before?"

"No, this is a first-time experience for me. My name's Samantha, by the way. It's so great to meet you."

A shadow moved subliminally in Colleen's peripheral vision; something passed quickly on the other side of the doorway. But looking through the open door, Colleen saw nothing but darkness. She shuddered.

"What's wrong, Colleen? Everything okay?"

Colleen realized she must have been staring through the doorway a little too long. "Being back in this place…. Guess I'm seeing things. I thought I saw—"

"Now," Dr. McDowell said, catching everybody's attention suddenly, and breaking up all the little conversations that had been going on between everybody, "I propose this question to you all now. Should we stay in the Engstrom House, or would any of you prefer to leave now, and forget about this house entirely?"

Furtive glances were exchanged amongst themselves.

"No," Colleen said, the first to speak. "I don't want to go."

"Neither do I," Pixie Cut said.

"Me Neither," Samantha said.

"I'm staying," Scott said.

"Me too," Jane said.

"Excellent." Dr. McDowell reached into one of his card board boxes, then he collapsed.

He convulsed on the floor and everybody rushed to the front of the room to help him. Margaret told everybody to stand back and to give him space. Everyone was unsure what to do, and the only thing that could lift their eyes from the fallen doctor was the slamming of the heavy door behind them; it perpetually opened and shut on its own.

A furious chill rushed through the room and put out the fire.

Dr. McDowell was trying to stand, and Colleen noticed for the first time that he had hit his head so hard on the ground that blood was spurting out. The doctor attempted to balance himself by putting a hand on the wall, but he collapsed again, falling to his knees and holding his head in pain with both hands.

"Go ahead. Try to run," Dr. McDowell said. His sickening laughter chilled the room. "I'll kill all of you before you reach the front door."

His eyes were permanently black. Margaret backed away from the doctor, as did all the other women in the room. Scott was the one to step forward, his expression never changing—as if this whole ordeal had been a common situation he had faced many times.

"Listen, doc, you've faced these things before. We can get it out of you. I need you to fight it."

The doctor laughed. "You think *you* can stop me? You think that the doctor can *fight me?* The doctor is mine and the rest of you will be. Let's see where all your training gets you when you stand up to the devil himself."

Scott remained calm. "If you're the devil then strike me dead."

The pure blackness in Dr. McDowell's eyes slipped away and his brown eyes showed again. He put a hand on the wall again and stood up with what little strength seemed to be left in him. Colleen watched Scott as he put an arm around the doctor and helped him to one of the chairs.

She thought about running out the door, she was right by it, but she was too terrified to look away.

"This house," Dr. McDowell trembled as he spoke, *"it's a menace like nothing I've ever faced before."*

"Let's get you out of here, doc."

"It's too late for that, Scott."

"Doc—"

"Run." Dr. McDowell turned his attention from Scott to the women. *"Get the hell out of here."*

Margaret, Jane, Samantha, and Pixie Cut obeyed. Colleen lingered.

Dr. McDowell stood up from the chair, and Scott put his arm around the doctor again. "I'm getting you out of here."

The door had stopped viciously slamming once Dr. McDowell had snapped out of the house's grip, but at that moment it slammed again, sending splinters of wood flying in all directions. Colleen shielded her face from the splinters, and when she caught a glimpse of Scott and Dr. McDowell again, Dr. McDowell threw Scott down with such force that Scott was knocked unconscious. Dr. McDowell, his eyes flashing between normal and pure black, opened his suitcase that was on the table in the front of the room.

Dr. McDowell put the end of the gun in his mouth. For the first time since giving the warning, he acknowledge Colleen. They locked

29

eyes. Colleen's heart skipped a beat. She didn't know what to do or say, especially when Dr. McDowell took the gun from his mouth and pointed it directly at her.

With a split second to react, Colleen fell down, attempting to obscure herself from the doctor since there were a dozen chairs in between them. He fired again with some accuracy and the bullet zipped past her shoulder—an inch closer and it would have penetrated her body.

Colleen was absolutely positive that she was dead. She was sure another bullet would come in the following second, and was surprised when her life had not yet started to flash before her eyes like she had so often heard preceded death. There was no such flash of her life, no such light at the end of the tunnel, there was only uncertain stillness, a terrifying stillness that may have been the final moments of her life. How long was left?

"I can't fight it much longer. Get out of here."

It was then that she noticed the door had stopped moving, and Colleen ran for it, taking no chances at lingering in the room, and it wasn't until she was in the hall that she caught a glimpse of the doctor. He was trying to aim the gun at his head in his right hand, but his left hand was trying to force the gun away, as if each arm had a mind of its own—as if two spirits were fighting for control of his body.

Colleen ran.

BANG! BANG!

Two gunshots echoed through the hall.

We're all going to die.

6

JAMES MCDOWELL SLAMMED THE gun on the table. It skidded over the edge and a few feet away under a chair. The room was dropping in temperature by the second so that he could see his breath. His mind was spinning and he was dizzy again. It was hard to distinguish his own mind from the dozens of voices screaming at him.

He kicked the chair out of the way then reached for the gun. Scott's hand grabbed James's wrist and pulled his hand away from the gun. James broke free of Scott's grasp, picked up the gun by the barrel, then smacked it across Scott's face.

Scott moved away from James and shook his head. "Doc, use that big head of yours. How do we get rid of it?"

James set the gun down. *"Get it the hell out of my head."*

The fireplace was raging abruptly again without any human hand having touched it, and James saw all the events unfold in front of him as if he were in a dream, watching the world move through a chaotic uncertain control, and there was no waking up, no changing it, no controlling himself.

With unnatural strength, James clasped his hands on Scott and lifted him up. Scott struggled against James—or rather, James's fleeting mind thought, the body that *used* to be James, but now it was completely out of his control. And it was taking Scott to the fireplace.

Scott's flooding screams had no effect on the possessed monstrosity he was fighting against.

James was forcing Scott head-first into the fire. The flames were so close to Scott's head that the edges of his hair were singeing. Scott twisted, and as James's spirit was regaining control of his body, stretching his soul to refill the spaces of his torso that the spirit had controlled, he loosened his grip on his friend.

James retrieved the gun then extended it to Scott, who was still in front of the fireplace. "Kill me."

Scott ripped the gun from James's clutches in a heartbeat. He kept it aimed away at a wall. "Cool it, doc. It's the ghoulies in your head speakin' for you."

James shook his head. "The *ghoulies* won't win if I'm dead. Scott, the demons of hell have a vendetta against me for exposing them. The Engstrom House has been awaiting my arrival. If you kill me, it loses."

"You're talking nonsense. I don't believe you. You've written about exorcisms before—hell you've *seen* at least one. I was with you."

"Don't you understand?"

"Doc you ain't making much sense."

"Hell is sending all of its fury. All those other demons were teddy bears compared to what's taken me. Work fast, Scottie, I can't hold on much longer."

Scott aimed the gun.

Silent seconds passed. James waited for the release of death. It would be better than the flames of hellfire that were blistering his insides, searing his soul with the heat of a hundred infernos. From hell, the screams of endless damned souls were screaming into the darkest regions of James's mind; it was a preview of the hell that was awaiting him. The little devil that was inside of him was determined never to let go.

Scott lowered the gun. "Doc, no. There's a way."

James lunged at his friend, both of his hands twisting Scott's wrist to steal the gun. James landed a punch with his free hand across Scott's face, but it had no effect; James felt no pain. In the struggle, Scott's finger squeezed around the trigger and sent a bullet zipping above James's ear; he had almost gotten his wish.

Scott held in his scream and pushed through the pain of James's fingers digging deeper into Scott's flesh; with any more effort they'd not only pierce his skin but probably find their way to the bone. His friend's eyes were black as an abyss, and the man he had once known was entirely gone. An evil agent of hell was holding onto the body and not letting go.

Maybe, Scott thought, doc was right. Put a bullet in his head. Don't let the demons of the Engstrom House win.

But there must have been another way. There was always another way.

Scott used all the force he could find in the less than optimal position he was in to slam James into the wall near the fireplace. James's eyes turned back to brown, and the piercing grip he had on Scott receded. There were bleeding crescent-shaped scars along Scott's arm but he didn't pay them or the incredible burning pain any attention.

"Maybe, doc, if you keep this up I'll finally listen to ya. But I'm not giving up on ya this easy. Let's take a minute here and think."

James ran straight at him. Scott staggered aside at the last possible second. When James faced him again, Scott realized he had no idea how to defend himself. He didn't want to hurt James—and it wasn't really James, wasn't really his spirit in control—and killing James would defeat the demon but would also mean the death of a friend. James—or the thing in front of him that had been James up until he stepped foot in the dreaded Engstrom House—wanted Scott dead and was vicious.

"You delusional fool." James's voice was deep and plagued with menace. Not only were his eyes black, but his face was slightly misshapen and contorting into a creature that was less than human. *"You think* you *could defeat* me?"

Scott stumbled. Was doc right? Was it the only way to release the demon from its grasp? With doc's knowledge, how powerful could a demon become? Scott's hand was slick with sweat and growing hotter around the gun. How many bullets could be left? One? Two? He had to be careful and couldn't take his chances. If he really did have to put a bullet in this creature that was once his friend, he might only have one shot at it, and that was if there were any bullets remaining…

The sickening creature controlling James laughed. *"I am the taker of souls. I am the king of all damnation. Others tremble at the mere whisper of my name. And* you *are going to defeat me?"*

Scott had to be strategic. He couldn't blow this. Maybe if he kept the creature talking, he could find a way to bring doc out long enough to find a solution. Some ideas were stirring in his mind; maybe he had a trick up his sleeve after all.

"What do you want with Dr. McDowell?"

"You think I answer to you?"

"What's his soul to *the* 'taker of souls'?"

"You'll join him in damnation."

Scott aimed the gun. *"Here's to you, doc."*

"Human weapons. They're nothing against me."

Scott shook his head. "I guess we'll put it to the test."

"Fool."

Scott moved one step forward. "Look how far all your *'power'* has gotten you. The king of damnation can't overtake a pudgy fifty year old man and his friend."

The James-Thing smiled wide. *"A treat like this comes once in an eternity. I'll savor tearing his soul apart."*

"What if I offered you a trade?" Another step closer. There must have only been five short steps between them. "My soul for his?"

"I don't need to strike deals. Both of you are joining me in my domain. Welcome to the underworld, Scottie."

Scott closed the gap between them. They were inches apart. Then he dropped the gun at his feet. "I'm ready. Take me."

James set a hand—a grotesque *paw*—on Scott's shoulder. *"I hope you enjoy your stay. You'll never leave."*

Scott's opposite hand dug into his pockets and pulled out his tangle of keys. His fingers fumbled to single out the wooden cross and hold it up and apart from all of his keys. He jammed it into James's forehead; the James-Thing pulled Scott's wrist away with a fierce pain that traveled up Scott's arm and spread with the beat of his heart.

Then he let go of Scott's wrist. James was back in control.

James stumbled across the room to the wall where the boxes for his presentation were stacked; they had all been filled with supplies, devices, and tools for the investigation. They might still come in handy, Scott thought, taking precise and careful steps behind his friend. Suddenly Scott realized the gun was still aimed, and he pointed it down at the floor.

"What are you doing, doc?"

"Can't... fight... long... but if there's one thing that... always works..." James pulled a rotting slat of plaster board that was exposed from the deteriorating wall. He leaned it against the wall then reached for a second one. "God have mercy on my soul."

James laid the two slats down in the shape of the cross then he fell to his knees and collapsed over it. His body writhed and his eyes were splitting against between brown and complete darkness. Steam uprose from James's skin as if a red-hot poker had been set on it instead.

Seeing that there was rope in one of James's presentation boxes, Scott acted quickly, and he set the gun down so that he could restrain the doctor and tie him to the cross to keep him subdued. In the process, James's eyes became permanently brown. By the time

Scott finished tying the knot, James was slack, his eyes shut, and his breaths ceasing.

He checked for a pulse; doc was still alive, thank God.

Scott removed the wooden cross from his keyring then worked it onto the necklace that James had been wearing under his shirt: a silver chain that was devoid of any pendant until the crucifix had been added to it.

"Just in case."

7

SCOTT KEPT THE GUN in his pocket. He hoped he wasn't gonna have to use it.

Then he dragged James to the living room where he found that Jane was passed out on the couch and Samantha was looking after her. Scott didn't pay the two ladies much attention; he kicked the table at the center of the room aside and put James in its place. James was still unconscious, and Scott checked for a pulse again. It was getting stronger.

Doc's shirt was completely torn and hanging on by threads; it was seared around the remaining edges from the power of the cross burning his possessed flesh. The rope might've been a little too tight, and Scott debated loosening them, but if he undid the ropes even slightly then it would give the damned spirit another chance to kill James—and kill the rest of them too.

"James..." Samantha said distantly.

"Where are the others?"

"They've left."

"It's okay. It's you I need most of all."

"For what?" Samantha said on the brink of tears.

"Doc wasn't prepared for the wrath of this house. Playing with demons finally caught up to him." Scott left the doctor where he was then joined Samantha at Jane's side and kissed Samantha on the cheek. "Just like old times, huh?"

"I'm not the expert psychic you think I am. I spoke with a dead uncle once. My mom wanted to know where Grandma's wedding ring was."

"There was one other time. I've seen what you can do."

"I wish that time would stay in the past."

"The past doesn't always go away," Scott said then went to the front door. "Let's see if anyone's still around. Maybe they didn't get so far. Keep an eye on doc, sweetheart."

Scott felt Samantha's eyes on him as he passed through the front door. And he was right—the others hadn't gotten very far. Margaret, Joy, and Colleen were arguing down the pathway at the shut gate.

"Listen here you dingy bitch," Joy's hands were in fists. *"I'm getting out of here, and I'm going to the police and there's not a damn thing you can do to stop me. Give me those keys."*

"The police can't do anything for you." Margaret's hands were on her hips. She looked Joy up and down as Joy moved closer. *"The doctor paid for your expenses and time and now you're gonna help him."*

"I'm not gonna listen to his whore of an assistant. How much does the doctor pay you to go away in a miniskirt to lonely buildings with him? What sort of things does he pay you to investigate? Huh?"

"Give her the keys." Colleen was standing with her back against the gate and hanging her head in disbelief. *"This was all a mistake."*

Margaret ignored her. *"I don't have to take this from some beach-blonde piece of sh—"*

Joy wound her hand back then slapped Margaret across the face. Margaret grabbed two handfuls of Joy's hair and yanked. The girls screamed and clawed at each other. Scott didn't intervene—not yet. He was too amused. None of the three women had noticed him coming up the path. Colleen continued hanging her head, Joy kicked Margaret in the stomach, and once Margaret let go of Joy's hair, Scott stood between them.

After Margaret caught her breath, she said, "What are you doing?"

Maybe it was a bad idea, but it would be the best way to convince them. Scott pointed the gun at Margaret. "Well, doc's inside and needs our help. I don't think you need any convincing." Next Scott aimed the gun at Joy. "Joy, why don't you come on up to the house."

"I'm going to the police."

"Yeah, sure. Now come up to the house."

Colleen looked up for the first time. "I want no part in any of this. You people are crazy. I want to go home. Let me go."

"You're the reason we're in this whole mess. Now up that path you go. Come on."

Colleen didn't need any further convincing and was the first of them to listen to Scott's demands. Margaret followed. Then Joy reluctantly gave in. Using the gun wouldn't be necessary, so Scott put it back in his pocket. With the possibility of only having a bullet or two left, he really wasn't going to use it on any of the women, but it was the only way to get everybody to join.

He was going to need everybody possible to help.

Back inside the Engstrom House, Jane was conscious again and was sipping water from a glass cup that Mrs. Wilson—Scott had forgotten all about her—was giving her, sitting at her side and putting a hand on her arm.

Samantha had taken the time that Scott was outside to diligently prepare for the rituals. Long white candles were lit and surrounded the doctor. Adjacent to him was the table that Scott had kicked, which Samantha had now straightened out and set chairs around it. There were seven chairs—enough for everybody. The only thing on the table were Samantha's Spirit Slates. They were two four inch by six inch chalkboards with wooden frames. During seances, they were pressed against each other, and once pulled apart, a message was revealed from the spirits that had been contacted.

Scott knew it wasn't going to be enough. It wasn't what Samantha needed to do.

"Everybody, gather around."

Samantha sat at the head of the table. Scott sat on her right. Joy was on his other side. Nobody was in a hurry to sit down, and were taking long looks at James who was still unconscious.

"That man needs a hospital," Joy said. "Why aren't you getting him out of here?"

"What I say goes," Scott said.

Joy shook her head. "I can't believe this."

"Shut your mouth." Scott slammed a fist on the table. Then, to Samantha, he said, "Go ahead. Do your thing, Sam."

"Join hands," Samantha said. A flicker of shadows from the nearby candles glided repeatedly over her face.

Everyone took hands at her instructions except for Joy. *"This is ridiculous. Why doesn't anybody do something?"*

"Knock it off," Scott said.

"Why can't you think about anyone but yourself, Joy?" Jane said. "As soon as we get this over with you can go."

"You're not making things any easier," Colleen said.

Joy was the last person to join hands. Samantha began speaking but was cut short by the crucifix on the wall that flew from its rusted nail and swung through the group at the table and crashed into the wall at the other end of the living room. It snapped in half. Everybody let go of each other's hands, but the house was furious, and it was too late to calm it down. The Engstrom House was shaking.

Scott's first instinct was to check on James.

James jolted awake and twitched side to side under the grasp of the ropes. *"Release me from these restraints."*

"Listen to him." Samantha yelled, having fallen from her seat. Tears were flooding from her eyes.

"We have to do this!" Scott said. *"It's the only way."*

"This wasn't in the handbook!"

"What handbook? What are you talking about?"

Samantha grabbed a small black book with a painting of a candle on the cover from under her chair. While she flipped through it, Joy and Margaret were fighting again while Colleen ran out the front door. Scott stumbled across shaking ground to look at the book with Samantha.

Handbook for Beginning Spirit Mediums.

He snatched the handbook from Samantha's hands. Flipping through the pages, both of his hands were struck with a mighty whack—Samantha's Spirit Slates had lifted from the table with a mind of their own and slammed themselves against his hands.

Samantha picked the slates up from where they landed. Inside was written in chalk: *YOUR FATES ARE SEALED. YOU ALL BELONG TO ME.*

Samantha wiped the words away then shut the slates. Behind them, despite the shaking house and all the strange noises within, Scott could still hear the sounds of Margaret and Joy hitting each other and cursing each other out.

Scott found the pages he was looking for. He pointed at a section; Samantha's eyes followed. "Says here we can communicate to the spirit through a vessel."

"I can't do it, Scott."

"Samantha look at what's happening. Maybe we can reason with it."

"You can't reason with demons! I shouldn't have started the ritual."

The two of them went silent.

"Scott," James whispered, *"untie me. Please."*

"Not until we know that demon's out of you."

"I've lost all feeling in my arms. It's getting hard to breathe. Loosen these ropes."

"Do it." Samantha grabbed Scott by his shoulders and shook him.

Scott fumbled through the shaking house to James's side. He looked his friend in the eyes—James's eyes were overpowered with pain. Scott loosened the ropes a little bit, but not enough so that James could free himself. James's arms were purpling, and so was his face. A sickness was forming in the pit of Scott's stomach; any hope for saving James—or getting out of here alive—was dwindling.

"Why don't you let me out?"

"Because I know that little gremlin is still in your head. Samantha's gonna help us get it out."

"What if I don't do it?" Samantha said.

"Then I'll shoot you in the head."

"You won't do it. Then you wouldn't have anyone else who could perform the ritual."

The house stopped shaking. It came at such a shock that even Margaret and Joy had stopped their fight mid-action and calmed down. But that did not mean things were over—not by a long shot.

Scott kept his eye on James. James was grimacing.

"I'm fine now, Scott. Truly."

Scott shook his head. "I don't buy it."

"What do you mean you don't buy it?" Joy said. *"Just look at him."*

Scott fixed a chair that had been flung across the room and tossed upside down by the shaking of the house. Mrs. Wilson was hiding in the corner; Scott grabbed Mrs. Wilson by the wrist and pulled her from her hiding place, then he pushed her into the seat. She was so frightened of him that she didn't dare argue.

Scott looked around the room and counted each person. "Two short," he said. "Samantha, chef here's the one. Our vessel to speak with the other side like I told you. Like it said in the book."

"Boy," James said, *"stop digging yourself further into this mess. We can leave now. Untie me."*

Scott didn't acknowledge him. He went to the front door and opened it. Jane and Colleen were shaking the gate and screaming for help; there was nobody near enough to the house to help them because the house was high up on a hill and near a farm and was set apart from the town of Ashfall.

"Colleen, Jane, get your asses back in here. Stat."

The girls looked at him with crestfallen eyes sparkling with tears.

"Get moving."

They had no choice but to listen.

Mrs. Wilson's hands wouldn't keep steady. Hot wax spilled over the edges and dripped onto her skin. Samantha had a seat next to her, dangling her pocket watch in front of Mrs. Wilson to begin the process, while the others were sitting on the other side of them and holding hands. James had given up his begging. Everybody else had given up trying to argue with Scott—even Joy had kept her mouth shut while everybody was setting up the chairs and candles to continue the rest of the ritual.

Samantha took a deep breath. "Here we go. Mrs. Wilson, I'm gonna begin this by…"

Suddenly James was laughing. All eyes turned to him.

The final bullet of James's gun blasted through Mrs. Wilson's face. Brains squirted all over Samantha and drenched her clothes. Everybody but Scott was frozen with terror; his hand reached for his pocket to find that the gun wasn't there anymore—that was why James wanted him to come closer, so that he could swipe it from him. Scott hadn't been careful and now somebody was dead.

Scott took two steps toward James; James threw the gun and it hit Scott in the forehead, opening a small wound that bled into one of his eyes. With a hideous pounding headache, Scott watched James levitate from the ground and float above their heads. The house was shaking powerfully again.

Sudden new pain was exploding in Scott's left side. He turned his attention from James momentarily to the new pain; Joy was punching him in the side so he smacked her then pushed her away.

"You're getting us all killed! It's all your fault!"

"She's right, boy," the James-Thing said. *"You've damned them all to hell."*

"Doc." Scott stepped forward. *"Doc, you've seen men overcome demons. There's a way past this."*

"For the love of God," Colleen said, *"let me out of here."*

The James-Thing shifted so that it wasn't laying on its back while in midair, rather now it was levitating right-side-up. Its eyes changed from black to James's brown eyes again, and his thin lips pulled into a frown.

"It won't work, not for me," James said. *"The house has a vendetta against me. Scott, you told the demon I was just another soul. I've exposed the secrets of the devil before, and that's why this time there's no winning—I'm not just another soul."*

"Get a hold of yourself, doc."

"I'm sorry to all of you. I know that means so little now, under the circumstances, but I truly am sorry."

The two slats of plaster board that James McDowell had shaped into a cross snapped. Their jagged edges plunged into his skin and stapled him to the wall near a painting of a waterfall. James shut his eyes; screams as sharp as glass left his lips and pierced the room. Then James leaned his head forward and brought it back repeatedly, slamming it with tremendous force into the wall so that it cracked and sent down handfuls of dust that sank into the gathering blood beneath him. James's arms contorted until they snapped; lengths of sharp bone extended through torn flesh. Screams continued leaving his throat, each one straining him more and more than the last.

Scott looked away from James's misery to the gathering blood. It was alive. As James's head whacked into the wall again, more flakes of dust fled to the *boiling* blood. Scott turned his attention back to James, and a bucket of blood squirted from the slats near James's chest and oozed over the red cross symbol that the slats themselves had branded into his stomach and chest like the iconic symbol of some comic book superhero.

Hellish torment spread through James and split his flesh open directly through the symbol of the crucifix on his torso. His skin was pulled completely from his body to display his weakly pulsing heart and other organs. As blood spilled by the gallon, Scott wondered how much more blood was left in the doc's body—and doc was still alive as if the house had found a way to prolong death and allow James to feel the incredible pains that no other man had ever experienced.

The boiling blood grew in size and spread through the floor and dispersed itself through any crack or crevice it could find.

James's skin was torn in patches and moved over the Engstrom House's walls as if miniature hands were inside of the thin layer of skin and used them to stretch over broken patches of wall that exposed the inner plaster boards and other materials. The torn skin mutated; changed; shifted until it became one with the Engstrom House and covered up most of the torn sections of walls in the living room.

Pulsing organs floated from James's living corpse and stretched midair; the only organ left in his shell was his heart which was trickling out spurts of blood. Each organ snapped into tiny pieces and were absorbed into the house. James's liver filled a mousehole near the fireplace; his intestines spread into the cracked ceiling; his veins found the remaining open stretches of wall and slithered serpent-like inside of them, and where they ended up was completely impossible to determine.

Bones snapped; sinew split from joints; muscles tore in thick strands. All of James's remains were pulled by unseen hands from his body and thrown against the living room walls. Scott watched with disbelief as all the pieces of James McDowell were absorbed into the house, becoming one with it, sometimes repairing it and sometimes becoming lost in it.

All that was left of James was his head, his heart, and his central nervous system. His heart was the first of the three to be taken; it was severed from his body and flew into the fireplace. Flames rapidly and urgently raged and filled the cold room with blistering heat.

The central nervous system crawled like a spider out of the living room and vanished.

James's head was still alive, still screaming.

Where it ended up, Scott did not know. He turned his back on James. He was the last of the group to leave the Engstrom House.

8

Officer Thompson and Officer McKinley were coming back to the station after a robbery at a thrift shop and stopped at a red light when the frantic lady came to their car and slammed her fists on the passenger window. Instinctively Officer Thompson reached for his gun, then drew his hand back. McKinley put their car in park then they both stepped out to address the woman.

She raised trembling hands and put them on Officer Thompson's shoulders. *"Do something! Do something quick! He shot her at the Engstrom place!"*

Officer Thompson removed the lady's hands from his shoulders. "What are you talking about?"

"Who shot who, lady?" Officer McKinley asked.

The lady looked back and forth between them and wept. *"The doctor shot the chef!"*

"Wait a minute, Thompson, I recognize her from the paper. About a year ago she was the broad claiming her husband disappeared at the old Engstrom place."

"What are we waiting for? She says a man's been shot. Step on it, McKinley."

As they drove, Officer McKinley said, "You believe her?"

Officer Thompson looked at her through the rearview. She was sobbing in the back seat. Her hands were cuffed behind her back as a precautionary measure because of her severe frantic state. "Why not?"

"They never found the husband. I say we should've brought her back to the station. Girl who cried wolf. The owners of that old place should put a better lock on their gate to keep crazies away. Not to mention squatters and looters."

"Sure, sure."

"You'll see," the woman quietly said. "I'm not crazy."

Officer Thompson pressed the button on his radio. "This is Thompson, I'm here with McKinley headin' up to the old Engstrom place. We've got a lady here pretty shaken up saying there's been a shooting."

"Roger that," a voice said back. "Do you require backup?"

"We've got it under control for now."

Officer McKinley parked at the base of the hill. There was a blonde lady with a pixie cut descending the slope. Presumably she was on her way to her parked car and on her way out of here, but with a potential dead body, they couldn't let a likely witness leave.

"What did we get into, Thompson? An assembly of the crazies?"

"If it were up to me, they'd tear this old place down."

Officer Thompson handled the blonde while McKinley brought the crazy lady out of the back of the car. He stood between the blonde and her Buick Super as she fumbled in her purse for her keys.

"Put the keys away. You won't need them for a while."

"Are you crazy? You can't stop me from getting in my own car. Move out of the way."

Officer Thompson nodded toward Officer McKinley, who was ascending with Crazy Lady. Crazy Lady was begging him not to take her back up there and to uncuff her.

"Way I understand it," Officer Thompson said, "there's a dead body up there. What are you fleeing from?"

"They're all insane. They want to get us all killed. If you were smart you'd turn around and pretend none of this ever happened."

"Come with me, lady. What is your name."

"None of your business."

"What is your name? Or you'll be making a trip down to the station for further questioning as a murder suspect."

"Joy."

"All right, now we're getting somewhere. Come on up there with me, Joy. Let's see what all the fuss is about."

Everyone was rounded up in the living room. Officer McKinley looked over the dead body while Officer Thompson stood in the doorway and watched McKinley's back by monitoring all the strangers. The murder weapon—or what Officer Thompson assumed was the murder weapon—was lying on the floor. Nobody had wanted to hide any potential evidence. Which one of these people was a coldblooded killer? Officer Thompson didn't have a guess.

"Give it to me from the top." McKinley looked over the crowd of strangers along with Thompson. "Come on, out with it."

"Dr. McDowell did it," Crazy Lady said. "Dr. McDowell shot her."

"You McDowell, son?" McKinley asked the only male suspect.

"No, sir. James McDowell is dead."

"Somebody better start makin' some sense around this place."

"He shot her in the head then the house tore him apart." The girl with long dark hair was crying into her hands. *"Dr. McDowell was ripped to pieces. You won't find his body because it doesn't exist anymore."*

"Wait just a minute," Officer Thompson said. "Who tore him apart?"

"The house."

"So that's how it's gonna be?" Officer McKinley looked each of the suspects in the eye one at a time. "Who are you all covering for?"

No answer.

"You all expect me and my partner Thompson here to believe that a woman's laying on the floor dead, none of you touched her, right there's the murder weapon, but the man who did it has *vanished*. Pretty likely story coming from the same woman who said just about the exact story a year ago. Well there was at least one of you who was eager to get out of here." Officer McKinley pointed at Joy with his thumb. "What was your rush, chick?"

"My rush is getting away from this nuthouse! Can I go now, 'officer', or are you and your partner gonna keep holding me against my will?"

"What was she doing in this chair anyways?" Officer Thompson asked.

"A séance." The dark haired girl stopped crying. "We were trying to get the demon out of Dr. McDowell."

Officer McKinley shook his head. "Come on, Thompson, there ain't enough room in our little car for all six of them druggies, let's call the boys."

"Please believe us." One of the girls stood up.

"Sit down." Officer Thompson took a big step in her direction. "Nobody moves a muscle. They've got ways of making you talk down at the station."

The girl obeyed. *"The doctor was possessed. The house took control of him. You can trust me—I'm the doctor's assistant. My identification is in my purse."*

"Do you people take me and Thompson for a couple of damn fools?"

The room was eerily silent.

McKinley walked back around the body. "Somebody stands here, shoots this innocent tied up woman while you all watch, then you all say he was 'torn up and eaten by the house', and we've got a suspect eager to make an escape from town. You could see why it sounds so *silly* can't you? But since I'm a nice guy, and so's Officer Thompson here, we'll give you folk one more chance to clear your names and tell us what happened. And if any of you here are guilty, maybe—just *maybe* we can lessen your sentences. I know Thompson here's a man who's been able to pull a couple strings in his day."

"No, no, McKinley, we've been kind enough. I say we call in that second car and handle this the old fashion way."

"Sounds like a plan to me, my friend." McKinley put a hand on the wall near a painting. "If these walls could speak, I wonder what they'd say."

"He's in the walls." Crazy Lady stared at her feet. She couldn't meet anybody else's eyes. She spoke in a scared whisper. *"He's part of the house now."*

Officer McKinley snapped an exposed plaster board slat and was sprayed with a thin mist of blood. A heart was attached to the inner structure of the wall and thick tangles of veins were pulsing and attaching in and out of other slats and sections of wood. The silent room was filled with the heart's prolific beating.

One of the girls—the one with big eyes—was struck with terror and ran past Officer Thompson and out of the Engstrom House. The door closed on its own behind the fleeing woman.

"Quit standing around, Thompson. Go get her."

Thompson drew his gun and opened the door, running straight through the threshold without a thought, and becoming tangled in the web of human flesh. Sinew and skin were madly stretched like a web to fill the doorway; the girl's dismembered parts hung by veins and leaked blood prodigiously.

There were screams coming from inside the house. McKinley was telling everybody to shut up and stay put. When he joined Thompson outside, he was also covered in streaks of filthy scarlet and tiny lengths of skin and flesh.

McKinley pushed the button on his shoulder radio. "This is Officer McKinley, do you read me?"

Static.

"This is Officer McKinley, I'm with Officer Thompson at the Engstrom place. We've got two dead bodies on our hands. Do you read me?"

Still his words only received hushed static in reply. It was useless.

Thompson tried his own. "I've got no signal either."

"Look, one of us needs to stay here with the crazies, the other needs to get backup." McKinley handed Thompson the keys. "I can handle this group on my own."

"You sure?"

McKinley nodded. "If the boys ask about the blood, don't give them any straight answers. Who the hell knows how we explain that one. And for it to happen on our watch—damn."

Thompson went down the path to the gate, and traveled only a few feet down before stopping. Moving any further would be useless. The squad car was coiled in chaotic vicious hydrillas that dragged it across the hill and around the side to the back of the house.

"McKinley, get over here," Thompson said, back through the gate and halfway up to the house.

"What is it?" McKinley stepped out. "Out with it. Can't leave them alone too long."

"Our car's gone."

"The hell you mean it's gone?"

Thompson led McKinley down the hill to see the last glimpse of their squad car as the hydrillas took it away.

"Whose Buick is that out front? Give me your keys."

"You have got to be joking." Joy stood up and put her hands on her hips. *"I'm not giving you two… pigs anything. Let us go."*

"There are two fresh corpses in a room full of prime suspects, ma'am. And all of you suspects will be treated as such." Officer McKinley looked at the dead body again. "The boys are gonna have a field day with this debacle."

"Yeah, yeah, yeah. Who do you think you are, Mike Hammer?"

"Quit it, lady. Hand over the keys."

"I'm not handing over my private property to someone who—"

"You must not be aware of how the law works. As a police officer, I have the right to commandeer your car."

Officer Thompson put a hand on McKinley's shoulder to pull him out of the conversation. "Let her alone. There's no reasoning with someone like her."

"Aren't you convinced?" Colleen said. *"Don't you realize we didn't do anything? You two saw the heart in the wall. And none of us could have hurt Jane. Oh Jane. Poor girl."*

Officer McKinley retraced his steps back to the plaster slat he had torn off minutes ago. The heart was gone. "Fool me once but you won't fool me twice. I say all of you belong in the nut house, and personally I'd put you all there myself."

"What do we have to do to convince you we didn't do anything?" Colleen asked.

"Tell the truth for one," Thompson said. "And if the so called *'doctor'* were responsible for the dead woman in front of me, one of you better fess up to where he is."

"You, Miss Assistant," McKinley said. "Tell us where he is."

"Well, officers, it was fun." Scott stood up. "I think it's time you two walk out of here and never speak a word of this to anyone ever again."

McKinley grabbed Scott by the wrist, knocked Scott into the wall, then pulled both of Scott's hands behind Scott's back. McKinley handcuffed him.

"Take your paws off me."

"We could sure use the keys to that Buick now."

"I just want to get out of here." Colleen screamed. *"You can take my keys. Just get me out of here already."*

Thompson was ahead of the group. McKinley walked behind. They were leading everybody down to the lot when the hydrilla vine wrapped around Thompson's ankle and pulled him down hard on his shoulder and jolting him with harsh pain. For a second he found his footing after ripping off the hydrilla, but it wrapped around him tighter and pulled him backwards, crashing the back of his head hard into the hill.

McKinley made his way past the group and to Thompson's side, but Thompson was being pulled away by the continually coiling hydrillas wrapping tighter around his body. They were halfway up his torso; blood seeped between them and streaked the grass below him as his body was tugged further backwards.

"Help me!"

Tremendous pain burned into Thompson's body by the hundreds of cuts the snakelike hydrillas were opening in his flesh as they compressed. His vision was blurring, but he could still see the outline of his approaching partner.

McKinley caught up to Thompson before Thompson could be taken completely behind the Engstrom House and into the mysterious other side that lurked behind the dreaded building. McKinley grabbed his partner by the hand, which was the only thing besides

Thompson's face that was left uncovered by the twisting monstrous plants.

"Can't… breathe…"

McKinley pulled; it was effortless.

He was letting go and retreating when separate hydrillas came for him. They started on his legs and slithered over his body, writhing as they crisscrossed his torso, then they wrapped around his neck and sank into his mouth. McKinley choked, screaming, and fell over. The last thing Thompson saw, the hydrillas were stretching through McKinley's eye sockets.

9

COLLEEN NEEDED TO GRAB her bags from her room in the Engstrom House. Archaic chills pulled over her skin and sank through her body. The hallway was pure darkness and she only had a small candle to guide her. As she opened the door, she had a premonition that something was lurking in the impossibly black room; some hideous creature that was going to plunge its grotesquely long teeth into her flesh.

The door creaked open on its hinges. Colleen stepped into the room. Her hand slid along the wall for a light switch that she discovered did not work at all.

Small steps closer to the bed.

Her bags were gone.

Colleen knelt at the foot of the bed in her Engstrom room. She pulled the covers back so that she could see beneath it, and slowly she lowered herself.

Dense darkness stared back at her, and Colleen had a creeping sensation that there was something else under the bed with her; something ancient and evil stalking her with the veil of murky gloom that spread throughout every inch of the room.

Her next destination to check was the closet. It was partly open and she nervously tiptoed to it.

CREAK!

Something moved behind her as she passed by the bed.

Colleen abruptly turned. A scream was building in her throat and daring to escape; she held it in when she saw that there was nobody there with her. Old floors can do that—can make sounds all on their own. There was nothing to be afraid of, she thought. Get the bags and go back home.

Her heart beat furiously in her chest. Colleen raised her free hand to the door and pushed it fully open with her fingertips. Inside she found boxes, but none of them belonged to her.

Where were her things? The thought hardly passed through her mind when she was chilled by the same creaking she had heard seconds ago. Furtively she looked over her shoulder; the room was still empty.

Nothing will get me.

There was another place in the room that she could check; the bathroom that joined her bedroom with the neighboring room. Colleen wrapped her fingers around the cold doorknob and turned it. The switch just inside the doorway did not work either.

Colleen prayed her bags were in here and that it wouldn't take long to find them and get out of the Engstrom House.

Her bags were not behind the door, nor were they around the sink. She felt stupid checking in the bathtub, but she had to be certain not to leave any place unchecked. She was leaving the room when she heard the creaking sound again. This time it was coming from within the bathroom.

The powerful scream was resurfacing.

At the other end of the bathroom, the door leading to the adjacent room was open a short length, and a big vicious eye gleamed under the light of Colleen's candle.

10

"SHOT OF BOURBON," SCOTT said. "Keep 'em coming."

The bar wasn't far from the Engstrom House. Everybody had split ways, and here Scott was drinking alone.

The bartender put the shot down in front of Scott then went to the other end of the counter and served a pair of giggling chicks.

Scott picked it up and thought, *Here's to you old friend.*

He was mid-drink when somebody sat down on his left.

"Didn't think any of the others were still in town," a somewhat familiar voice said.

"I didn't have a chance to buy a return ticket yet. What are you doing here?"

"My employer's dead. Guess I need some time to get things figured out."

"Hey pal, didn't I say keep 'em coming?"

The bartender came back and poured Scott a second shot.

Scott slid it to Margaret. "This one's for you."

Margaret downed it. "I take it you don't have anything to look forward to back home either?"

Scott said nothing.

"Or else you'd be gone."

"Back home I work in construction. My girlfriend that I don't even like is living with me in my cramped apartment. A change of scenery can do a guy a lot of good."

"You know how easy it is to find secretarial work? I'll be employed the minute I get back home."

"And you don't like it?"

"Not in the slightest, but that's the way things go, isn't it? You settle for something because it's easy instead of following your dream because it takes a lot of work. Since I was a little girl I wanted to be a doctor. I guess I just *kind of* wanted it. When you get to my age, how do you rethink and replan your entire life?"

"I bet you won't guess what I studied my first year of college."

"What?"

Scott laughed. The bartender came by and poured a third shot. After Scott drank it, he said, "I went to seminary for a year."

"You? In seminary? You must be joking."

"Nope."

They were both silent for a little while until the bartender came around again and Margaret ordered a water. Then she whispered, "I wish James never brought us here. I wish you had been right when you said we could've helped him."

Scott stayed silent, then drank another shot.

"I wish…"

"Keep wishing. Go ahead and drive yourself crazy."

"What?"

"Get over it. You're a nice girl. You'll figure things out."

Margaret picked up the shot glass when the bartender filled it again for Scott. "Mind if I have this one?"

"Go ahead."

"Thanks," Margaret said. After she drank the shot she put her hand over Scott's. "Do you think James's soul… do you think he's at peace?"

"No. Not at all."

Margaret frowned. "I wish we could help him."

Scott wrapped his hand around hers. "There's a chance we can. We still have that house for another three months."

11

Scott went up to his bedroom. Margaret wanted to take a few minutes to go through Dr. McDowell's things so she went to the doctor's room. Since he had been late to arrive at the house, she had picked it out for him. His papers and typewriter were on the desk in the corner. Just days ago she had finished turning a dozen pages of his awful handwritten notes into readable pages...

KNOCK! KNOCK! KNOCK!

Margaret shuddered. Who was visiting now? So late at night, after she and the others had all parted ways...

She crept from the doctor's room to the living room and peeked outside. A fat lady was knocking.

Margaret opened the front door just a crack. "Yes?"

The fat lady raised her gun and pushed past Margaret. "Ashfall PD. Let me in."

Margaret put her hands up and moved out of the lady's way. "Take it easy."

Fat Lady looked around the living room suspiciously, taking in the torn up walls, ancient furniture, and crooked paintings. The house needed serious renovations.

"You know, you don't look like a cop."

"My husband is in the patrol car in case you're not cooperative."

"Geez, don't point that at me every time I speak."

Fat Lady lowered the gun. "Sorry. It's my first time doing something like this. I'm usually the phone lady, but since we're unusually short on cops…"

"Two officers disappeared, you said?"

Fat Lady squinted. "Don't think I said a number. Tell me what you know."

Scott stepped into the room. "What's going on in here?"

Fat Lady stepped toward him. *"Oh hello."*

"I wasn't expecting a guest this late or I'd have cleaned up a little."

"I'm with the Ashfall PD. Two of our officers said they were coming up here and no one's heard from them since." Fat Lady raised the gun at Scott. "Don't think I'm fooled by a pretty face."

"Well, as you can see," Scott raised his hands, "there are definitely no officers around here."

"Are you sure you saw no officers today?" She lowered the gun.

"What would officers be doing here?" Scott kept his hands raised even though the gun had been lowered.

"They said something about a shooting. Um…"

Scott lowered his hands, laughing a little bit, then pointed through the entryway into the rest of the house. "As you can see, there's nobody around here that's been shot. You can check all the other rooms if you want, but it would take you all night to get through one floor alone."

"That's okay, it's getting late anyways…"

Scott showed her to the door. "Have a good one, lady."

It stormed all through the night. Margaret had too much on her mind to sleep.

She crept out of bed. A flash of lightning brightened the ancient room momentarily. The room was strange but rather pretty. Wide open spaces. Vintage wood. It felt like a place that could only be reached through dreams.

Margaret crept from her room and went to the living room. She had a maroon Philco tube radio that picked up a local station after she retuned it. Music flowed softly and stretched from wall to wall. Then she struck a single match from the box that was on the table and threw it into the fireplace. Logs that Scott had brought in earlier caught fire.

Scott and I shouldn't have come back. It was the bourbon talking.

Margaret laid on the couch. She tensed up when there were foot-steps. Then she sighed in relief when it was only Scott. He sat on the couch over on the other side of the room without anything a word to her.

"I didn't wake you, did I?"

"Your radio isn't loud enough to reach me on the third floor."

"I couldn't sleep because I kept thinking about everything. This house is so powerful. Could we ever help James? Was it a mistake to come back here?"

"No. No mistake."

"Are you sure?"

"What do you want me to say, Margaret?"

Margaret sat up. "I'm lost. I'm completely lost. James is dead, and when I leave here I don't know what I'm gonna do with my life."

Scott kept quiet.

"I feel so alone."

Scott went across the room and sat next to Margaret. "No. You're not alone."

She looked deep into his eyes. "Scott…"

His hands were on hers. Margaret trembled under his touch. He slid his hands along her arms to her shoulders, then he pulled her to his lips and kissed her. She wrapped her arms around Scott's body and laid on top of him. The radio lost its signal and turned to static, but she didn't notice for a while.

Scott fell asleep first. His bed was warm, and with the downpour outside his window, it was easy to be relaxed and fall asleep. The radio was going in and out of music and static, and Margaret's mind was hanging on to the glimpses of words loosely.

She was on the ledge of sleep when she felt a sudden chill crawl through the room.

Then she heard his voice.

She jolted awake. She checked on Scott. He was still asleep. She sat up and listened closely. Rain spilled outside. Songs played in hushed fragments. Static hummed.

Maybe Margaret had been wrong.

She shut her eyes and laid down, moving Scott's arm over her body, fitting her body to press against his. The merger of soft noises made her sleepy again. She fell easily through the threshold of sleep.

"Help me."

When the doctor's voice came again through the radio, nobody heard it.

12

IT WAS A PRETTY day in Raven Hill.

Samantha was finishing up with a client; a lady in her eighties that had been referred by a friend. Samantha flipped tarot cards and told the old lady across from her about the good fortune that was coming her way; the cards spoke of love and money that were destined to come her way. The old lady paid then left.

There were no more appointments for the day, but Samantha took walk-ins. Her office was in the living room of her home, and she had big signs out front for psychic readings. Sometimes people would come in and ask her to talk to their dead parents or dead friends that weren't really dead, but she could tell when those people were lying and trying to expose her as a fraud because she could feel it in the cards or feel it in whatever kind of spiritual ritual they were doing.

Maybe I'll close early, she thought. *Maybe I'll get ice cream. Go to the park.*

She left the table at the center of her living room and locked the door which led from there into the rest of her house. She went up to her bedroom with her metal box of money and sorted and counted it. She was almost done when there was a ring of the doorbell. Of course when she wanted to wrap up, there was a walk-in. At least it was during her short business hours that were posted on the door, and not some nut who visited at two in the morning like she had gotten four or five times in the past.

The bell rang again. Whoever was waiting for her was insistent.

Samantha put the money back in her box, locked it, then put it in the safe in her closet.

She went down the stairs and the bell rang again. It made her a little nervous, but she couldn't say exactly why. Samantha peeked from the curtains in her living room. The person out front was a woman in black with a straw hat. The lady was walking away.

Samantha opened her front door. "Hey. Sorry about that. I had to step away."

"I was hoping we could talk."

"That's what I do best. I make my living talking. But I've done a lot of talking today, why don't we slow down over a cup of tea?"

"With everything that happened, we didn't get a proper goodbye."

"I hope you didn't come all the way to Raven Hill to tell me goodbye. Hey, come in, come in. Where are your bags?"

"In my motel room."

"You didn't have to spend the money on a motel room. You could've stayed with me."

While Samantha put the kettle on the stove, Colleen stood in front of the fridge and saw a photo of Samantha's small family. "Your daughter is so pretty. She has your eyes."

"If she were here she'd be dragging us off to have playtime. She's spending the weekend with her grandma."

Colleen was quiet.

"Do you have any kids?"

"One. I had one. She's in heaven now."

Samantha put a hand on Colleen's arm. "I'm so sorry, I didn't know that."

"It's okay," Colleen said. Samantha thought she saw a tear forming in Colleen's eye.

When the tea was ready they sat together at the kitchen table.

"Do you want to go to the theater? They're showing *Arsenic and Old Lace.*"

"That sounds like a fine idea and all but there's something I came here to ask you that I don't want to put off. The only reason I ever accepted McDowell's invitation was to find out what happened to my husband. Can you help me?"

Samantha sipped her tea then set it down; Colleen still hadn't touched hers. "Sure I can."

They went through the doorway and to the table where Samantha did her readings. Colleen's eyes curiously took in all the details of Samantha's living room-slash-workplace. Samantha shuffled her deck of tarot cards then laid them out on the table in a three card spread.

"How much would I have to pay you to tell me what happened to Ambrose?"

Samantha rested her hands on the sphere at the center of the table. "Tell me about your husband."

"How much will it cost?"

"Don't worry about it. Why don't you tell me how you two met? Tell me about your first date together."

"We knew each other all our lives because we grew up next door to each other. Our first date was to Roy's Ice Cream Parlor where he had a strawberry cone and I had chocolate. He was nineteen I was eighteen."

Samantha rubbed her sphere. It was a transparent purple glass at first, but as she rubbed it, wisps of smoke intertwined and stretched throughout it.

"I didn't think Ambrose could be alive this whole time sealed up in that room, but McDowell's letter had given me hope. With what happened, I never had the chance to learn any of the answers surrounding my husband's disappearance. But… but you always believed me, didn't you?"

"Yes I did."

"Does this really work?"

"Don't tell me you came all this way for something you don't truly believe in."

"To tell you the truth…. I was almost thinking about going back. To find out the truth once and for all. Since Dr. McDowell didn't have the chance to help me, but maybe I could figure it out on my own."

Samantha shut her eyes. Warmth uprose into her hands from the crystal ball. She felt Colleen's eyes staring at her. Poor Colleen, she thought—just a poor girl whose life went horribly wrong. She didn't deserve to lose her husband, especially in such a wicked way.

Samantha opened her eyes. "Let us look into my sphere."

Colleen moved an inch closer and leaned on the table to see into the glass. As the two women studied it together, the wisps of smoke pulled away and revealed Dr. McDowell's face twisted in fear and his lips pulled apart into a scream.

The sphere shook. Samantha was petrified; Colleen pushed her chair away from the table and watched with horror as the doctor's head turned completely around to face her. His eyes were wide with pain and his torment never wavered.

"Help."

Samantha screamed as she pushed the sphere off the table. It landed upright.

"Amb—rose."

CRAAACK!

The window nearest to Samantha cracked and in a split second it shattered and propelled into the room. A three inch long shard was headed for Samantha's face; in the two seconds she had, she lifted her arms up to shield herself, causing the long piece of glass to cut across her arm instead of her cheek. It was dangerously close to her wrist; it had missed by inches, and the cut curved around the side of her forearm.

Colleen helped Samantha wash the blood off in the bathroom sink. Both women were sobbing as they did it.

"I think there's a piece of glass stuck in me."

"I am so sorry Samantha."

"Shut up and call my doctor. Hurry. Check my phonebook."

"I've got this. Do you have any iodine?"

Colleen patched Samantha up without having to get Samantha's doctor involved. When it was all over with, Samantha took a pill for her headache then laid down on her living room couch. Colleen kept apologizing. Samantha told her she didn't need to.

Colleen sat at the foot of the couch. "It's not gonna stop."

Samantha said nothing.

"We have to end it. The evil of that house followed us all the way here."

"We can't end it. There's nothing we can do besides leave it alone."

"That house wants us dead."

"You know how far we are from Ashfall? That house can't hurt us here."

"What about the window? What about McDowell? Yes, Ashfall is hundreds of miles away, but how far is this evil willing to travel to get to all of us?"

"It didn't happen until you showed up."

"So it's my fault?"

"Goddamn, I don't know. I don't want to talk about this."

Colleen stood up and left. "Next time, it won't just be a little cut."

Samantha almost stopped her, but there was no point.

Alone in her living room, her mind wandered to that dreaded day a couple months ago. Everybody's life changed in a split second. Dr. McDowell was dead. Jane was dead. Two police officers were dead. Colleen never found out the truth about her husband and the disappearing door. And who knew, Samantha thought, how it had affected Margaret, Joy, and Scott...

13

MARGARET SET UP THE darkroom.

After she and Scott extensively photographed the places where James McDowell's body had been torn apart and absorbed into the Engstrom House, Margaret put their film through the development process. She was alone in the darkroom, waiting for Scott to come back, and opening the film cassette when she heard the hushed faint scream.

She listened closer, setting down the film cassette and the opener in her hands. The scream came faintly again. She left the darkroom and was heading for the living room, but the scream came again from the other direction. This time it was louder.

"Heeeeeeeeeelp!"

Margaret followed the cries to a door that led into the basement. The steps were worn and looked as if they'd fall apart under her weight, but there was a screaming child down there and she had to help her. At the bottom of the steps, Margaret briefly looked for a light switch, but there was none; there was only the faint light from the open door that strained to descend the stairway and spread, and a vague source of light coming from one of the only windows that wasn't obscured by mountains of boxes or various items that the previous families had left behind. Somebody could have made a fortune, Margaret thought, going through all those antiques and selling them—on one old dresser, covered in dust, was a gold necklace, but she dared not to touch it.

A ray of light from the window up ahead widened over a gap in the floor. An entrance into depths unseen. And Margaret would have never gone anywhere near it, if it hadn't been for the little girl's screams uprising. Margaret kneeled; darkness was too strong within to see the girl.

"It's cold down here. Help me. Heeeeeelp."

The girl was splashing around. There was water down there, but Margaret did not know how deep.

Margaret felt around the entranceway until she found a thin extension of metal to grab onto. She lowered herself and moved down the small ladder into the cistern. There was a semipermeable wall separating the room into two; one place for the sediments to be left from rainwater, and the side she was in, which was for the water to build up in. The water wasn't deep at all—it had all gathered into one far corner and lengthened against the wall under the in-wall drainage pipe.

There was no little girl.

"Hello?"

Silence. Stillness. Margaret stepped closer to the puddle. Was it possible to drown in such shallow depths? There wasn't much water accumulated at all—somebody would have to lay on their stomach and willingly hold their face down in order to drown in it. And there was nobody doing that here.

"Help me."

Faint whispers.

"It's so cold in here."

Margaret balanced herself with her right hand on the wall then got on her knees. She broke the surface of the water with her other hand, testing how deep the blinding pool was. The palm of her hand touched the floor through the numbing water. She slid her hand from side to side searching for any child that could be in an unseen pocket of water, but she found no such child.

Margaret's heart was beating fast. If she hadn't heard a drowning child, who had she heard?

She pulled her hand from the water and rubbed it on the side of her outfit to dry her hand. She pressed her back to the wall. The cistern was silent for a few long moments outside of the constant drip of water from the ceiling into the nearby water.

Then there was the cry again.

Margaret pushed her hand back into the chilling water, searching for the child, but there was nothing to find in the shallow depths, except for the hand that grabbed her back. Margaret pulled her hand abruptly out of the water, bringing with her the hand of a child that was clinging painfully tight to her wrist. The filthy black nails on that little hand pierced the surface of Margaret's skin; drops of blood merged into the ugly cistern water.

Margaret pulled her left arm in an abrupt desperate thrust that couldn't remove the child's hand. Taking her right hand off the wall and losing her balance, Margaret fell forward a few inches into the shallow pond of water, afraid that she'd drown—afraid that the unseen child would pull her face in and she'd drown. She wrapped her right hand around the child's hand and pulled it off of her, sending it back into the stygian regions of unknown depths that existed below a mere puddle in the cistern.

The child's own cries had stopped, but Margaret inched away crying and screaming.

Margaret went up the metal ladder quick. She ran away from the cistern entrance without looking back and bumped into a man whose hands grabbed her tight. She was still screaming and trying to pull away from him when she realized it was Scott.

"What the hell happened?"

Margaret was speechless. She ran past him and up the stairs; he followed behind her. She went to the nearby bathroom and washed her wrist off in the sink. Scott found peroxide and poured it on her wound.

"What were you doing down there?"

Margaret said nothing as she put Band-Aids on her cuts.

"Margaret?"

"Whatever you do, don't go down there."

"What the hell is going on?"

"I thought a little girl was drowning. It was a mistake."

"What little girl?"

"No. No little girl."

"What the hell?"

Margaret leaned on the sink. Tears dripped from her eyes. Every time she blinked she saw the child's arm sticking out of the water from the elbow up. She shuddered; the chills from the cistern had never left her.

Later on, the photos finished developing. Scott and Margaret laid them out.

"Once," Margaret said, "James and I discovered the hiding place of a family fortune by doing this."

"Did they tip well?"

"Not a cent."

Together they inspected the images with magnifying glasses. The initial photos were of the meeting room; nothing strange appeared in any of them. Following those were pictures of the living room; the wall where the doctor's beating heart had been revealed, and where his body had been pressed against when he had levitated.

Still the pictures revealed nothing.

Margaret moved some of the pictures around. "This doesn't always work. I know this is something the doctor wanted to do with Colleen."

Scott put his hand on a picture to stop Margaret from discarding it. "Don't be so quick. See that? Under the couch?"

Margaret moved her magnifying glass to where Scott's finger pointed. A wisp of purple smoke under the couch. It was about half a foot in length, twisting in a strained S-shape. Margaret looked at the photo taken before this one, which also showed that same couch, and there was no such wisp of smoke in it.

"I think one of doc's veins had gone under there," Scott said.

The next picture was of the fireplace; nothing unusual about it.

"Double check that one," Margaret said.

"Nothing," Scott said. "What's any of this mean anyways? Purple smoke?"

"There's not a handbook. We're trying to find anything we can."

"How did it work out when doc found that hidden family fortune?"

"James found a hidden inscription in one picture and the face of a relative in another. One thing led to another and James found the treasure in a hidden room sealed off by bricks."

"Seems like it always comes down to a hidden room."

"Houses like these had plenty of them. You know what else gives me the creeps in places like this? When they..."

Scott was turned away from her, picking up a picture that had fallen. "When they have what?"

Margaret was frozen as she examined the next picture. The darkroom went cold. Scott pried the picture from her hands and looked it over. The expression on his face never changed—he was always relaxed, always calm, even when the fat lady held the gun to his head the day before.

"I'll be damned," he said.

Scrawled on the ground in the picture in James's handwriting was one word: *help*

14

JOY PAINTED THE ENGSTROM House from memory on a big four foot by six foot canvas. The door was open but only darkness was within. The upper windows glowed with yellow light, but nothing was clearly defined within them. Hydrillas at the sides of the building threatened to strangle any passerby, like the Shadow Man she had painted at the edge of the gate. Behind the house, the sun was setting.

Since she lived in a small apartment, her painting room was also her bedroom. She put her paints and brushes down, then across the room she opened her drawers and found new clothes. She had hardly noticed it was nighttime; painting could make an entire day go by in a blink.

She turned the shower knob to the left then she undressed while the water ran.

Joy stretched under the waterfall and yawned. When she shut her eyes to wash her hair, all she could see was her painting and all she could think was that there were so many places where it could be touched up and improved and fixed. And maybe this one would sell. The only way that she was able to afford her rent was with the check that Margaret had given her on behalf of the late Dr. James McDowell. And that money was running out quick.

The trip was terrifying, and for a while, Joy had doubted she was gonna escape the house alive. And when the cops had been taken by hydrillas and murdered, Joy was sure that the rest of them could never leave; they'd also be taken by the—

Joy's eyes snapped open at the sound of creaking floorboards.

She stood motionless in the shower, waiting to hear the sounds again. They never came. It must have been imagination, Joy thought to calm herself. She must have been hearing things. A little at a time she moved her body again and stopped being scared.

The water was running cold, despite the fact that she had only been in the shower five minutes or less. She turned the knob to the left some more and it didn't pick up in temperature; it was lukewarm and running a little cold.

Joy finished washing her hair then turned the knob all the way to the left. A little better, but hardly above lukewarm. She grabbed the bar of soap and rubbed it against her skin and heard the creaking footfalls approach the bathroom. Joy recoiled in fear and covered herself with her arm. Since she lived alone, the bathroom door was never shut and locked like it would be otherwise.

"Who's there?" Joy shivered as she whispered. The water was freezing cold and her teeth were jittering.

Joy shut the water off. She wrapped a towel around herself and opened the cabinet under her sink. Her hand rushed to grab the hammer that was lying next to a box of nails and a screwdriver. She carried it out of the bathroom in both of her hands like a baseball bat.

"Is there somebody out there? I have a weapon and I'm not afraid to use it."

Upon inspection, Joy found nobody hiding in her small apartment. She double checked her front door and it was locked; nobody would have gotten in without her hearing. She went back to the bathroom, threw her towel over the rail, then wiped the steam from her mirror. Dr. McDowell's eyes were watching her.

She shrieked and turned but he was not in the room with her; he wasn't anywhere around her. Joy was seeing things.

"Oh God, what's wrong with me?"

Joy put the hammer away under her sink then she left the bathroom and went to her bed. She almost touched up the painting, but if she started now she'd be up all night, she could never leave a painting alone. She admired her work for a second, then turned away from it so that she could walk over to the light switch, but something caught her attention in the painting; something in the corner of her eye that moved so fast that she almost missed it.

Something had moved in one of the glowing yellow windows.

A chill brought out gooseflesh on Joy's arms.

Joy waited to see if something moved again in her painting of the Engstrom House. Nothing did. It remained still because it was only a painting, and paintings did not move. Paintings were a frozen moment in time.

She hit the lights then laid in bed.

Two seconds later the sound of creaking floorboards passed through Joy's bedroom. She tensed and furtively looked over the edge of her covers into her void bedroom. Nobody was in here with her. It was only her and her bed and the painting. Nobody could get in through the front door because it was locked. She was only hearing things...

Joy turned to her other side. She was trying to get comfortable when she heard somebody whispering her name.

Her heart was ready to leap from her throat.

Joy's eyes swept across the room and ended up locked on the painting. She moved across her bed, jumped off of it, then turned on the lights. Blood was leaking from the front door of the Engstrom House in her painting.

She shivered. A chill rushed through her bedroom and shook the trees in her painting. Then the blood that had leaked from the door moved across the painting and reformed itself into the words: *help me*

A scream was hidden very deep in her throat. Joy clutched a knife she found in her kitchen then came back to her bedroom. Her hands trembled as she approached the painting. Joy plunged the knife through the canvas into the top right corner of trees. Red paint seeped along the tear. Joy dragged the knife halfway through the painting when she saw Dr. McDowell's face momentarily appear in one of the glowing yellow windows.

The knife fell from her hand. She grabbed it again and finished cutting up the canvas. She broke apart the wooden pieces into smaller ones that would fit inside a trash bag. When she was done she crept outside with a big black bag full of what had once been a beautiful painting.

Hoping she wouldn't wake anybody, Joy quietly tiptoed to the first floor then left through the back door to get to the dumpster. She threw the bag in then crept back inside the apartment building. On the second floor, one of her neighbors opened their door.

It was old man Hernandez. The grumpy guy who complained about everything and everybody. "Burning the midnight oil?"

"Sure." Joy didn't want to say much. She wanted to get past him and forget any of this had ever happened.

"Well keep it down." He slammed his door.

There was no way that Joy was getting any sleep tonight. She boiled water and made tea to soothe her sore throat that was strained from holding in all of her screams.

She felt guilty, as if she had just buried a body.

Joy shuddered. How could it be possible that her painting become a doorway between her home and the Engstrom House? How could anything she had just seen have been real? She didn't want to believe it but it was real.

The letter she had received from Dr. McDowell was kept in her phonebook. She took the letter from it then tore it up into little pieces and tossed them in the trashcan. She should have done that months ago.

"I wish I never would have gotten this letter."

15

KNOCK! KNOCK! KNOCK!

It didn't really register as Colleen laid in the motel's bed.

KNOCK! KNOCK!

Colleen opened her eyes.

KNOCK!

She shifted, sat up, and watched the door. Shivers traced her body. She crept out of bed and crept across her motel room to the door and looked through the peephole. Samantha was standing there with two cups of coffee and a little paper bag.

Colleen opened the door. "How did you know I was here?"

"I don't know if you had a good look around when you drove into town, but this was sort of the only motel around."

"Uh, is your arm okay?"

"You did a good job patching me up. I'm feeling better already." Samantha handed Colleen a coffee cup as she came into the room. "This is for you."

"Oh, thanks." Colleen took a small sip then set it down on the motel room's dresser.

Samantha opened the paper bag. "Donut?"

Colleen took one without a word.

"Look, I wanted to apologize to you about yesterday. You were right about everything. When we were in the Engstrom House I felt its power. That house is *alive*. It can reach us no matter where we are, and there's nothing I want more than to be done with it."

The small building was alone on a long dirt road and it didn't have a name anywhere that Colleen could see. And there was nobody behind the counter when she and Samantha went inside. Posters filled up the dismal walls; Wallace the Magician, Houdini, Howard Thurston, George Melies, and others.

Samantha placed a few fifty cent coins on the countertop. "My father brought me here all the time when I was a little girl. All the magic within these walls are fake, but this is the place that got me interested in what could be *real*."

As they walked through the entranceway that led into the building Colleen said, "Are you sure we can walk straight in?"

"Don't worry, I'm sure Howard's only taking a break."

A big sign hung around the room they came to: *THE RAVEN HILL AMERICAN MUSEUM OF MAGIC!*

Nearest to them was an ancient book on display under glass with archaic illustrations explaining a trick to 'cut off one's head.'

"Probably shouldn't lean on the glass," Samantha said.

Colleen moved off of it. "What is this?"

"This book is hundreds of years old. It was supposed to save accused witches from execution because it exposed all these magic tricks."

"King James tried to burn every copy of that book." The rough voice of an old man said. The man walking up to them was dressed like a magician in any of the posters on the walls; white shirt, white bowtie, black suitcoat, black pants. He was shuffling a deck of cards. *"The Discoverie of Witchcraft.* It's a miracle that book survives to this day. Samantha, it's good to see ya. How's that little girl of yours? It's about time you bring her by for a magic show—I apologize I don't have much of an act lined up for you ladies today, but Mondays were never our busy days."

"Howard, meet my friend Colleen. She's visiting from out of town and I couldn't let her leave without stopping by the best attraction in Raven Hill."

Colleen reached for a handshake. "Nice to meet you."

Instead of shaking her hand, Howard brought it to his lips and kissed it. "The pleasure is mine. Would you like to see a little trick?"

"Um—"

Howard broke the card deck in half and riffled them on top of the glass containing the ancient book. Then he spread them out and nodded to Colleen. "Pick a card, any card, any card at all, little lady."

Colleen picked the nearest card to her hoping to get this over with.

"Take a look, make sure you remember it now."

Colleen glanced at it but didn't bother to remember what the card was.

Howard split the deck in half. "Now place the card back in."

Colleen did so.

Howard did an overhand shuffle and mixed the cards up real well. "See? Nice and shuffled. Now." he selected the top card then turned it around and held it an inch from Colleen's face; she stumbled a step away from him. *"Is this your card?"*

Colleen didn't really know if her card was the 'eight of hearts' or not. "Sure is."

"See, Samantha? Your ole pal Howard's still got it. I'd love to give you girls the grand tour but I'm about to take a little lunch break, and Samantha I know you could do it just as well as I could. Have a good time looking around and don't break anything. We here at the Raven Hill American Museum of Magic have a strict *'you break it you buy it'* policy—replicas aren't cheap, you know. Some of these things cost me an arm and a leg—good thing I've got plenty of spare legs stashed away in the back somewhere, but arms, let me tell you, those aren't so easy to come across."

Colleen and Samantha went through the room.

"That guy was so weird." Colleen whispered even though Howard was far away.

"He's a sweet guy. He just likes putting on a bit of an act for his guests. Hey, was that really your card?"

"I don't know, I didn't pay attention."

"He's tried to guess my card ten times at least since I've been coming here. Each time he gets it wrong."

Between two glass cases of vintage trinkets, antiquarian books, and memorabilia was a metal structure almost barrel-shaped with rusted padlocks. Next to that was a hollow plastic construct with three sides that was only big enough for a little kid to stand inside.

"What are these?"

"Well that metal thing's a replica of Houdini's milk crate. Could you imagine being locked inside of that thing, handcuffed and under water? Now crouch in that thing there," Samantha pointed to the three-sided plastic display piece next to it, "and you'll get an idea of just how cramped Houdini was. Blind. Under water. Handcuffed."

"Did he really do that? You magic people are crazy. Hey, what's this?"

To their right was a tiny stage with a red curtain. A few props were inside of it scattered on the floor or leaning against one of the walls: a full-body mirror, a hat, a dozen red balls, a walking cane, and a cardboard box of trinkets.

"Magic Box Theater. When I was a little girl I did a little show in here myself. Howard puts a few disposables in here and kids can do acts for their parents."

"No, not that," Colleen said. "That display in the corner next to it."

"Oh, *that.*"

The devil winked at them. His head was attached to a square metal box with stars painted on it. Attached to the body was a thin metal plaque which read:

ASK ME A YES OR NO QUESTION

DOES HE/SHE LOVE ME?

WILL I BECOME RICH?

IS MY FUTURE BRIGHT?

And below that, on a separate thin piece of metal:

1¢ MYSTIC SEER

On the right side of the body was a slot of a one cent coin and a little lever.

"Wanna try it out?" Samantha set her purse on circular diner table that was home to the Mystic Seer. "I've got some change in the bottom of this thing somewhere."

Colleen grabbed two cents from her pocket before Samantha could find any in her purse. She handed one to Samantha. "Let's each ask it a question…. You go first."

"Is today my lucky day?" Samantha put in the coin then pulled the lever. A small piece of paper came from a slot at the top of the machine. Samantha flipped it over. YES in big letters. "Your turn."

"Will I find Ambrose?" Colleen put the coin in. She caught a worried glance from Samantha that she quickly tried to hide. The paper emerged in the slot; Colleen tore it from its perforated edge. YES in big letters.

Colleen put the slip of paper into her purse.

She wanted to ask it more questions, but Samantha was walking away from the machine so she followed her into the next room; more artifacts from years thousands of nights lost were on display. Samantha explained to her the significance of some of the things they saw and what they meant.

After that, they went to the final section of the little museum, which was the giftshop. Howard was already in there at the register eating a sandwich and reading a newspaper. He didn't pay any attention to them as they went around the racks and looked at the knickknacks and magic toys.

Colleen picked up a red plastic vase about four inches tall. "What's the trick?"

Samantha took the top off to show Colleen that there was a ball in the vase. "Now watch me make it disappear. Abracadabra." Samantha put the lid on the vase then removed it instantly. The ball was gone. She reached into her pocket and pulled out an identical blue ball. "Here you go."

"That's it?"

"What did you want me to do? Pull out a rabbit?"

"Could you?"

"I could try." Samantha picked up a magician's wand from a cardboard box overflowing with them. She tapped Colleen on the head. "Hocus pocus."

Something shiny caught Colleen's eye at a small spinner rack at the counter by Howard. A green amulet.

"How much is this?"

"For you…" Howard whistled. "For a pretty lady like you, you can take it."

"No, really. How much?"

"A dollar."

Colleen opened her wallet and gave him a dollar bill. "Here you go."

"Would you like a receipt?"

"No thank you."

"Good, because as you can see," Howard tapped a little white sign, "all sales are final. That includes the cursed objects we sell in the back."

16

SNAP!

Joy was blinded by incoming sunlight as her eyes creaked open at the little table in her apartment. The pot of coffee she drank had failed to keep her awake all night like she had planned. She shut her eyes and rubbed her temples hoping that her headache would be gone soon.

SNAP! SNAP! SNAP!

What was that noise?

Joy sat up, yawning, and turned. The terror was back.

SNAP!

The torn remains of the painting were morphing back together. The broken pieces of wood were snapping back into place and the threads of the canvas were attaching themselves back to each other. The yellow lights in the upper windows of the painting flickered; the hydrillas writhed and twisted awaiting a victim. Any trace of McDowell that had seeped out of the painting while Joy had destroyed it was gone, as was the Shadow Man at the edge of the gate.

With nothing but her purse in her trembling hands—and without stopping to put on shoes—Joy ran away from the painting and out the door of her apartment stepping in warm paint that was trailed from the dumpster all the way up to her home. Joy was halfway down the stairway that led from the second floor to the first floor when she felt somebody watching her; unblinking eyes chained to her. Then she saw it. A living shadow. A *thing* that was human in outline but had no features. It receded into the amorphous shadows cast onto the wall by the stuttering lightbulb above her.

Joy was frozen.

The Shadow Man.

She moved backwards and never looked away from the indistinct formation of unusually shaped shadows. Deep within them Joy had the sensation that the Shadow Man was moving with her and creeping through the other shadows.

"What do you want from me?"

No answer. Joy stepped backwards up the stairs. The Shadow Man moved within the expanse of shadows. The lightbulb above her flickered and flickered and when it completely died she turned and ran with her frightened heart beating a hundred miles a minute back up to the second floor, nearly slipping and tumbling down the whole flight as the paint on her feet made each of the narrow steps very slick.

Old man Hernandez leaned out from his door and yelled at Joy. *"Keep that racket down. Quit slamming your feet. Pendeja."*

Would her shut and locked door keep the Shadow Man out? If he was a shadow he could find his way in no matter what. A shadow didn't have any form that was bound by physics. A shadow could fit through any length of space no matter how tiny. Nothing was stopping him from crawling under her door…

Joy shivered.

And facing her apartment, the painting was gone.

It left a trail of thick red paint leading into her bedroom. She followed it, her heart still racing badly from the stairway, knowing that there was no escape from the painting or the evils of the Engstrom House, and found the painting back in her bedroom where she had created it. It was hanging on the far wall.

"Just leave me alone." Joy whispered. *"Leave me alone."*

The painting creaked and leaned to one side. A thin stream of blood dripped from the seams where it had patched itself back up. The blood gathered at the base of the painting and from there crept in a slow ooze onto the wall and contorted into a big *DIE*.

Tears overflowed in Joy's eyes. *"Please go away."*

Joy walked backwards crying. She was about to leave her room when the shadows on the wall, cast from her partly open blinds, came to life and rearranged themselves into the word *DIE*. Then something *else* moved sinisterly within them; a glimpse of the Shadow Man.

Tormenting pain pulsed through Joy's body and she let out a scream.

Immediately she left her bedroom and her apartment; she instinctively shut the door behind herself although there was no point in doing so because a shadow could move through any thin space and there was no getting rid of the Shadow Man. But maybe it would throw him off, Joy hoped.

Around the corner and into the neighboring hall, she slammed her fists on Veronica's door. Veronica opened the door and before she could get a single word out to her friend, Joy pushed past her and shut and locked the door—maybe locking a door to keep a living shadow out would be pointless, but she had to take every precaution if she wanted to live.

"Joy, oh God, you scared me half to death. What is wrong with you?" Veronica put her hands on her friend's shoulders.

Joy was out of breath and strained to speak. "Don't—look—out—there."

Veronica looked through the peephole in her door. "Do you need me to call the police?"

Joy pulled her away from the door. "No. Nuh-uh. Don't call the police. Please."

"What is wrong with you?"

Joy was crying. "My art is gonna kill me."

"Oh Joy—I told you it would all work out in the end. Are you having trouble with a painting?"

"Veronica you don't understand, it's really gonna kill me."

"Do you need help with the rent again? Look I can talk to my husband. Maybe we can help you again... but you still owe us a couple dollars."

"I don't need money. That's not it. My art is gonna kill me."

"Are you sure you're feeling all right?" Veronica put the back of her hand on Joy's forehead. "You've got a bit of a temperature. Want some medicine?"

"I need to stay here for a little while."

"They didn't evict you, did they? They can't do that to you. You know what? I'll talk to the—"

"No, I'm not evicted. It's just my art."

"Joy, you need to start making some sense. Are you drunk?"

"No I'm not drunk. My art... *please believe me.*"

"I'll make us some tea and you can start over from the very beginning, okay? Do you need me to call somebody?"

Joy crossed her arms and frowned. "No."

Veronica went from the front of the apartment to the kitchen in the back. It was a nice place, somehow cleaner and more perfect every time Joy visited; there was never anything out of place, and never anything that Joy could help her friend with. It was perfect—one of those places that there must have been a hidden fault in somewhere. Veronica lived here with her husband, who was gone working an early shift at the factory.

As her friend opened the cabinet for the teabags, Joy filled a pot with water and set it on one of the front burners.

"It breaks my heart to see you like this, Joy. I know things weren't going well and it's been months since you've sold a painting, but things will turn around. You still have that job at the bakery, don't you? You know, you came back pretty early from that trip you said you were taking—I had expected you to be gone months. Did anything ever come of that?"

"I wish I never went on that damn trip."

"I'm sorry to hear that. You know, we love the painting you did for us so much we keep it hung above our beds."

"Veronica. I don't think we're safe here. Let's forget the tea. Let's just go."

Veronica squinted. "Really I don't know what's gotten into you but you're scaring me. Is it that serious?"

"Uh-huh."

Veronica looked Joy up and down. "Geez, you're not even wearing shoes. Is that blood on your feet? Oh my God Joy are you hurt?"

"Paint. Not blood."

"Wait right here, I'll get you shoes, I have a few spares."

The teapot was boiling. Joy was about to add the tea when she saw that steam had gathered on the nearby kitchen window and written within it was the word *DIE.* Then there was a crash and a scream of torture coming from Veronica's room.

Joy felt reality breaking into pieces. She had brought the monster to her friend, and there was no escape from its grasp.

A lamp had fallen from Veronica's nightstand and projected the distorted reflections of her and the Shadow Man. His hands punctured her skin and ripped apart handfuls of flesh; Joy watched it all in shadow then took one discrete step further to find Veronica struggling against an unseen attacker. She was on the floor of her bedroom, hands reaching up at nobody and attempting to hit an unseen attacker. Looking back at the shadows cast on the wall, Joy saw the Shadow Man prying open Veronica's jaws. Then, slowly turning her attention back to her friend, Joy saw that Veronica's lower jaw was torn completely off from her face.

Veronica's flesh was peeled away in handfuls repeatedly, sending a flow of blood to Joy's feet. The misery and suffering in front of her was never ending. Veronica's stomach was sliced open by one long nail—a nail which was seen only in shadow on the wall; no attacker was ever visible in Veronica's demise—and her organs were crushed.

Joy had assumed her friend was dead, but there was one small groan of pain—the only sound Veronica was able to make since her throat had been pulled open and she had lost the ability to scream. The Shadow Man grabbed Veronica's head in both of his hands and twisted it carefully, savoring each of the steadily passing seconds, so that Joy could see the final fading glimpses of life left in Veronica's blue eyes.

The Shadow Man's outline of a face was laughing at her in its shadow cast on the wall. Taunting her. Joy had been the one to create it, but it had all the power in the world over her. She wasn't safe anywhere she went—a shadow could follow her anywhere and forever.

"She was a good person. Why did you have to kill her? Why? Why? Why?"

The Shadow Man kept laughing, kept taunting.

"Why? Why? Why?"

The Shadow Man raised his right hand. His fingers were unnaturally prolonged and slithered like snakes. They formed into the words *KILL YOURSELF.*

"Is that what's gonna make you go away?"

His fingers transformed into the word *DIE.*

Joy wept.

"Please don't do this. Don't make me kill myself."

His fingers were transforming into another word or set of words, but Joy looked away too quickly to see what those words might have been. She kneeled over Veronica's dead body. It couldn't be real. She was just here. She was just alive. In a few moments everything had changed, and Joy had been responsible for her friend's demise.

"I'm so sorry Veronica. It should have been me."

She didn't look at the Shadow Man again. She went to the kitchen and pulled a knife out from the knife block. Joy pressed the chilling metal edge to her throat. If it was the only way out of this, then she had to do it.

17

THE BOYS WALKED UP to the Raven Hill American Museum of Magic. Bobby was holding a gallon of water in each hand. Theodore brought along two gallons as well. And Chet had an arm around Arnold's neck telling him, "Quit being all nervous, new kid."

"What is this place anyways?"

"Old man Howard runs this place. He's the guy you gotta prank to prove you're one of us."

"I dunno guys. I gotta bad feeling about all this."

"Quit sounding like a chick," Bobby said.

The boys used the back exit to enter the building so that Mr. Howard wouldn't see them or the gallons of water. Chet took his arm away from Arnold's shoulder and held the door open for Bobby and Theodore. He let go of the door as Arnold entered and it squeaked on its hinges and struck Arnold in the back of the head. He wobbled a step and rubbed his skull where the door had hit him.

"What was that for?"

"An accident, I'm sure," Bobby said. "Ain't that right, Chet?"

"You betcha."

"Guys I don't wanna be a buzzkill," Arnold said, "but I've got a bad feeling about this. I've only been here two weeks and I'm sneaking in to places—I don't want to get in trouble with my parents or nothing."

Theodore set a gallon down so that he could slam his palm rather hard on Arnold's back. "Lookit the momma's boy afraid of his parents."

"Ouch."

"I hardly touched you."

"Who's in there?"

"Guess Howard heard us," Bobby said. "Quick Theodore, let's hide these gallons."

Bobby and Theodore moved the gallons of water behind a shelf. Howard entered the room the moment after they were done. He had a newspaper rolled up in one hand as if he were ready to hit a dog with it, and a candy bar in the other; a little piece of chocolate had fallen from it earlier and melted on his all-white shirt and stained it.

"Hey, Mr. H," Bobby said. "How's business?"

"Bobby Powell and the gang. Hope you're not setting off stink bombs again. Although there's no customers here for you to scare away, seeing as how we're coming up on closing time."

"This is Arnold, Mr. H." Bobby pointed his thumb. "He's new here so we were giving him a grand tour of the neighborhood. What better place to start than with this tomb of all-American magic history, huh?"

"Bobby, my boy, it's about time you bring me some new business. Maybe I should put a lock on that back door so there's no sneakin' in any more. Since you've only got fifteen minutes til close, I'll only charge you kids half price. How about that?"

Everyone dug in their pockets for change and gave it to Howard. He put it in his back pocket without counting it. He thanked the boys and walked away, presumably to begin the closing procedures for the day, and the boys pretended to be interested in the displays until he was fully out of sight.

Bobby, the ringleader, was the one to break the façade and whistled for his friends to come to the metal milk barrel display. The plaque told about its significance and what escape had been performed on what day, but Bobby had his own alternate history on the milk barrel to tell Arnold:

"It's been a tradition going back a couple years now that each of us had to get in this thing to prove our loyalty to the group. I did it first, ole Theodore here almost backed out but he came through, and strongman Chet—believe it or not—fainted while he was in this thing but made it out all right. Only the toughest men can pull off something like this. Think you've got what it takes, Arnold?"

"I—I think I do, but what's this got to do with loyalty?"

"To the untrained eye, pal, it may seem like a challenging feat, but if you stay calm and trust in your brothers then you can stand up and climb right out, and your loyalty is easily proven. All you need to do is climb in there, stay still while we dump the water on you, and last one whole minute with that top sealed. You might feel a little scared in the dark, you might even feel like you're running out of air, but these gallons of ice-water's not enough to drown you and it'll come up to your tippytoes at best."

"Can—uh, can... can a guy really, uh, fit, uh, in that small thing?" Arnold tapped his knuckles on the metal surface. "And there's a display rope around it, isn't this thing off limits?"

"Don't worry about it, Mr. H is cool."

"He's cool?"

"He was our mentor in the Magic Fun Club in elementary. We would meet every weekend. He knows we do this sort of thing. Doesn't he, guys?"

Chet and Theodore agreed.

"I dunno…"

"If you wuss out," Chet said, "we'll put you in there upside down."

"Yeah, and then you won't even be part of us," Theodore said. "So do it our way or the hard way."

Arnold gulped. "I'm in."

"Let the games begin." Bobby moved the ropes out the way. "Theodore, Chet, grab the water."

While they retrieved it, Bobby stepped up to the barrel and un-screwed the lid. He handed it to Arnold who was as red as an apple; he was having a hard time hiding his shaking hands. He looked like he was gonna be sick.

"What are you getting all worked up about? We've all done it, dude."

Arnold shrugged. "Nothing, don't worry about me. I'll be just… fine. I'll be fine. Right?"

"Right."

The others came back with the gallons and spread them out at the base of the milk barrel's display as if precisely setting up the elements of a ritual at an altar. Chet then came up to Arnold and took the lid from his hands.

"Few rules you need to know, new kid. First is no screaming—if you scream, you're out. Second, no calling for Mr. H or for anybody to come and help, understood? Third—and perhaps the most important rule of all—if you try and tattle on us, you're out, and we'll bring you back here and put you in upside down, you got me?"

"I-I understand you. I—I read you loud and clear."

"Excellent."

"Shoes," Theodore said. "And if you take off your clothes you'll have more wiggle room."

"Wuh-wiggle room?"

"Wet clothes are pretty restricting. Ever swim in a t-shirt?"

"Nuh-no I haven't, Theodore."

Arnold kicked his shoes off, then peeled off his socks. He put his pants and shirt into a pile next to the metal milk barrel. The others laughed as he did so, and held the barrel still so that Arnold could climb in. The look of terror on his face grew with every passing second. He rubbed small tears out of his eyes discretely, pretending that the others hadn't noticed.

"Are, um, are you guys sure there's enough room in here?"

"Just kneel down, dude," Bobby said. "How many times do I gotta tell you what to do? What are you, a baby? Do I gotta baby ya? Hey guys, maybe we made a mistake. Chet, Theodore, what do you think?"

"No, cut new kid some slack," Chet said, "he's not used to doing stuff like this."

"Yeah, Bobby, cut him some slack. I think new kid will definitely become one of us soon enough."

"Guess you two are right."

"Well… here goes."

Arnold kneeled into the barrel and said that he was ready. Bobby, Chet, and Theodore poured out the gallons into the barrel; the water chilled Arnold so bad that he was squealing. Arnold splashed around trying to adjust himself.

"Hey, new kid, you all right in there?" Bobby asked.

"Guys, guys, this fills up with way more water than you thought. And I think I might be stuck."

"But we've still got a little left, new kid." Bobby held it up. "Just a little more won't hurt."

"Bobby please. Don't."

Bobby dumped in the final gallon. Chet and Theodore gave him high fives. Theodore screwed on the lid, then the boys slammed their hands around all sides of the barrel and chanted, *"One of us, one of us, one of us."*

Bobby found a wand laying on the ground. He waived it around and said, "Abracadabra, let this whole place come to life."

Arnold slammed his hands on the inside of the barrel and let out some choked screams. Chet and Theodore grabbed their respective sides of the barrel and shook it around. Bobby collected the empty gallons and tossed them in the big trash bin near the exit door they had come in from.

"Guys, please—" Arnold gurgled the words out with mouthfuls of water. There was a deathly scream that erupted from within the barrel causing the boys to all freeze. They exchanged panicked looks.

"Arnold?" Bobby whispered.

A small step forward.

"Arnold? Arnold?"

Bobby tapped a hand on the barrel. "New kid?"

Theodore unscrewed the lid. They took turns looking in.

"Oh my God," Chet said. "What did we do?"

Bobby reached in and felt for Arnold. He had to reach so deep into the barrel that he felt as if he's fall in himself despite how small the inner space of that barrel was. He slid his hand from side to side and wondered if Arnold had performed a magic trick of his own—leaving the barrel without being seen. For a second he wondered if it had a trap door underneath that was built into the display, but his friends had been rocking the barrel back and forth, and if such a trapdoor were there, then water would've been spilling everywhere.

His desperate search came to an end when he found a handful of Bobby's hair submerged under what seemed to be an entire barrel of water—but that was impossible... they hadn't brought that much water with them. And their goal was never to drown him, they only wanted to scare him.

Bobby strained to pull up the slack body. He had to bring Arnold's freezing corpse halfway up, stop, regain his footing, then use both hands to pull the boy's upper torso up through the barrel's opening. Arnold hung over the lip of the barrel by his chest, with one arm in the barrel still and one arm limp over the side.

"Is he dead?" Theodore said.

Chet gulped. "We killed him."

Bobby stepped away. "It was—it was you guys that did it! Shaking the barrel!"

Chet paced back and forth in a panic. "Maybe he's still alive. Bobby, you've got to give him mouth to mouth."

"What? Why do I have to do it? I'm not giving him mouth to mouth."

"Well neither am I."

"I'm not giving mouth to mouth to another dude," Theodore said.

"Oh my God," Bobby said. "We killed him. We are *screwed*. Oh hell. Oh hell. Oh—wait just a minute. You guys. Mr. H—we say it was Mr. H."

"Okay, okay, we can tell the police that," Theodore said. "Let's go."

"We can't go! We gotta get our story straight! And if we leave now then Mr. H has the upper hand, he'll pin it on us. We gotta get him before he gets us. Don't you guys understand?"

"Well get it straight quick."

"Oh no, oh no," Chet said. "This can't be happening.

Suddenly came Mr. H's voice from within the museum: *What is going on?*

The boys were frozen again, but this time not as long. They bolted from the milk barrel display to the Magic Box Theater stage; a small stage with red curtains and basic props. As kids their parents had brought all of them to Mr. H's museum, and they had played on this stage putting on little shows for their parents and the parents of other little kids who had played here with them.

Bobby shut the curtains. The boys were even redder than Arnold had been. They sat down on the floor and were sobbing, reflecting on how screwed up their lives would be if anyone found out what they had done. There had to be a way to pin it on Mr. H, Bobby thought. There had to be a way...

"We have to kill him."

"What the hell are you talking about, boy?" Chet said.

"There isn't any other way. If Mr. H takes the fall, we have to kill him."

"We've killed one person and now you want to kill another? Where does the madness end?"

Theodore slammed his fists on the floor. "I can't believe this. I cannot believe this. Bobby we can't kill again."

"Say he attacked Arnold. Say he put him in that thing."

"And what were we doing meanwhile?" Chet said. "Standing around with our thumbs up our—"

"I don't know! That's why I said let's get our story straight, you knuckleheads."

"You're messed up, Bobby," Theodore said. "Real messed up. Who's to say you aren't gonna kill one of us to get you out of a jam?"

"It's Mr. H. No one will miss him."

"He has a family! He has two kids! I think he might even have a grandbaby!"

"It's him or us. We have our whole lives ahead of us."

Howard's booming voice echoed again and chilled them: *"I know you're in here."*

"Oh no," Bobby whispered. "It's too late. He knows we're hiding. He knows what we did to Arnold." He paused. Nobody else spoke. Then he said, "We need to split up. Make a run for it. He can't chase all three of us."

Theodore gulped. "Well isn't this just *dandy.*"

Behind Bobby was a yellow rectangle box on wheels. The *'I will now saw my lovely assistant in half'* trick that he had seen performed many times in the Magic Box Theater. A favorite of his and many of the other local kids. His knees creaked as he stood up. As he opened the lid, Howard's voice let out another awful scream: *"Oh my God."*

"I'm hiding in this thing. You two make a run for it."

"There's no way you're hiding in there, Bobby," Theodore said. "You're too tall for it. I'm shorter than both of you. *You* make the run for it."

"No way."

Theodore crept across to Bobby and slapped him. Bobby was in the middle of throwing another punch, but Chet came between them both and held him back.

"We can't fight with each other right now. This won't do us any good."

Bobby did not argue. Theodore opened the box and climbed in. Bobby wondered what he would do now—where he'd hide and how he'd get the story straight. It was too complicated to think of a solution half-heartedly. He'd need to put a lot of effort into it but he couldn't think straight. Arnold was already dead. Mr. H was screaming, and somehow Bobby needed a way to get Mr. H out of the way and put all the blame on him.

Then he was faced with a new problem: Theodore was in agony. The moment the lid shut, there was a burning shout and then blood spewed from the box. Chet was terror-stricken; and watching him move was like watching reality unravel in slow motion. None of it seemed real: not the situation they were on, not the tears in Chet's eyes, and not Theodore's body that was sawed completely in half and convulsing.

The next screams they heard were their own.

Bobby and Chet raced each other out of the Magic Box and realized that Mr. H's screams were coming from another room; he had not discovered Arnold's body at all. For a moment Bobby wondered how he could use that to his advantage, but there was almost no possible way to get out of this situation without Mr. H dead—he knew Arnold and Theodore had been here with him, and Bobby would take the blame unless the old man was out of the way.

Mr. H's scream were overbearing. The boys followed them into the other room to see what was happening to him. They found him huddled in a corner sobbing weakly. His body was convulsing. Bobby and Chet shared an uncertain look then moved a little closer to the sobbing Howard. Coming closer revealed bruises and cuts all along his arms and parts of his body that were revealed through his torn shirt.

"Mr. H?" Bobby whispered.

Chet took a step past Bobby and closer to Howard. "What happened to you?"

Howard's neck twisted slowly to face them. His eyes were bulging in their sockets and his lips were pulling into a menacing smile. He laughed hideously and grabbed Chet's wrist. Chet attempted to pull away but Howard was too strong for the kid. Bobby instinctively raised a fist; something else grabbed him first: a long gooey tongue.

An army of windup frogs hopped from the giftshop entrance into the room and spit up their tongues at Bobby. Sticky, slimy, and *pulsing* as if the tongues were coming from real animals, but he could see the windup dial on the side of the toy that never did need to be wound up for these frogs to move. No matter how hard he struggled against their restraints, there was no loosening himself away from them, and he was unable to help Chet as Howard dragged him across the room.

On one wall, in the center of clustered posters, was a target board used for knife throwers at carnivals or magic shows; green balloons were already taped to its surface. Typically the person tied up by ropes to the target board were pretty blonde women with big chests, and who were dressed in next to nothing. That wasn't the case this time. Howard pinned Chet to the board and tied the ropes dismally tight around Chet's wrists and ankles.

Chet begged Bobby for help but there was nothing Bobby could do against the constantly tightening grasp of the frogs; with each passing second he felt his skin about to burst.

Howard gave the wheel a nice hard spin, then opened a case to find the set of knives. His first throw missed Chet by inches on the left side of his face.

"I'm sorry Chet. My eyesight's not what it used to be since the diabetes set in."

The second throw landed to the right of Chet's face. Another very close call.

Chet wasn't so lucky with Howard's third throw. The third dagger landed in Chet's thigh; following was a knife that landed straight between his legs—nobody's scream in the entire magic museum bloodbath had been worse than Chet's when that happened.

Howard stepped away from his knife set to give the board another spin. Chet's blood leaked down his body and ran to his face. He grimaced against it, trying to keep it out of his eyes and nose and mouth but failing.

POP! POP!

Howard's subsequent two throws landed in balloons.

The next one landed deep in Chet's stomach.

SPLURSH!

Knives repeatedly struck Chet in the stomach and chest and arms. It ended with what must have been the final knife in Howard's set penetrating Chet's skull straight between the eyes. The wheel stopped spinning; Chet's corpse was hung upside down like a hog in butchering time. Blood spilled down to completely cover his face.

Howard stood over Bobby.

"What are you going to do to me?"

Howard laughed. "I've saved the worst for you."

Bobby was preparing for a knife, preparing to drown, preparing to be torn in half, but Howard stood still. The wickedness in his eyes receded and his demeanor changed. He was stricken with guilt and fright.

"What have I done?"

Howard stumbled away from Bobby and caught himself on a glass shelf. He was breathing heavy and shaking bad. He put a hand on his face then collapsed. Howard stayed completely still without saying a word.

Was he dead? Was that what a heart attack looked like? Bobby had no idea. While he was fixated on Howard's lifeless body, waiting for it to come to life and attack him, the restraint of the frog toys receded.

The toys backed away from him and retreated to their normal positions and places. Bobby went into the gift shop and picked up one of the frogs to examine. The tongue was hard plastic and did not move. When he wound up the toy and set it down on the counter, it moved in an unsteady motion.

Had any of it been real? Had he hallucinated it? Had he been responsible? Had he killed them all?

Bobby did not know what to believe anymore.

Maybe that was his torture; maybe that was how the evil of the magic museum was going to kill him—it was going to drive him to insanity. He had not killed a single soul but there were four dead bodies and he was the only survivor, and nobody was going to believe him that he didn't have anything to do with it.

The only escape was suicide.

Bobby shuddered.

That really was the only way out of this mess, he thought. How bad did he really want to avoid being blamed?

He examined all the bodies again. Maybe there was still a way to pin it on Mr. H, he thought. Theodore cut in half—but Bobby could not find a blade anywhere in the magic box. Maybe he could say that Mr. H disposed of it somehow. Arnold drowning—how could Bobby blame that on Mr. H? How could Bobby and the others stand around while Mr. H drowned their friend? Chet impaled multiple times… how could Bobby even begin to make up his explanation of it all?

And Mr. H. Was he even really dead? Or was he just passed out?

Bobby kneeled at Mr. H's body.

Mr. H jolted abruptly. He was completely deranged—his eyes were impossibly wide, and his mouth was contorted into an uneven smile. Bobby staggered away as Mr. H reached into his suitcoat pocket and pulled out a plastic gun. He took aim.

"Buh-bye, Bobby."

BAM!

The pull of the trigger released a length of worn plastic; the cloth around it unraveled. One word on either side: *BANG!*

Bobby had played with the toy before. None of those times had ever made anybody's head explode with the lack of bullets.

At first there was no pain, only confusion at the spray of blood. Bobby stumbled, grabbing onto a display case to keep himself from tipping over. His consciousness was fading fast and being replaced by a burning sensation in his skull; a fire that kept growing and consuming his body.

The world slipped out from under Bobby's feet.

His life did not flash before his eyes; his vision was obscured by the thick river of blood that spilled over his face.

18

The headline: **SUSPECTED CHILD PREDATOR ACCUSED OF QUADRUPLE MURDER!**

"It's not true, you know. What they're saying about him."

Colleen put a hand on Samantha's shoulder. "I know."

"He's innocent."

"I know."

They waited in silence to be let in. Colleen kept trying to find words to comfort Samantha with, but every time she faced her, her mind went blank. How many times could she keep telling Samantha that she was sorry? There was no way to make this any easier on her.

When it was their turn to see Howard, he had been completely changed. He was trembling even after the guard stepped away and allowed them privacy; Colleen was surprised he could hold the phone on the other side of the glass steady when he lifted it to speak to them. There was something strange in his eyes—was it guilt? Colleen couldn't put her finger on it. There was something deathly wrong with him.

He clutched the phone receiver with both hands and fidgeted with a loosened end of the spiral cable wrap.

"Howard look at you. You're a nervous wreck."

"Kill me. I want to die."

"What?"

He couldn't look Samantha in the eye. "I want to die. Please kill me."

"What are you saying?"

"I'm guilty." Howard did not wipe away his tears. For the first time, his eyes met Samantha's. "And your little girl is next. What was her name again? Brittany?"

Samantha dropped the phone. Colleen picked it up and straightened the cord. She was about to say something but Samantha grabbed it back from her.

"How could you do this?"

Howard smiled. His tears were drying up. His eyes looked back and forth between both Samantha and Colleen. "Let's call it a matter of revenge. There was so much work left for me to do, and there I was... floating... without a body."

"What are you talking about?"

"A certain matter of a ritual. An exorcism of sorts in which you helped your friend Scott expel me from Dr. McDowell's body."

"Go to hell."

"Your friend Howard, he watched while I tortured and butchered the innocent. And he'll watch while I rip apart your baby."

"Don't do this."

"Hahaha, you stopped me, Samantha."

"Our Father, which art in heav—"

"Hahaha, we're praying *now? You think that will save you? Go ahead. Keep praying for the souls I've dragged to hell—you two will be joining them soon."*

Colleen was chilled as Howard's eyes locked onto hers. She could do nothing but cry.

Suddenly Howard said, *"You need to kill me."*

"We can't kill you," Colleen whispered.

"I still hear from your friends in the Engstrom House. Mrs. Wilson, the chef. That pretty young thing Jane. They're screaming."

Howard put his hand on the glass divider. *"I am so sorry Samantha. Please believe me. I don't mean you or your girl any harm. But I did it—oh God, I did it. I killed those kids. God help me, I killed those kids."*

"I want to help you."

"There's no helping someone like me. I'm sick. There's something wrong with my head, Sam. But I want you to know I've always loved you. You've always been a daughter to me."

"Howard what are you saying?"

Howard's lips extended back into that disturbing smile. *"He wants to fuck you, you filthy whore."*

Samantha wept. Colleen put an arm round her.

"Samantha," Howard said. The evil in his appearance was gone. *"Put me out of my misery. I want to die."*

Samantha was at a loss for words.

"What's the matter? Cat got your tongue?"

"Let's go now," Colleen whispered.

"I want to help him. Maybe we can figure it out with my sphere."

Howard tapped on the glass. "I hate to see you girls go. Can I show you one little trick before you leave?"

Colleen's guts twisted.

Howard had unraveled a length of the chrome cable wrap and pressed the exposed jagged edge to his throat; in his eyes up until that moment was the devil, but as his hand pulled the sharp metal through his jugular vein his own spirit regained control of the body and felt the remaining moments of his life leak away. Blood splashed the glass divider and ran down in long streaks. Colleen and Samantha could not stop their screams.

Alarms blared. There were about five other booths with inmates in them talking to visitors through phones. The two security guards who were watching over the inmates ran to whichever prisoners were nearest to them and pulled them away from the visitation windows; six more guards entered behind them with urgency to secure all the remaining prisoners. Nobody helped Howard.

"Do something!" Colleen yelled at the cops. Her voice strained under the sound of the alarms that screamed with a deafening ring.

"Save him!" Samantha slammed her palms on the divider glass.

All the cops were ignoring them, carrying out their duties and making sure the situation was under control. Samantha and Colleen continually begged them to help Howard.

"We can't do anything," a cop with grey hair finally addressed them, *"we have to wait for the medics."*

Two or three minutes later the medics arrived. But it was obvious by the way they handled Howard's body and the stiff way he turned under their touch that he was dead. Colleen put her arms around Samantha; the two women were pulled apart by Raven Hill Police Department officers who escorted them outside of the building,

Colleen and Samantha sat on a bus stop bench and sobbed.

We're doomed, Colleen thought. But she was too afraid to say it. They were a million miles from Ashfall, but the Engstrom House still had a grip on their lives and would never let go. Now innocent people were dead.

"If I had listened to you…"

Colleen said nothing.

"If I had listened to you, this wouldn't have happened."

"What happened to Howard isn't your fault."

Samantha rubbed her eyes. "We have to go back. I'm going with you."

"You've had a traumatic day. Take some time to think this through."

"That *monster* in there is after my little girl. It followed me here all the way here from Ashfall, and if I leave now it'll follow me away from here and my family will be safe."

19

VERONICA'S BLOOD DID NOT wash off so easily. Joy scrubbed hard under the stream of burning water in her shower. The heavy suffocation of guilt stunted her breathing. Nervousness pulsed through her body with the beat of her heart.

There was no time to waste. After a passable job at washing her skin from her friend's blood, Joy dried off with the nearest towel that her unsteady hands could find. Then she added that same towel to the garbage bag in the corner of her bathroom.

The bag with Joy's bloodied clothes went down the incinerator.

On the way back to her apartment, she saw police officers coming in and out of Veronica's apartment. Her body had been discovered quicker than she thought—perhaps Joy had forgotten to lock the door. Perhaps somebody had come to check on Veronica after hearing her scream.

Guilt smothered her again.

Joy felt too hot. She wanted to run back to her apartment and lock the door, but had to move slowly so that she would not draw the attention of the cops. It was like a nightmare when she wanted to run but could only walk.

She paced through her apartment and double checked every inch of it. No drops of blood on the floor. None in her sink. None in her shower. None visible on her face. Nervously she looked through her peephole to find out what was happening. A few doors down a police officer knocked on Mr. Hernandez's door. They exchanged a few words, then Mr. Hernandez let him in.

Joy had one hopeful thought: she wasn't suspected of murdering Veronica, or the police would have come to her straight away. Nobody could prove she was there anyways, and nobody would pin it on her. Unless she messed something up by the time the police came to her door.

And she had to get her story straight.

"No officer," Joy practiced in the center of her living room, "I don't remember when I heard from Veronica last. Oh no—did something happen?"

KNOCK! KNOCK! KNOCK!

Joy gulped.

Maybe if I don't answer the door he'll go away.

KNOCK! KNOCK! KNOCK!

Joy stood up with her hands clenched into fists. She took nervous steps forward, going over excuses and lies in her head. She opened the door partway. The officer was tall and handsome with dark stubble; bright eyes over a friendly smile.

He looked Joy up and down then showed her his badge. "Officer Chambers. I need to ask you a few questions."

"What about?"

"Mind if I come in, ma'am?" Officer Chambers pushed the door gently and looked past her.

Joy did her best to hide her discomfort. She forced a smile and moved out of his way. "Can you tell me what this is about?"

Officer Chambers stood in front of a collection of her paintings on the wall; Joy had dozens of paintings of all sizes scattered throughout her apartment on the walls, on tables, on practically anywhere she had space.

"I see you're an art lover."

"Actually I painted them."

"You're kidding. These are really good."

"Tell that to all the galleries that turned me down."

"I'm sorry to hear that, but I'm sure your paintings sell all the time, don't they?" Officer Chambers examined the next wall of art. "They're really good."

Joy shook her head. "Haven't sold one in months. It's a miracle I have any money saved to pay my rent."

Officer Chambers looked her deep in the eye as if expecting a confession that very second. "How long ago was it that your neighbor across the floor bought one? She has one of your paintings hanging in her bedroom."

Joy felt her cheeks growing red. Her guilt was choking her again.

"What's wrong Joy?"

"Nothing." She was quickly slipping away from the happy disguise she had presented to him. "I... gave that to her as a housewarming gift. I didn't know her well at all."

Her eyes looked past him to the shadows moving on the far wall of her apartment. Was it a trick of the light, or was the Shadow Man with them? She couldn't tell. Her knees wobbled and she staggered a step away from him and leaned on the wall.

Officer Chambers put a hand on her shoulder. "What are you afraid of? Does this have anything to do with Veronica?"

"What about Veronica?"

Officer Chambers grabbed a tissue from the box on Joy's table then handed it to her. "Nothing, ma'am."

Joy stayed leaning against the wall, wiping a few small tears from her eyes, as Officer Chambers continued to look around at her paintings. She had blown it—it was so obvious she was guilty. She wasn't going to get out of this alive. He was going to arrest her. She was going to get the electric chair. They'd think she was crazy if she told the truth about who really killed Veronica—the Shadow Man.

Officer Chambers furtively looked at her then back to a painting of rotten fruit under a tree on a bright summer day. He was toying with her. He had her where he wanted her. She had already said too much, and he was waiting to see just how much she'd say before he took her to the police station.

"Could I get you something to drink, officer? Want some water? Or I can put a pot a of coffee on the stove?"

He pulled back the window curtain and had a look outside. "No thanks. Hey, how long have you had this place?"

"About a year."

"Ever notice anything suspicious going on?"

"Nuh-never," she said. "Like what?"

"I think I will have that cup of water."

She filled him a cup then gave it to him. He held it but didn't drink any of it because he was too busy have a look around. "Are you married?"

"I broke up with my boyfriend six months ago."

"Does a pretty lady like you get lonely in here?"

"It's about time I start looking for a smaller place." Joy crossed her arms.

Officer Chambers drank a little water then set the cup down. "Thanks."

"So what were you saying earlier? About Veronica?"

"Not important." Officer Daniels left the kitchen. He ended up at her shut bedroom door and was intrigued by the bright pink flowers she had painted on it. "Your landlord let you paint the doors like that?"

"Sure."

"Mind if I have a look inside this room?" He grabbed the knob.

Joy put her hand over his before he could open the door. "Better not."

"Is that where you get your painting done?"

"That's where I sleep."

He slid his hand away from the knob but still held onto Joy's hand. "Pardon me, it isn't like me to ask a girl to her bedroom without catching her name. I've been walking all around your apartment and haven't even caught your name."

"Didn't you see my signature on the paintings? My name is Joy."

"Your handwriting's too sloppy to read, Joy. Joy. I think I like that name."

"But you're not sure."

"Maybe there's a way I could test it out." He nodded to her door. "If you know what I mean."

"I don't think so." Joy pulled her hand away from his.

"That's too bad, baby." Officer Chambers turned the knob.

"Don't go in there or…"

Officer Chambers opened the door and stepped in. Joy stayed in the doorway. Chills brought out goosepimples on her skin. Officer Chambers patted his hand on her bed. Then he saw the reassembled painting of the Engstrom House. DIE was still written in blood on the wall.

"Or what? You gonna kill me too? Just like you killed your friend?"

"No," Joy said. The coldness in her bedroom was growing. She pointed past him. "He will."

Officer Daniels spun around to face the Shadow Man. The Shadow Man's hands grew into the gigantic paws of an otherworldly monster with long sharp claws that plunged into Officer Chambers's chest. As blood spewed from his torn up body with every beat of his heart, the officer was thrown into Joy's wall and the back of his head split open.

The Shadow Man grabbed the officer's shadow and brought his head forward; just like with Veronica, his body moved although nobody was touching him. Then the Shadow Man pushed the officer's head back and it cracked again to reveal the bulk of his brain drooping between his skull.

A desperate hand stretched across the room for Joy. Joy stayed where she was and watched as the third and final pounding of Office Chambers's head into the wall split his head completely in half. His body twitched on the floor. He did not have long left.

The only sound in Joy's room was the clock on her wall ticking down the final seconds of the officer's life.

20

THEY DROVE THROUGH THE night.

"I have to confess something to you," Colleen said. "I hope you don't take this the wrong way."

"Huh?"

"I'm jealous of you."

"Of me?" Samantha shook her head. "You shouldn't be."

"I never told you about Amy. My only child. She's gone now, but I feel like she's watching over me. Seeing you with your daughter, it reminded me of the life I could have had."

They were quiet for a little while.

"If you knew everything about my life, you wouldn't be jealous."

The Engstrom House brooded sickeningly on its hill. The sky was dark despite the fact that it was early in the day; rain would be falling soon. Whippoorwills sang nearby. Something subliminally passed by the upper windows.

The house was alive.

Chills washed over Colleen as she and Samantha exited Samantha's car. Two other cars and the doctor's van were parked alongside them. Margaret must have stayed—must have been carrying on Dr. McDowell's work.

"Margaret's still here…" Samantha said.

"We'll need all the help we can get."

Samantha reached into her back pocket for her copy of Handbook for Beginning Spirit Mediums. "I crammed at all of our stops but there's nothing in this book that tells me how to deal with evil houses."

"Maybe they were saving that for volume two."

They went up the muddied path; it had rained the night before. The gate was cold in Colleen's hands. It creaked wide open under her touch, inviting them in. They stepped through together; the gate closed on its own behind them.

Samantha opened the front door and stepped in. "*Margaret? Anybody home?*"

The living room had been transformed. At its center was a wide detestable machine glowing with a sickly green luminosity; the intricate machinery's tubes, rods, and purposes were wholly strange. White electrode wires ran from the far side of the structure and were secured to the walls.

A floorboard had been removed and another machine was half-buried in the ground; a metal rectangle that looked hastily put together. Orange cords stretched from that and had been dragged from the living room to the entryway into the rest of the Engstrom House.

Samantha and Colleen stepped slowly and carefully through the living room to examine all the strange changes. Some of the patches of wall that had been torn or rotten and exposed plaster board slats had been fixed.

"She's been taking care of it," Samantha said. "Like it's her patient."

Colleen felt a chill. "What does this machine do?"

"I've never seen anything like it before."

"Was this not in the handbook?"

"Must be another thing they were saving for volume two."

"I didn't think you two would be back." Margaret had entered without a noise and hugged each of them. *"How have you been?"*

How to even answer that?

"We've made some incredible finds," Margaret said, not giving either of them time to respond to her question. "Oh, where are my manners? Are you two hungry? There's some *fantastic* restaurants nearby we go to all the time. What are you gals in the mood for?"

"We?" Colleen said. "Who else is here?"

"After everyone left me and Scott stayed around. We had some drinks at the bar and decided to stick to McDowell's plan."

"All this is to finish his book for him?" Colleen asked, turning her attention back to the strange machine in the middle of the room that glowed with that sickening green shine. "Is that what you're doing here?"

"Sorta kinda. There's so much more that can be done here than finishing a book."

Samantha wandered toward one of the electrode wires and touched it with her fingers. She was spellbound by the strangeness of what the Engstrom House's living room had become. "It's like this house is your patient. You've got it hooked up like a man in a hospital."

"Careful with those, Sam. It's important we don't move anything or loosen the wires."

"What do they do?"

"Scott can explain better than I can."

"Where is he anyways?"

"He's in the darkroom developing some photos. Let me go get him, he'll be happy to see you two."

Margaret left the room. Colleen and Samantha stepped over wires so they could sit on a couch together.

"Why is she so excited?" Colleen said.

"I dunno. And I can't believe they've been in here for over… what now, two months?"

A chill climbed up Colleen's back. "Something about this is giving me a bad feeling."

They were silent for a little white. Colleen left the couch and walked around the machine, examining it in further detail. On the side where the electrode wires extended, she discovered a white screen with a black graph moving up and down like waves.

Samantha followed the orange cords out of the room. "Come look at this."

The orange cords each went in other directions; some went up stairways, some turned corners and went into nearby rooms. One cord directly ran under the main spiraling staircase and was connected into a bizarre contraption; a dark pedestal about four feet off the ground, and on its surface was a cylinder holding a glass sphere identical to Samantha's. Within it was purple smoke.

"How do you like the place?" Scott said from the entryway into an adjacent hall. Margaret was with him. "Can't believe after all this time that anyone showed."

"What is all this?" Colleen asked.

"Months and months of hard work using all the resources that doc left behind."

"What do all these things do?"

"I don't have the explanation you want. It would take too much time to walk you through two months of research and experimentation and discovery. But what I can show you is perhaps the greatest breakthrough mankind has ever seen—the broken barrier between our reality and the other side. Doc would be very proud."

"Margaret, Scott," Samantha said, "there's some stuff you two should know. The house—"

"I apologize I wasn't quite prepared yet to give this presentation," Scott said, not allowing Samantha to finish. "You two wait for us in the living room. I have to throw a few last-minute things together."

"Listen to me," Samantha said. "The house followed us…"

There was no point in finishing. Scott and Margaret went away through a hall into a room whose door could not close because an orange cord passed through it and connected, Colleen assumed, to another unusual mechanism.

"What is wrong with them?" Colleen said.

"I've got an awful feeling about this."

Colleen and Samantha waited for the others in the living room. About a minute later Scott wheeled in a rusted cart—*Did they find that thing in the basement?*—with a white tarp thrown over it taking the shape of the containers and objects beneath.

"Prepare yourselves," Scott said, "some of this stuff is not done growing."

Margret reached under the covering and brought out a jar of red pieces of *flesh* that wiggled around the jar. *Pulsing. Moving.* Margaret held the jar out to Colleen who pulled back from it in terror.

"Muscle that is alive independent of a body," Margaret said, then she held it in front of Samantha next who had a similar reaction as Colleen's. "No heart, and yet the blood within it flows. It's alive."

"What the hell." Samantha shielded her eyes.

"But wait, there's more," Scott said. He brought out a small glass box containing a brown eyeball. The eye twitched. "We found this one in this very room."

Colleen's stomach clenched.

Margaret presented them another jar; this one contained a reddish oval-shaped organ. "His liver was growing out of the basement! This thing was a quarter of the size when we cut it out! And not only has it regrown in this jar, but it's still growing in the basement! If we mess up, we have a spare!"

"Doc will have a body back in no time."

"A body?" Samantha screamed.

"What are you two talking about?" Colleen said.

"This." Scott pulled the covering off the metal cart. A half-complete skeleton was surrounded by jars and boxes. Strips of skin and muscles had grown over the bones sporadically. "We're growing doc his old body back—maybe a little thinner this time. God knows he needs to lose a couple dozen pounds."

"I always told him to diet." Margaret nodded. "This must be the world's quickest weight loss program."

"You can't do this." Samantha left the couch and backed away from the atrocious display of dismembered parts. *"This house needs to burn down."*

"What's wrong with you?" Scott said. "It's only a body. We thought you two would be happy that we've made such progress."

"This house followed us. The demon that possessed Dr. McDowell possessed my friend then murdered four children. It threatened to kill my baby. We came back so we can destroy it once and for all."

"So what exactly do you want to do?" Margaret asked.

"Burn this house down," Samantha said. "End it all."

"We've got research to do and we're helping doc." Scott covered the body again with the tarp. "If you want to help us, you're welcome to stay. There's still some time left on the lease. If you want to leave, you know where the door is. But nobody's burning this place down. We're so close and cannot end it now."

"I don't think you're understanding me. Four children died. My friend died. It was the same demon that possessed McDowell. It isn't gonna stop until our lives area ruined and we're all dead. That *monster* you're growing is not the doctor. It never was and it's never gonna be."

"There's the door." Scott pointed at it with his thumb. "Let's not fight over this."

"You two have gone crazy."

"Crazy? This is science. Maybe I should have given you two some more explanations. Like I said, there's so many months of research and experimentation that would take too long to explain, but let me give you a brief rundown." Scott tapped his hand on the glowing green machine. "This thing was partially an invention of Dr. James McDowell himself, and perfected by me and my lovely assistant Margaret. Physiological Supernatural Interface—PSI for short. These wires are hooked up to the house so that not only can we monitor—"

BAM!

Everyone's attention was abruptly turned to the front door being kicked in. Joy was back. A shotgun in her hands and a barking Saint Bernard at her side. Both Joy and her pet were covered in thick blood.

"Go to hell," Joy said. She fired two shots into the PSI machine.

"What are you doing?" Scott said. *"Stop your fire! This machine's the only thing maintaining the house!"*

Joy kept firing bullets into the machine. Colleen, Samantha, and Margaret took cover.

"We've got to end it once and for all."

Scott reached into his back pocket and brought out the gun that McDowell had used to kill Mrs. Wilson. He pointed it at Joy and fired without aiming.

21

JOY'S CAR WAS APPROACHING eighty miles an hour. The last thing she had expected to have on her hands that day was two dead bodies. There was no getting around the fact that she would be found guilty. It would be impossible to convince anybody that she had not murdered Veronica and that she had not murdered Officer Chambers.

There was only one place to go, and Joy did not know which way would take her there. She drove away from her apartment without any set direction or route in mind. The only maps she had were left in her kitchen drawer in her apartment—the same apartment that was probably swarmed with police officers by now investigating the death of one of their own. Joy shivered. Her life was ruined. And the only way she could try to fix it was by going back to the Engstrom House and destroying the evil that possessed it. Joy knew that she was in the grasp of the house's vengeance.

She wanted to stop because she was thirsty, but she was paranoid. Would she make the news? Would the police suspect her already? She felt like an idiot—*Who else would they suspect?* She tried to rationalize a decision to stop, but her mind kept coming up with reasons not to stop.

I need water.

Don't stop. Someone will recognize you.

No they won't. I'm not on the FBI's most wanted list. I haven't been gone long, and news doesn't spread that fast. A police officer, I'm sure, dies every day and I've never heard about it. No one will recognize me.

But what if they do?

Joy shivered. *Then I'm shit out of luck.*

Nighttime came faster than normal. By six PM it was pitch black outside. She didn't know what town she was in; she was far from home, and who knew if she were headed in the right direction. The diner was the only thing she had seen in the endless stretches of land, so she stopped there. She parked her car at the end of the lot behind the building and was surprised to see there were five other cars already parked there.

This was as far as her car could take her. She unscrewed the license plates then used a file from the toolkit in her trunk to scratch off the vehicle identification number. Past the parking lot was a little swamp of murky water. Ducks swam. Bees hummed. For a place in the middle of nowhere, it was full of life.

Joy threw the plates in. They sank immediately. She walked away, stomach growling, then turned back around and threw her keys in after them.

Even outside the front door of the diner Joy could hear music playing through the speakers. Ethel Waters.

A couple men sat on barstools playing cards. A man and woman sat in a booth with a kid who was dozing off and leaning on the woman's arm. One waitress was refilling the men's coffee while the other waitress took empty plates off the counter from a customer who must have just left. Joy took a seat in the booth furthest away from everybody. It was nice to take a break from driving—the only breaks she had previously taken were to refuel—and it was nice to pretend, even for a few minutes, that things were normal still. But she knew she could not let her guard down. She had to stay on her toes.

She opened her small purse. Inside was hardly enough to order a small coffee and a donut when the waitress came by and asked her what she'd be having. Joy drank her coffee and leaned her head on the window. She was not only a million miles from home, but a million miles from her old life that she craved to have back and probably never could reclaim.

Her stomach growled. She searched through her purse again but knew that all of her money was split between her bank account and the in-wall safe in her apartment. There was no money left with her. Joy's heart broke at the thought that she'd either have to become a thief or would have to dive into a dumpster for her next meal. Which would it be?

She buried her face in her arms. The sobs were trying to burst out of her, but she held them back. The last thing she needed was to draw attention to herself in this diner while she was on the run—but she had completely failed.

Then somebody sat across from her.

"Hello," he said.

Joy lifted her head a little bit over her arms. The man must have been about forty. KEYSTONE FREIGHT on the shoulder patch of his uniform—a button-up shirt whose first two notches were unbuttoned. Below that was the name FRED sewn into his shirt. Fred removed his black hat and set it aside on the table.

"Pardon me, ma'am, for intruding. Couldn't help but notice you were sitting all alone. Mind if I join you?"

"Go ahead." Joy grabbed a tissue from the dispenser and wiped her eyes. She was embarrassed that a stranger had seen her cry.

"Did you already order supper?"

Joy nodded.

"What's good here, ma'am? It's my first time at this establishment."

"The coffee's good."

"That's all you had?"

"A glazed donut."

Fred found the menu, opened it, and slid it in front of Joy. "Please. On me."

"Oh no, I couldn't."

"Look, I can't let a lady sit here crying and do nothing about it. Let me help you out. Order whatever you'd like."

Joy ordered a burger and fries and a coffee refill. Fred had the same order.

"I can't thank you enough."

"Don't worry about it."

They were silent for a little while. A waitress came by and took their dishes.

"Hey," Fred said, "I'm no idiot. It looks like things are going rough. Believe me, I've been there. And I've seen it a helluva lot too—driving across America, you see just about everything. It'll turn around. Always does."

"Thank you so much. I can't thank you enough."

Fred put down the money for the meal and a couple dollars for a trip then checked his watch. "It's about time now that I get back on the road. It was nice meeting you. Say, I don't think I caught your name."

"Jessica."

"Pretty name. Have a good night, Jessica."

Fred put his hat back on and left. Joy watched him leave the diner. She couldn't stay here all night—the employees were already giving her strange looks. Nervously Joy grabbed the two dollar tip and put it in her purse without the waitresses seeing, then she slid out of the booth and smiled at the workers.

"Have a good night," the lady who waited on Joy and Fred said.

"Thanks, you too."

The headlights of Fred's truck were blinding. Joy waved and called his name but he hadn't seen her or head her, and pulled out of his parking spot and left. Joy ran after his truck with her arms frantically waving, shouting his name. The truck was partway onto the street when it stopped and reversed.

Joy was out of breath climbing up the little steps to the passenger side. She hopped in and shut her door using both hands.

"Somehow I knew I hadn't seen the last of you," Fred said.

"Thank you so much for stopping."

"Where you headed?"

"As far away from here as possible."

"I'm heading south. That good enough for you?"

"Sure. Actually I need to get to a place called Ashfall."

They were off into the night.

"Normally I don't pry, but a lady crying in a diner comes running up to my truck begging to go… anywhere at all. I'm not harboring someone I shouldn't, right? I'm not getting in the middle of something I shouldn't be in the middle of, aren't I?"

"No," Joy said, taking a few seconds pause to create the many lies she would need to keep track of. Already she had to keep reminding herself that she had lied about her name. "My husband left me after a nasty fight. That's all."

"You had a fight in the diner?"

"No. The diner's just where I ended up."

"What was your fight about?"

"I didn't love him anymore. There was somebody else."

"Someone else. Is that who you're gonna go see in Ashfall?"

"Uh-huh. So thank you. Without you I don't know how I'd get there."

"No problem."

"How long have you been a truck driver?"

"Coming up on year number nineteen. Might seem like a long time to somebody as young as you are, but it goes fast I tell ya. All those miles fly by. You know, it's nice to have someone with me for a change. This kind of job gets lonely. Sometimes more than anything, you just want somebody to talk to."

"I see."

"Yeah, but the job has so many great things going for it. The chance to see America and spend some time in each place you visit. I have at least one good friend in every state. Hey, Jessica, with all the turmoil you hear about in the news, you might think the world's gone to hell, but it does your heart some good to see the kindness that exists throughout our lovely nation."

"That's good to hear."

They were quiet a little while longer. Miles of road passed by. Fred switched lanes to cut off slow drivers. Joy shut her eyes and leaned against the window but couldn't get comfortable enough to sleep.

"You awake?"

Joy shifted to face him. "Not so easy to sleep with so much on my mind."

"Still thinking about that fight with your husband?"

"He said some awful things that I can't get out of my head."

Fred pointed his thumb over his shoulder. "Back in the cabin there's a few blankets. Feel free to take one. And don't worry about Bandit, he don't bite."

Joy wobbled past the front seat and into the cabin where she found a blanket neatly folded at the end of an inflatable mattress. Asleep against the opposite side of the truck was a Saint Bernard. Joy brought Fred's blanket back to her seat with her and curled up with it. It kept her warm but her mind still could not wrap around sleep.

"You can talk about it," Fred said. "If you want."

"Fred, let me ask you. Is there really goodness left in the world?"

"You've only gotta look around."

Joy stared deep into the farmland they were passing. "I don't see anything."

"Isn't there anything that gives you any joy?"

"Painting. But I quit that. It… stopped being fun."

"Maybe the change of scenery is what you need to get creative again. Once you get to Ashfall I bet you won't be able to stop painting. What kind of things do you paint?"

"Wildlife."

"What's your favorite animal?"

"Foxes. I like painting their fluffy tails."

Joy shut her eyes and tried to sleep again. This time sleep found her. It didn't last long.

Not much time must have passed because when she opened her eyes again the area was still dull farmland. The sky was still decrepitly black. She yawned and turned a little bit in her seat, rubbing her eyes.

"Morning, sleepyhead."

"How long was I asleep?"

"Twenty minutes at best."

Joy sat there without saying anything. Fred was quiet too. A few minutes later, they were coming up on a truck stop called THE GUZZLE. They were finally out of the seemingly endless ugly farmland that Joy detested.

"Get in there and get me a full tank on pump three."

"I don't have any money, Fred."

"Pretty girls like you don't need money to buy a tank of gas."

"You can't be serious."

"Gas, grass, or ass. Nobody rides for free."

Joy gulped. "I'll be right back."

She was the only person in the gas station. The guy behind the counter was a pudgy man in his thirties with a patchy beard. He looked her up and down.

"How's it going?"

"Good," she said. "I need a full tank on pump three. I don't have any money."

His smiled widened. He opened the employee-only door that led behind the counter. "That's just fine with me, gorgeous. That's just fine. Come on back here."

Joy hesitantly obeyed. "I don't normally do this."

"You don't have to pretend."

"I'm serious."

"Uh-huh." The man undid his belt then unzipped his pants.

Tears gathered in the corners of Joy's eyes. She dropped to her knees. Nerves tightened in her stomach; she was disgusted. Then, as the man came a little closer, something on the wall caught Joy's eye.

A shadow.

A living shadow.

The Shadow Man's head bent back on his long hideously bent neck. He was smiling, unveiling long fangs like those of a sabretooth tiger. The Shadow Man crept up to the gas station employee's shadow with his sharp claws ready to pounce.

Joy laughed at the shock and terror on the employee's face. Blood gushed from his body as the unseen attacker ripped his flesh apart. Life was leached from the man's eyes. During the chaos of the kill, Joy walked away.

She grabbed a handful of plastic 'Thank You' bags next to the register and went around The Guzzle filling the bags up with any food, candy, or drinks she could find. Sunflower seeds. Beef jerky. Lollipops. Anything would do, especially when on the run.

The Guzzle sold hot food as well. Hotdogs, nachos, breakfast sandwiches. She grabbed as much as she could fit into the bags and as much as her arms could carry.

A very successful trip.

Fred was filling up the truck at pump three. His back was turned so that he did not see her at first. He was whistling a song then stopped when he heard her footsteps. He faced her, asking how it went, then did a double take when he saw how many bags she walked out with.

"You got all that?"

"Yep."

"Hey, watch the truck, Jessica. I need to take a leak."

"The restroom's out of order. But here, I brought you back a cup." Joy set the bags down and reached inside for an empty cup. "Hope it's big enough."

"It'll suffice."

A couple minutes later they were back on the road. Joy ate a hotdog and drank an orange soda. Fred was giving her sideways glances; she wondered what he was thinking. Did he suspect her of something? Joy shuddered. There was no way he could have known what happened inside that gas station—the Shadow Man's attack came so quickly that his victim had no time to scream.

At a red light, Fred leaned close to Joy. "Geez Jessica, is that blood on your hand? Did you have to beat somebody up to get all of this food?"

"No, silly, that's just a little catsup from my hotdog." Joy dipped the hotdog in the blood on her hand then handed it to Fred. "Want a bite?"

"Don't mind if I do." Fred ate about half the hotdog in one bite.

HONK! HONK!

The light had turned green and Fred hadn't noticed. He put his foot back on the gas, and their travel into the night continued.

There must have been many more places in America that were long stretches of dull farmland than Joy had thought, because that's exactly where they were when Fred stopped again. A town about as small and as ugly as Ashfall. There were no diners or Guzzle truck stops or any signs of life anywhere around them.

"I'm getting tired. Even a trucker needs a break." Fred climbed out of his seat. "Bandit, come on, bathroom break."

Fred and Bandit walked from the highway a short distance to the grassy area that was the far side of a quiet farm. Joy stretched her legs far away from them, wondering how far she was from Ashfall, and if he were even taking her in the right direction. Would it be impolite to ask? He had already done so much for her.

"Isn't it peaceful out here, Jessica?"

"Sure is."

Fred and Bandit climbed up the steps back into the truck. Joy followed. She cuddled up on her seat again with the blanket Fred had given her earlier.

Joy wondered what was happening back home. Joy wondered what all of her and Veronica's friends were thinking about this situation. She wondered what theories they were sharing—theories, she assumed, that Joy was always jealous of Veronica, or having an affair with Veronica's husband and had to kill her so that they could be together. But there would be too many holes in those latter theories, like that Joy left town and Veronica's husband was still there. And then there was the matter of the dead police officer—they would have a hard time fitting him into their theories.

The officer was wise to the affair, Joy guessed one of them would say during all the speculation. *So she had to kill him.*

No, no, that doesn't make sense. What could the officer have said that was so bad Joy would kill him?

He knew what was happening! Joy freaked out!

No, that can't be it.

Joy thought about Officer Chambers and his family, and the pain they must be going through. It made her guts twist thinking about his life ending. She wondered if he was a father. It made her cry to think about a child losing a parent.

Joy hadn't realized she was so tired. Sleep was finding her easier than it had before. Then Fred broke it.

"You might be more comfortable back here. With me."

"What?" Joy said without turning back.

"You might be more comfortable on a mattress."

"I think I'm okay here. Thanks though."

A few seconds later, Fred was kneeling next to her seat, extending his hand. "Jessica. There's a lot of room for us both."

"I said I'm comfortable enough right here."

Fred put his hand over hers; she was too scared to pull it away. "Are you sure?"

"Uh-huh."

Fred moved his hand away. "If you change your mind, just come back here."

"How far are we from Ashfall?"

"I don't know exactly."

"Where are we?"

"Hollow Hill. Southern town. We're close enough. Maybe half a day's drive ahead of us, maybe a little more."

"Thank you. Goodnight."

"I know you've got somebody in Ashfall you're eager to be with, but you're not with your husband anymore. You're not even wearing your wedding ring."

Joy looked down at her hand. That was right—she lied about having a husband and hadn't even thought about explaining away her wedding ring.

"Fred... I don't see you that way."

"Jessica, I need this."

Joy pulled her hand away from him. "Please stop."

Fred left her alone. He went to sleep on his mattress. Joy couldn't rest after Fred touched her; she was too scared of what he might do to her if she fell asleep. So she waited there, not moving a muscle, staying completely still and quiet until the right opportunity came for her to sneak out. Until she knew he was asleep. She must have stayed frozen for two hours just to be certain he was asleep and would not wake up and talk to her, or try and touch her again.

She cringed opened the door. It made a little noise, but not enough to wake a man. She tiptoed out of the truck, leaving behind most of her Guzzle loot as an offering so that way Fred wouldn't be too mad at her.

She was free of Fred and his truck and his filthy touch. The sun was rising. The impossibly long night was over and done with. About a half a day's truck ride to Ashfall, Fred had told her at one point when she had asked how far she was from Ashfall.

A hand wrapped around her forearm; Joy screamed.

"Don't leave me, Jessica."

"My name is not Jessica!"

Fred pulled her back into the truck. Her fists beat weakly against him; she was too weak to overpower him. He dragged her past the front seats and into the back to the mattress then pushed her down.

"Why are you leaving? Didn't I treat you good?"

"Yuh-yes you did. You treated me very, very good."

She didn't know what to do; she was powerless and at his mercy. Fred opened an overhead compartment; Joy wondered if she could get past him while he was momentarily distracted. She decided not to make a move so fast; maybe she really could catch him while he was asleep, or abandon him at another truck stop—go into the washroom then climb out the window.

Fred pointed the shotgun at Joy. "I didn't want it to have to come to this."

"No no no Fred please—I'll give you what you want. Put that gun down. I'll give you what you want."

Fred lowered it but didn't put it away. His smile was ear to ear. He sat down next to Joy, shotgun pressing into her body, and kissed her. Joy wanted to pull away from him but knew that if she did, he would pull that trigger.

She shut her eyes and pretended she was somewhere else. Anywhere but here. Then she had a better idea. Maybe she could find a way to get rid of him.

Am I really a killer?

He had the shotgun in his hands. His grip was loosening as he was preoccupied kissing Joy up and down her neck. If she pried it away from him, could she fire in time? Was the thing even loaded? Joy had no idea how to tell, and had never fired a gun before.

Gently she pushed him away with the tips of her fingers. She had to play it cool. "Slow down a little, Fred."

"Uh-huh." His free hand ran along her leg. For the first time, the shotgun was pointed away from her so that he could inch closer.

Maybe soon, Joy thought, he'd let go of it.

He kissed her again. She kissed him back to give him the illusion that she was enjoying it. The whole thing happened a lot quicker than Joy could have hoped for: both of his hands lifting her onto his lap, then both of his hands traveled up her back and entwined in her hair. The gun was inches away. And Joy was determined to get it.

She pulled away carefully from the kiss then pressed the tips of her fingers to his chest. She pushed him calmly until he was laying down.

"That's it," Joy said.

She really sold it. As he laid down she kissed his neck just like he had kissed hers. He let out a moan—Joy buried her laugh in her throat and stopped it from escaping.

"Close your eyes, baby."

He did so.

Joy jumped from him and clutched the gun painfully tight in her hands. She kicked him and moved backwards over the mattress to put room between them. Fred's red face was twitching with anger.

"Hands above your head."

Fred did so. "You stupid whore."

Joy pulled the trigger. Nothing happened. Fred laughed and tugged the shotgun from her hands. Joy wept. Now what was he gonna do with her?

As tears swelled in her eyes, Fred was temporarily covered in a flash of light from the nearby window. Other trucks were coming down the highway and their headlights seeped into Fred's truck as they passed by.

Bandit was barking all of a sudden at the empty seats in the front of the truck behind Fred.

"To make a gun work," Fred opened the compartment again and pulled out a container, "you need bullets."

Light poured into the truck again. Fred could stuff all the bullets he wanted into that gun, but they'd all be useless against the formless terror he was about to encounter. A million shots wouldn't put one bullet hole into the Shadow Man.

Fred pointed the gun at Joy again. "Let's see if you'll be a good girl this time."

"Uh-huh. I promise I'll be on my best behavior."

"Excellent."

Three steps. That was as far as Fred had gotten. And for a split second, until the Shadow Man wrapped a hand around Fred's newfound shadow cast by another oncoming truck, Joy thought that she had only imagined the Shadow Man's presence here with them in Fred's truck. The Shadow Man twisted Fred's wrist completely around; the shotgun fell to his feet.

Bandit pulled against his restraint; he was tied up and couldn't move. He wanted to help his master, but there was nothing he could do.

Joy went down the steps and out of the truck.

What she had not accounted for was the absence of oncoming trucks. With no light flowing into Fred's truck from the lack of passing headlights, Fred had no shadow, and the Shadow Man couldn't harm him.

Even with that broken wrist, Fred moved quick. Joy ran, but he was easily catching up with her.

"Jessica! Jessica! Get back here!"

Two trucks came up the road. Joy didn't need to do anything but watch.

The Shadow Man reappeared and dug his elongated fingers deep into Fred's flesh. The Shadow Man timed it perfectly. When the second truck was within a few feet, he tossed Fred in front of it, creating an explosion of guts. Blood rained down and soaked Joy. The truck that had disintegrated Fred swerved into the other lane and turned over sideways.

Joy brought Fred's shotgun back into Fred's truck with her and sat in the driver's seat. She cleaned off the blood that had splashed her, then she adjusted the seat and mirrors. She drove off drinking another soda. It was going to be a long drive ahead of her.

22

THERE WAS ONLY THE haze and the darkness behind her eyes.

Joy's eyelids wouldn't open. She'd never see again. Pain drummed through her body. Her spirit lifted then fell like a long wave washing against a withered rock. Sounds drifted around her, but they were broken; they fell on her ears but did not process, did not make sense.

Her head pulsed. She told her hands to move to her temples and rub away the pain, but they did not respond. She had no control over any part of her body. All she could do was lay there—lay there and pray that none of her pain and immobility was permanent.

The sounds flowing around her continuously became distant. A door opened then shut. She wondered what was happening around her.

It was a long time before her fingertips could move. And even longer before her hand could turn into a fist. Slowly her hand un-clenched. Her hand carefully lifted and reached her temple. Her eyes creaked open.

She was in bed.

A room in the Engstrom House. She was halfway covered with a blanket, but the room was burning hot so she lifted it away and tossed it aside. Her clothes stained with Fred's blood had been stripped off of her and tossed on the floor. She was in nothing but her bra and panties. Bandages were wrapped around her left shoulder; as she adjusted her body in bed, pain pulsed with vicious torture through her torso.

"I hate you, Scott."

She laid down momentarily. The urge to destroy the house helped her get back up. She shifted to her right—her good side that wasn't inflicted with the pain of a gunshot—and slid out of bed. Where was the shotgun? None of her things were in the room. Where was Bandit? Where was Fred's Chicago Cubs hat she had found in his truck and worn through the rest of her journey to the Engstrom House?

Darkness met her on the other side of the door. She kept her right hand on the wall for support as she passed through, following drifting voices that were as indistinct as she had heard them in the haze.

A glow seeped into the hall.

Joy peeked around the corner. All the others gathered together next to the spiraling stairway. Scott and Margaret on one side of the glass sphere and its pedestal; Samantha and Colleen on the other side.

Scott rubbed his hands on the glass sphere. "We've been able to make a little contact with doc through his own invention here. It's been... iffy but maybe I can get it to work again. Allow me to demonstrate. *James McDowell, can you hear us? It's me, Scott. I'm here with Margaret, Colleen, and Samantha. Are you with us?*"

Wisps of smoke inside the glass sphere intertwined and spread. The lights on the ceiling above them flickered. Goosepimples rose over Joy's body at the sudden rising coldness.

"Doc. Come on. Where are you?"

Flames spewed within the glass; Scott never moved his hands away. *"Doc?"*

Chilling screams uprose from the blaze inside the sphere. Two charred hands pounded on the walls of the glass from within it; skin was torn away from the palms and sharp edges of broken bones scraped against the ball.

Scott pulled his hands away from the ball. The tormented screams and all the glimpses of hell receded into nothingness. It was all a reminder of what Joy had come here to do; she had to put a stop to the hellishness in the Engstrom House's walls.

All eyes were on her.

Samantha walked over to her. "Joy, it's good to see you're feeling better. You gave us quite a scare."

Colleen followed her. "My clothes are in Sam's car. I think they'll fit you."

"Where is my shotgun?"

"We put it away," Samantha said.

"Where is it?"

"You don't need that shotgun," Scott said. "You almost destroyed all of our research with it. Do you even understand how much time, money, and effort has gone into this research? And you almost wasted every last cent we've spent, and all the countless hours Margaret and I put into this, not to mention everything the doctor did beforehand. You think all this was easy? Doing all this just the two of us and no—"

"Do you know how many people this house has killed?"

"Don't worry about the doctor, Joy. We're bringing him back."

"You can't bring him back, you psycho."

"Since you no longer have that gun of yours, we can show you what we've been working on without worrying about you tearing it to pieces." Scott stepped away from the machine that had shown a glimmer of hell. "Come with me."

"Where's Bandit?"

"Is that your dog?" Margaret said. "'Bandit is down the hall.'"

The room was the very last one in the hallway that they took Joy through. Scott pushed the door open and its hinges squealed. The room spacious room was filled wall to wall with equipment; radios, machinery hooked up to the walls as they had been in the living room, and a glass case in the center of the room that housed a human skeleton. Pieces of flesh stretched over the skeleton—pulsing. Squirming. *Alive.*

An eyeball in the case rolled out of the skull's eye socket and slid along the body until it came to the edge of the case closest to Joy. The brown eye was hooked to her, observing her reaction to the room that belonged to a madman.

A shelving unit had been set up on the far wall; flesh and muscle and tendons writhed as they had over the skeleton in the display case. Fingernails tapped against their glass prisons. Black hair overflowed from its container and wiggled out from under its lid. Some of the jars had electrode wires attached to them, generating reports on a machine whose needle moved up and down.

Chills slithered on Joy's back. There was so much to take in that she noticed Bandit last. His collar was attached to a spike in the wall that kept him from moving. Between his teeth was a piece of flesh that one of the monsters running this place had fed him.

"I know you're upset," Scott said, "but nobody was hurt to get these specimens. Well, that isn't so true. The doctor was hurt, but he's getting his body back. Remember when we saw his beating heart in the wall? His whole body's been spread throughout the structure of the house just like that."

"This isn't natural, this isn't right. Whatever you make in that glass isn't gonna be the doctor."

"How do you know?"

"This house has driven all of you insane."

"This is a scientific breakthrough that you almost destroyed. We've blurred the lines between life and death. We've talked to somebody on the *other side*. If James stays dead then this house wins. Now, I'll tell you what I told the others: if you don't like it, then you can walk out of here and never come back. Nobody is making you stay here."

Joy smacked him.

Scott's fist was about to hit her between the eyes, but Margaret held him back.

"You're gonna kill us all. You can't raise the dead."

Bandit spit out the meat he was chewing and barked at Scott; he pulled against his restraint, bending it in the wall but not breaking free.

"Joy, we're on the brink here. A few more days, tops. Don't do anything stupid."

Colleen laid down one of her outfits for Joy on the bed. A black skirt and a white shirt. She helped Joy put the shirt on because Joy couldn't do it herself. Samantha brought all of them coffee and a box of cookies.

"Scott and Margaret won't listen to reason, but maybe you two will. The house's evil followed me to my home. It made one of my paintings come to life and it killed my friend. Then it killed a police officer and I fled. It even killed the trucker who gave me a lift."

"We know exactly what you mean." Samantha put a hand on Joy's shoulder. "It followed me and Colleen to my home too. Somebody close to me died because of it. I came back here to end it once and for all."

"Then why are you two letting it continue?" Joy moved Samantha's hand off of her shoulder.

"Joy," Colleen said, "we have to think this through. That's where Dr. McDowell went wrong. He underestimated the house. We all showed up without a plan."

"You want a plan? Let's pour gasoline on the floors then light a match. Don't tell me really think those two weirdos can bring the doctor back to life."

"But you saw the doctor behind that glass ball."

"This isn't about the doctor to you, Colleen. You only care about that door your husband disappeared behind. But you're never gonna find that door and you're never gonna save your husband. He's dead."

23

THE HOUSE WAS QUIET that night. Margaret didn't quite like it—no matter how much time she spent in here with Scott, the quietness of the house in the dead of night disturbed her. She shined her flashlight across the hallway; all alone. The bulb brightened the stairway that ended the hall. Margaret descended with a strong grip on the railing.

The suspicion never lessened even with endless nights in the Engstrom House that somebody was watching her; that dozens of bulging eyes were always stuck to her. Margaret furtively peeked over her shoulder; all alone. But maybe, she thought, deep in the impenetrable darkness, creatures were lurking.

In the kitchen she turned the faucet on and filled up her cup. Icy cold. It soothed her throat on the way down. She filled the cup to the brim then went back to the stairway. Scott had woken up while she was gone; she could tell because he was playing one of the doctor's records—the sound drifted through the house and down the stairs. Beethoven's ninth symphony.

On the second floor Margaret found the library. Every inch of space in the room was cramped with bookshelves. On the old wooden desk—next to which was the turntable—were many notebooks open with diagrams of the machinery they used, like the Physiological Supernatural Interface, and stacks of books they had studied and highlighted many sections of.

Scott wasn't there. Margaret sat on the chair behind the desk to wait for him. She turned the pages of the notebooks, going over diagrams and the doctor's little notes and his quickly jotted entries. As she read them, the music mutated. Its rhythm stuttered and the tempo altered. The distorted sounds frightened Margaret; sharp worry choked her.

The record screeched under the splintery scratch of the needle.

A voice hissed. Indistinct at first, then becoming more clear as the transformed screech of a twisted symphony continued to play.

"Stay away."

The doctor's voice. Unmistakably the doctor's voice.

"Margaret," he said, his voice full of pain, *"stay away."*

"From what?"

"Don't... open... the gate..."

"What door? Doctor? What door? Doctor? Doctor?"

The hideous noises from the turntable subsided. In its place was the music that should have been there all along. Beethoven's ninth symphony. No hissing, no morphed noises, no distortion. Margaret lifted the needle from the record.

A book fell from the top of one of the bookshelves. Margaret knelt to pick it up; a stream of warm liquid trickled down onto her hands. She stepped back, grabbed one of the seats that were across from the desk, and set it in front of the bookshelf. Standing on it, she found a new organ growing out of the bookshelf; she couldn't quite identify it yet, but it was almost transparent. Stringy. Smelled awful. And clear liquid continually leaked from it.

Margaret was excited to add this new find to the reconstructing body. She crept quietly through the hallways to the stairway, where she saw Colleen coming the other way, presumably also heading for the spiraling stairway.

"I didn't think anyone else was up," Colleen said.

"I couldn't sleep. Now I'm burning the midnight oil doing research. Where are you going?"

"That door that Ambrose vanished behind had to reappear sometime. It was around this time when I lost him. Maybe it comes back every night at the same time. With what happened to the doctor two months ago, I never had the chance to find out." Colleen plugged her nose. "Oh God, what are holding? That stinks."

"Part of the doctor, I just found it in the library. Colleen, hold on, don't go looking for that door."

"Excuse me?"

"When I was in the library the doctor gave me a message. He said don't open the door."

"He said for *me* not to open the door? What are you talking about? What do you know that I don't know?"

"No, he didn't mention you. It was quick. He said to stay away from something, and when I asked what he meant, he said don't open the gate. That was the end of it."

"He could've been talking about anything."

"What else could he have meant?"

Colleen crossed her arms. "You're not stopping me from finding my husband. If it weren't for me you wouldn't even be here."

"Yeah, and the doctor would still be alive."

"You are *not* gonna blame his death on me. He knew this house wasn't normal. It's his fault he didn't prepare."

"Didn't prepare? What did you think he was doing the whole time leading up to our arrival? Dr. McDowell was meticulous. He planned out his days down to the minute. These whole three months were planned out before he ever reached out to you. And it doesn't seem to me that you wanted to find your husband much at all, where have you been for the past couple months while Scott and I worked our butts off to help the doctor? We had to clean up your mess."

"None of this is my mess."

"The doctor doesn't want you to open that door. It's a gateway. He must have said that for a reason."

"What reason?"

"I don't know."

"Then why are you yelling at me?"

"Because the doctor said not to open it."

"Prove it."

"I can't."

"Then I'm not gonna listen to you. You're a hypocrite. You're allowed to try these unnatural experiments to resurrect the doctor, and I can't open a door to find my husband."

"If your husband can be found then why haven't we seen any sign of him or that door? Me and Scott have been here for months, and we never saw any single sign of Amb—"

"You weren't even looking. You two were obsessed with your experiments. I bet you never thought once about helping me find my husband."

"Well it wasn't my job to look for your husband. All I'm saying is we've come across more than just the doctor in this house, and not one single thing in this endless place pointed toward a weird door or the man who supposedly disappeared behind it."

"Supposedly?"

"Uh-huh."

"Is that what this is all about? You didn't believe me that Ambrose disappeared."

"Let's see. You say your husband disappeared, but the room doesn't exist. Strangers found you on the side of the road miles from here and you said you had no idea what happened after you two split. Me and Scott spend months here and don't find one clue about your husband, but we find a million about the doctor."

"The doctor is growing out of the walls. And you can't believe that my husband disappeared?"

"Look, the doctor said not to open the gateway, so—"

"Isn't that proof enough for you? You said the doctor means the door my husband disappeared behind, then you said my husband never disappeared. Which is it?"

"You're putting words in my mouth."

"Are not."

"But you just said that I said—"

"I don't care what you think I just said you said, I know what you said, and you said that—"

"Shut up."

Arms wrapped around Margaret and pulled her away. Scott's familiar arms.

"What are you two yelling about? God Margaret what is that? It smells like piss."

"A new part of the doctor. It's from the library."

"Is that his bladder?"

"Let's add it to the body."

"Sure," Scott said. "Colleen, are you okay?"

"Yeah, thanks. Have a good night, Scott."

"Night."

Colleen went up the stairway. Margaret and Scott went into the Assembly Room as they called it.

Scott opened the skeleton's case. Margaret set the bladder in and it inched out of her hands and into place. The other pieces of flesh on the doctor's skeleton stretched and expanded. They seemed to generate quicker when more new pieces were added.

"So what was your fight about with Colleen?"

Margaret leaned over the glass container, observing the body parts while she talked. "I heard the doctor's voice in the record player. He said don't open the door. He didn't say which door, but I just thought, Colleen, you know, that's what she's here for. Is it a warning about that door?"

"Leave her alone. We're almost done here. When doc's put back together again we'll get out of here. Then Colleen can walk around here opening all the doors she wants."

24

COLLEEN ARRIVED ON THE third floor; her flashlight dimly cut through eternal darkness and brought her to the same place where she stood on that awful night nearly a year ago. The door in the corner of the wall was back.

Someone was crying.

Colleen lowered her flashlight. A little girl with her face buried in her knees, barely peeking over them to look at Colleen, was sitting in front of the door Ambrose had vanished behind. Her long hair was clumped with dirt. Stains all along her tattered clothes. The sobs never stopped.

Colleen knelt next to the child. "What are you doing here?"

"Please don't open that door." The girl's hair covered most of her face, but her sad blue eyes stuck through. "What you want isn't behind it."

"What's your name?"

"Teresa."

Colleen took the girl by the hand. "Come with me, Teresa."

Teresa stood up. "I hope when I grow up I can be as pretty as you."

They came to the main stairway. "I'm going to take you to meet some friends of mine."

As they descended the steps, a sickening scream ripped through the house.

His veins reassembled themselves and blood trickled through. Over time they filled until blood pumped regularly through them. His muscles took the shape of the bones over which they were placed. Skin pulled painfully tight over his new body. The organs were assembling themselves, connecting to each other, creating a system that could sustain life.

The production of a new body was always at work. At all seconds of the day, cells were generating, searching for the distant simultaneously forming components of the reconstructing corpse. The essence of a dead man becoming whole again under glass and heavy observation.

A past life was a dream.

When he closed his eyes and fell through the darkness behind them, he could almost bring himself back to another life. Another time when he had been whole. When he had been alive. Now he didn't know who he was. The memories in the back of his mind were eager to escape, but had not been reassembled yet.

Voices argued in his head. Who were they?

An unusual sensation touched his exposed nerves; his body convulsed at the sudden touch of cold.

His hands raised to his face. With his one eye he studied the regenerating pieces of himself that his caretakers had found. Nine out of ten fingers, mostly flesh now with only small sections of exposed bone. His arms were only a third of the way through the process of repair.

Muscles in the process of coming back into existence, tearing, healing stronger, lifted the glass casing from above the creature that had once been a man. The partly-formed body strained to sit up and set the lid aside without breaking it. Carefully he crawled out of the prison and left the room.

The house was his.

Long empty halls. Amorphous shadows taking unusual shapes. Floorboards creaked under his steps.

In the living room his memories were trying to form. Who had he been? What was he trying to remember? What had happened in this house that was so important? Perhaps when the brain inside his head grew to its full form, he could finally know.

Fists on the door. Somebody desperate to get inside and out of the storm.

The muscles in his hand instinctively knew how to grab a door-knob. He twisted it open. The man with the umbrella entered and did not see him.

"Anybody home? My apologies but my brother and I need a place to stay for the night. My name's Jack. Can anyone hear me?"

Creeping steps. He tiptoed up to Jack.

Jack stepped through the living room. "My apologies, I know it's late. Is there anybody in here? I saw some cars parked down in the lot."

The hands of the monstrosity jabbed into Jack's back and a stream of blood erupted. Agonizing screams fled Jack's lips. The monstrosity dug his fingers deeper and ripped Jack open wider. Jack swung his arms desperately to hit his attacker but never came close.

Jack's legs went slack and Jack toppled over. The monstrosity turned Jack on his back. There were footsteps racing all around the house; he had to work quick. He ripped away lumps of meat and snapped Jack's bones until he found Jack's heart.

Feebly beating. Giving out.

The monstrosity pulled it out of Jack's chest and bit into it. A growing body needed to eat.

Colleen and the girl were the first ones in the living room. The remains of a dead man were slumped in the center of the room. His chest torn open. His heart missing. Colleen shielded the little girl's eyes and turned her away from the harrowing remains of the stranger.

Who was he? What was he doing here? Tall man. Blond hair. Lanky. Ripped apart in seconds. The house, she knew, had claimed another victim. Poor stranger. His blood seeped in a slow crawl in every direction.

Margaret and Scott were the next to arrive. Scott had a gun ready in his hands. Joy and Bandit were next; Joy still didn't have her shotgun, and Colleen had no idea where Scott had hidden it. Samantha was the final one to enter the room.

"What happened?" Joy asked.

"We don't know. This is how we found him."

"Who's the girl?" Scott lowered his gun. "Christ, get her out of here."

"I found her upstairs. The door is back."

"Did you open it?" Samantha put her hand on Colleen's shoulder. "What happened?"

"I'm not opening it. I've seen how easily this house kills people, like Jane or this man here. But we've got all this equipment, let's do the research we came here to do. Let's test it and when it's safe I'll open it."

"You've put us through all this hell," Margaret said, "and you're not even gonna open the door?"

"An hour ago you didn't even believe there was a door. And Teresa wouldn't let me open it."

"Wait wait wait let's take a scientific approach to this," Scott said. He kneeled next to Teresa. "Teresa, tell me what you know about the door. Did you come from the other side of it?"

Teresa pointed at Jack. "He was a very bad man."

David, carrying two suitcases, pushed through the storm and ascended the hill. The gate was open. He set down the suitcase in his right hand and twisted open the knob, then picked the suitcase back up and walked inside to find the corpse of his dead brother, where four women, a little girl, and a man had gathered. The room was unlike anything he had ever seen before; a big machine hooked up wires to each wall, and orange cords ran from this room and through the entryway into the rest of the house. David dropped his bags and fell next to his brother's body, holding him and crying.

"Which one of you psychos did this?"

"It wasn't us. It was the house," the man said. "I'm sorry."

"Was it you? Did you kill him? Jesus Christ!"

One of the women crossed her arms. "Why are you blaming us? It was the house. Don't you know where you are?"

"Is all of you insane?"

The lady with glasses, who was holding hands with the little girl, put her hand on David. "I'm so sorry about your friend. But this house, you have to understand that it's—"

David hit her hand away. *"This is my brother! What have you all done?"*

"Don't hit her," one of the women said. "You ignorant—"

"Who killed my brother?"

"Just calm down," the lady with glasses said. "The house has hurt all of us. It took my husband away from me. But we're trying to..."

"Is anyone gonna tell me what goddamn happened?"

"We don't know," the man said. "Margret and I had just left the Assembly Room and were back in bed when we heard your brother's scream."

"Who are you people?"

"Researchers," the man said. "I'm Scott, this is Margaret, that's Colleen, Samantha, Joy. We were assembled here to research the house because Colleen's husband disappeared in here. Now we're trying to save the soul of the man who brought us all together—Dr. James McDowell. Are you familiar with him?"

"Who the hell is Dr. McDougall?"

"It's McDowell."

"What are you going to do to me?"

Scott laughed. "We aren't gonna do anything to you. We already told you we didn't hurt your brother. Do you need a room for the night?"

The room that Scott brought David to was on the first floor. David dragged his two bags to the edge of the bed then sat down. Tears still dripped from his eyes. Scott leaned against the wall near the door.

"Sorry again about your brother, man. I really am."

"Are you serious about this house?"

"It's alive. I've found a way to subdue it, but my system is faulty since Joy put a few bullets in it. You should've seen her on her rampage."

"How did this happen?"

"Dr. McDowell was possessed by a demon. It ripped him apart and the house absorbed him, and since then I've been working on a way to save him. He's contacted us from the other side."

David paused to run it all through his head. "Is there really life after death?"

"If this experiment goes as planned, there's resurrection after death. Want to see what McDowell's been up to since the house ate him up?"

Scott brought David to another room on the first floor. The Assembly Room Scott called it as he opened the door. David's stomach turned; body parts in jars. A partially constructed lifeform in a display case in the middle of the room. The work of an insane man. David did his best to hide his disgust and wondered if Scott could tell how sick David really felt by seeing the single eyeball move in the skull of the living dead carcass. Something sinister was in the veins of that creature; something menacing in its smile; something David could only define as the touch of the devil.

"This… this is McDougall?"

"It's McDowell."

David backed away from the glass case containing the *creature.* "How can he be alive?"

"Those details, well, I can't be certain of them yet. I suspect that when the house absorbed the doctor, his spirit lingered. The human body has all sorts of regenerative properties, like a broken arm that heals or a tear in your skin that clots. Willpower combined with those properties… maybe human beings are more capable of these sort of things than previously thought. Which, I hypothesize, could explain miracle cases in hospitals—cancer that suddenly disappears, patients with incurable diseases given six months to live but continuing a normal and healthy life for decades after their diagnosis. If we can understand how the human body regenerates, we could cure all diseases."

David pretended to stay calm as he headed for the door. "This is all too much for me. I'm going to bed."

"Have a good night. My condolences about your brother."

David stayed in his room for hours, waiting for the chance to escape. He peeked out the cracked door, suspicious that the insane group of people in this house might be watching him. David had a suspicion that the guests of this damned house had taken apart the man in the Assembly Room down to his skeleton, and perhaps they'd do the same to him. He couldn't stay here.

His grip was sweaty around the suitcase handles. He prepared himself to see his brother's corpse in the living room, but it was gone. Not a drop of blood left behind. In his mind he saw Scott and his deranged friends taking Jack apart. Playing with his body parts in the Assembly Room.

Out the front door. Nobody saw him. Nobody followed him. David was free.

Passing the gate he took one sickening last look at the house. In an upper window flashed a familiar face for one hurried second. His brother. Just as quickly as Jack appeared, he vanished.

At the base of the hill, David threw the bags into the car and slammed his foot on the gas. Even as he entered the Ashfall Police Department parking lot, he was going well over the speed limit. A speeding ticket was a very minor inconvenience if he were to get one; somebody had to put an end to the madness in that house.

An officer was entering the building with a coffee in each hand. Sawyer on his badge.

"You have to help me! They killed my brother! The McDougall cult!"

"McDougall cult? Out with it."

David paused momentarily to gasp for breath.

"Boy!"

"That house! On the hill! They killed my brother! Hid his body and cleaned up their mess! I would have been next if I hadn't escaped!"

Officer Sawyer and his partner, Officer Hooper, were on it. They drove back to the house with David in the back seat.

"Please let me stay back at the station. I want to be as far away from these wack jobs as I can."

"Can't do that, sir," Officer Hooper said. "You need to show us where the body is. You're a witness. You can't stay behind."

"How do you like this, Hooper? Our first couple weeks on the job and we're already being called up to the Engstrom House. How about that?"

"Rumor has it the reason there was even a vacancy for our positions is that the last couple cops who went up here vanished. Had I been there, let me tell ya, the loony cult would not have stood a chance."

"Yeah, yeah, Hooper. Keep dreamin', man."

"Bam!" Hooper threw some pretend punches. *"And it's a knock-out! Nobody can beat me because I am the greatest! They're not worthy of being my competition! No one is! Hooper always knocks them out with one punch! Maybe two if I go easy on 'em!"*

Officer Sawyer shook his head. "Get in the ring with my grandma and she'll pin you in fifteen seconds tops."

"Your grandma is eighty-seven."

"So? She can still get in the ring."

"I won't take it easy on her. She'll need a new pair of fake teeth when I'm done with her! She won't be able to open her mouth for a week!"

David had enough. *"You guys, tell me what happens now. Are you going to arrest them all?"*

"Depends how it all checks out," Sawyer said. "We'll have a look around so long as Hooper here can keep himself under control. He's the type to shoot first and ask questions later."

"Shoot them. Shoot them all. They killed my brother those psychos."

"Quiet down with that sort of talk," Hooper said. "You're sounding about as crazy as you claim those people in the house are."

David shut his mouth.

They arrived at the Engstrom House.

Chills crept under David's skin. He never wanted to see this house again, but here he was back within an hour.

The trees swayed although there was no wind. The brooding house welcomed David back with the flicker of a light in one of the lower windows.

His mouth was dry. The officers led the way. David wished he had a gun of his own to protect himself with, but having two armed cops along with him was better than nothing.

I'm so sorry, Jack, he thought.

Officer Sawyer was first through the unlocked door that was halfway open despite David having shut it when he left. The house was eerily darkened; the officers shined flashlights to reveal the apparatus that hooked up cords to the walls. The officers inspected closely. David stood near the door the whole time, ready to run outside if things went south.

"What do you suppose it is, Sawyer?"

Sawyer stayed silent for a few moments as he touched the wires. "Must be some deathtrap. Something the cult uses to torture their prisoners with. Tell us again how you escaped, David."

"I... walked out the front door. The bedroom they gave me was down the hall."

"They let you walk out the front door? What kind of cult is this?"

"Could be a satanic cult," Hooper said.

"See!" David said. "I told you something freaky is going on out here."

"Show us the body, David," Sawyer said.

"It's probably in the Assembly Room. That's what they called their torture chamber. Down the first hall to the right."

The officers followed his instructions. In the Assembly Room there were living body parts in jars on shelving units. Jack's bloody clothes on a metal cart. David staggered backwards as the repulsed officers took in the details of the squirming living pieces of flesh and the other horrific sights of the lab that could only belong to somebody demented.

Sawyer joined him at the door. "Let's sort it out down at the station. I want to get out of here."

Hooper was the last one to leave the room. "My God. I've never seen anything like this demented place."

Hushed steps through the hall. Fast passing moments of silence. The last peaceful seconds before Hooper's screams spewed into the temporarily quiet hall.

Sawyer drew his gun. David was stunned.

Faint light illuminated Jack pinning Hooper on the floor with both of his hands tightly grabbing hold of Hooper's head. Blood was already trickling through Hooper's thick hair. Jack's face drooped and a smile strenuously attempted to form. His body was disintegrated; torn and bleeding. Bones exposed.

"No! Buddy! They're here to help!"

Sawyer's gunshot missed.

"Don't shoot him! That's my brother!"

"That's my partner! Oh my God he's killing him!"

Jack lifted Hooper's head as Hooper strained to escape his grip, then madly smashed Hooper's face into the floor. Jack lifted Hooper's face again, Hooper gasped for breath, and perhaps Jack would have split his head open if Sawyer's next shot hadn't met Jack square in the chest. Blood spattered from the wound but had no effect on Jack.

"Put your hands where I can see them."

A short leap from Hooper to Sawyer; Jack snatched the gun with a jerk and twist out of Sawyer's hands then tossed it down the hall. He squeezed Sawyer's neck so tightly in a split second that Sawyer's eyeballs bulged in his skull and popped from their sockets; they dangled as Sawyer ran blindly and screamed. Hooper hardly had time in the madness to scramble up from the ground and grab his own gun. He took aim at Jack in the darkened hall.

David stood between them.

"Don't shoot! Don't kill him! We can save him!"

"You nitwit! That thing ain't your brother no more!"

As Sawyer collapsed and screamed in agony, choking for another breath, David and Hooper lost sight of Jack. Hooper picked up Sawyer's dropped flashlight and searched for the half-living monstrosity. It found him instead.

It lurked in the unseen corners of the hall and suddenly attacked Hooper from behind. Jack sunk his teeth into Hooper's neck and mutilated him. A mouthful of flesh. Jack drank the pumping blood that erupted from the wound.

David backed into the wall and sank to the floor.

When Jack was finished with Hooper, he crawled to Sawyer. Sawyer was praying.

"*Hail Mary,*" in a whisper, "*full of grace…*"

David watched between his fingers. Jack breaking open Officer Sawyer's chest. His heart's remaining beats reverberating in Jack's torn up hands. Deathly shivers pierced David's skin; he couldn't bring himself to look away. His brother ate the officer's heart.

Jack dragged his tired body to David's side.

"I don't know what they've done to you, but we're gonna get you some help."

Jack looked David in the eye. David put a hand on his brother's shoulder. Slowly Jack's face slid off and plopped to the floor revealing the same detestable skull as the one in the glass display case in the Assembly Room.

David's heart raced. He staggered an inch back on his hands and knees. "*You're not Jack.*"

The creature smiled.

Jack screamed. It was the begging shout of a dead man.

During the chaos, everybody slept peacefully.

Scott and Margaret were in each other's arms.

Joy slept with Bandit at her side.

Samantha dreamed about leaving the Engstrom House and going back home.

And Colleen dreamed about her little baby girl. She dreamed she was sitting in front of the fireplace, rubbing life back into her from the heat of the flames.

25

COLLEEN AWOKE TO THE sound of footsteps outside her bedroom door. Teresa was asleep next to her. She kissed Teresa's forehead then left the bed. The flashlight was on her dresser. She crept into the hall. Nobody was there.

The dim flashlight cut into darkness. It seemed that no source of light could ever completely pierce the Engstrom House's darkness as strongly as it could break into darkness elsewhere; there must have been things that the house wished to remain hidden.

CREAK!

CREEEAK!

CREEEAAAK!

Old floorboards weak under Colleen's touch.

Coldness curled around her skin. Footsteps in the murky darkness that her flashlight failed to illuminate. Colleen followed the steps through darkness until a green glow brightened the hall. The door was open again.

Colleen was breathless. She followed the hazy shine and set her fingertips on the door. She was going to push it open when an unbearably freezing hand gently touched her arm and brought it down. Ambrose looked as if he had not been gone a day. He was in his same outfit she had last seen him in. It was as if he had been transferred one year into the future but all that time had passed for him in a single minute.

His hand slid along her arm, up her neck, and to her cheek. "I knew you'd be back."

"I never stopped thinking about you."

Colleen kissed him. His lips were icy and numbing.

"What's in there?"

Ambrose shut the door. "It's best you don't look in there."

"What's in there?"

Ambrose grabbed her hand. "It doesn't matter anymore now that we're together. I'm so sorry I've been away from you for so long."

Together they walked through the third floor until they came to the spiraling stairway. They sat down on its steps together. Colleen leaned on Ambrose's shoulder. The coldness in his body never diminished.

"We can start over now," Colleen said. "We can have another child. We can be a family again."

"There's nothing in the world I want more than that." He squeezed her hand.

Another kiss.

"Why are your hands so cold?"

Ambrose said nothing.

Colleen grabbed both his hands in hers to warm them. "I wish we never spent a moment apart. Why did it take you so long to open the door?"

"None of that matters now that we're together. Let's enjoy this."

Silence fell over them. Colleen shut her eyes. It was heaven.

"There's a little girl that I found. Her name is Teresa. You'd love her. She has pretty blue eyes just like Amy did."

"Uh-huh."

"Let's take her with us. This is no place for a little girl. Why wait for morning? Let's leave now. Let's go get her. Let's drive away from here and never come back."

Ambrose stood up, still holding her hands. "Lead the way, my love."

Colleen led him a few steps away from the stairway when the child's scream erupted. It was coming from below. Colleen rushed down the steps with Ambrose. Her guts twisted sickeningly. They followed the miserable cries to the ground floor. They were coming from the living room.

The fireplace was enraged with wrathful flames stretching abnormally far. The irregular flames seemed to be the only kind of light that could ever slit open the Engstrom House's corrupt darkness. Within them, two hands were struggling to crawl out of the destructive inferno. Each attempt failed.

A stretch of flames receded momentarily to expose Teresa's face.

The same laughter of children echoed from the night Ambrose disappeared. The house was mocking Colleen again.

Teresa's skin melted in the blaze. There was no saving her.

Colleen buried her face in Ambrose's chest, shut her eyes, and cried. Tiny hands crawled over her arms. She brushed them away.

"I can't sleep."

Colleen's eyes opened for her to find that she had been dreaming. Teresa was at her side shaking her.

"Me neither."

Colleen looked around the room. It had felt so real. She could still feel the chills from Ambrose's cold touch on her hands.

"Come with me, Teresa."

"Where are we going?"

"I need to check something."

They went to the third floor. The electrode wires were connected to the door. It was completely shut. It had never been opened. She still hadn't found Ambrose. It had been a dream. A stupid dream. She was tempted to open the door already, but both Teresa and Ambrose had warned her.

It's best you don't look in there, Ambrose had said.

Colleen put her hand on the knob.

"Don't do that," Teresa said. "You'll regret it."

"Why? Why would I regret it?"

Teresa dragged her pointed finger across her throat.

A whisper behind the door. *"Help me."*

Colleen pressed her ear to the door. It was as cold as Ambrose had been.

"I know you're there. Help me, my love."

Colleen sobbed.

Teresa grabbed her hand and helped her away from the door.

Samantha looked into the glass sphere Scott had used to contact the doctor. She rubbed her hands on it and watched the smoke change and morph inside. A message was forming within; she was close to finding it when her little girl Brittany came to her from the living room.

Samantha picked up her four year old child. "Brittany? Where did you come from?"

"Daddy said we're visiting."

"Oh my God. You shouldn't be here. Where's your father?"

"I dunno."

Samantha shuddered. She stepped into the living room since Brittany had come from that direction. "Mark? Where are you? Damnit where are you?"

"Mommy you said a bad word."

"I'll put a dime in the swear jar later. Are you sure you don't know where Daddy is?"

Brittany tapped her chin with her pointer finger. "Upstairs maybe."

Samantha hurried up the spiraling stairway. *"Mark where the hell are you? What are you doing here? Oh my God we need to leave."*

On the second floor she heard bedsprings. A distant moan. Her gut twisted at the awful memory. Tears dripped from her eyes; she shifted Brittany in her arms so that she could wipe them away. The worst thing she had ever experienced—worse than anything that had happened to her since accepting Dr. McDowell's offer to come to the Engstrom House—was her husband's betrayal. Being unfaithful in their own bedroom. Samantha had tried her hardest to keep their marriage going. To keep her family together.

She found the hallway where the moans were coming from. The little girl Teresa was kicking a ball around at the other end. When Teresa saw Samantha she picked up the ball and came her way.

"Hi Teresa." Samantha set Brittany down. "Can Brittany play with you?"

"Of course she can."

The girls kicked the ball around. Samantha reluctantly approached the room. She turned the knob. Mark and Joy were making love on a dusty bed in an empty room. Neither one acknowledged her when she opened the door. Neither one seemed to know they had been caught.

Samantha slammed the door shut. The tears were so prolific in her eyes that everything was a blur, and she couldn't tell who or what she had bumped into. She staggered back with pain pulsing in her heart.

She wiped her eyes. It was Howard.

A smile on his face. A scar on his neck.

He put his arm around her. "I'm sorry."

They walked down the hall. Teresa and Brittany were kicking the ball around still. Teresa kicked it hard past Brittany, and Brittany chased after it.

Samantha wiped more tears from her eyes. "I thought he had changed. I thought he loved me again."

"I'm sorry."

Samantha's hands turned into fists. She moved out from under Howard's arm and beat her fists on the wall. "Why can't he love me? Why did he do this again?"

"I'm so sorry."

Samantha hit the wall with her fist again. *"I don't care if you're sorry. I wish I never tried to keep this marriage going. I wish I never*

*forgave him. I hate him. How could he do this to me? I wish… I wish
he'd drop dead."*

"You know what your problem is? You're a psychic that can see
everyone's problem but her own."

Samantha said nothing.

"You and your neighbors every time you got together, you always
picked the winner of every ballgame or Kentucky Derby," Howard
put his arm around her again, "but you couldn't tell your husband
was having an affair with the hostess. What kind of psychic are you?"

"I hate him."

"Were you just a good guesser?" Howard tapped her head with his
pointer finger. "Or was there somethin' special in here?"

Samantha was crying hard.

"The Samantha I know's special. She can do things others can't."

A door opened and shut and drew Samantha's attention. Joy
walking the other way down the hall; she was still half dressed.

Samantha's hands turned into fists. She found Mark in that bedroom again. He was asleep with the cover over his torso. Samantha
raised her hands from the doorway and his eyes snapped open. She
spun one finger and Mark's head turned in the same rhythm against
his will. His throat stretched painfully for his head to face her. His
eyes were wide in pain. He couldn't move under the power of her
invisible grip.

Her hands moved rapidly with their newfound power and Mark
was pulled from the bed to the floor. A smile across Samantha's face.
Her left hand turned into a fist again; Mark's hands wrapped around
his throat as he gasped for air. Her right hand struck, and Mark was
slammed into the wall head-first; blood spewed on impact.

When her left hand unclenched he could breathe again.

A quick fist again. Mark choked.

Her fingers tensed; incisions on Mark's chest. Blood trickled.

Samantha put her two fists against each other at her thumbs and gestured them into a *SNAP!* so that Mark's right arm broke. His eyes begged her to stop.

"Mommy! What are you doing to Daddy?"

Brittany was at her side.

"Your daddy deserves this."

SNAP!

His other arm.

"Say goodbye to Daddy, Brittany."

Samantha squeezed tight. Blood gushed from Mark's mouth.

Strange power circulated her veins. With every new movement her grip on Mark from across the room became stronger. Invisible hands burrowed into his skin and pulled apart his feet. Blood splashed through the room. Mark gasped and choked.

Samantha laughed madly. All at once his body parts were severed; his fingers, his joints, his eyes. He was being completely dismantled. Then Brittany ran between them.

"Stop hurting Daddy! Mommy stop it! Stop it!"

The otherworldly power was uncontrollable. There was no way for Samantha to shut it off. Brittany was caught in the middle of the display of power. Simultaneously as Mark was hacked apart, Brittany's head was pulled from her neck then her torso was severed in half.

Father and daughter together in pieces. Their blood gathered below their remains.

A scream left Samantha's throat.

Howard was at her side, holding her face straight so that she couldn't look away.

"Don't you feel better now that he's dead? You got your wish."

Teresa kicked the ball into the room. She was unaffected by the pile of bodies.

The interrogation room was dark. Joy couldn't break free of the awfully tight handcuffs.

The officers across from her struck matches to light their cigarettes. Joy hated smoke and choked on it when it drifted her way.

"Did you or did you not paint this confession?" One of the officers reached below the table and brought out a painting. Joy throwing Fred in front of an oncoming truck. Bandit barking in the foreground.

"No I did not," Joy said. The nervousness in her stomach grew. She had been caught.

"Your signature's in the corner of the painting," the other cop said. "You were very proud of your work."

"I didn't paint it. Honest. I don't know where that came from."

"The killer always returns to the scene of the crime."

"I didn't hurt anybody."

"We'll let the judge and the jury decide on that."

"Please believe me."

"Maybe you can tell us where this came from?" The second officer reached below the table and brought out a glass soda bottle. It was brimming with blood. He turned it over and dumped it on the table. An eyeball was within. "We found this at The Guzzle. Recognize a certain employee working the late shift?"

"I swear I didn't do anything."

"The evidence against you is staggering."

"There is no evidence."

"Maybe this will convince you otherwise," the first officer said.

He opened the door. Behind it was only darkness. From within, squeaky wheels ran over a creaking floor. A woman dressed in black with long sable hair draped over her face to conceal her identity pushed a cart into the room. There was a white sheet over it.

"Exhibit A," the second cop said, lighting another cigarette.

The lady with Sable hair pushed the cart until it was inches away from Joy, then she disappeared walking backwards through the threshold. The door stayed open.

The first officer pulled the sheet away. Veronica's mutilated naked body.

"It wasn't me it was the Shadow Man. It was the Shadow Man. I didn't do this."

"Let's see what she has to say about this."

Veronica's eyes opened. She moved grotesquely like a stiff marionette. Her joints cracked as she climbed out of the cart.

"Get away from me! Get me out of here! Stay away from me! I didn't kill you!"

The officers stood together at the door.

"We'll let you girls have a little time alone to figure it out," the first one said.

"I'll bring you back a hot coffee and an apple pie," the second one said.

The door slammed.

When Joy looked back at Veronica, she was gone.

Stillness in the room.

"Veronica I didn't kill you. It was the Shadow Man. I never wanted anyone to hurt you. You were my best friend."

"You were never sorry." Veronica's chilled words could have come from anywhere.

Joy stood up. Her hands were still handcuffed. Where was Veronica? Joy backed away into a wall, her eyes sweeping across the room, but there was nobody with her. She ran to the door and pulled it open to find Veronica waiting for her.

Veronica reached with a decomposing hand; Joy stumbled away and avoided her grasp.

"You'll be much happier if you come with me."

"I didn't kill you! I'm innocent!"

Joy stepped backwards again; it wasn't enough to keep her out of Veronica's chilling grasp. Veronica lifted Joy into the cart, then was setting the sheet over her when the officers came back with coffee. No apple pie.

"We'll take over from here."

The officers wheeled Joy on the cart out of the room.

Suddenly they were in court. Joy was on the stand.

"Please rise," an officer said to the empty room, "for the honorable Fred Evans."

Fred was a mangled from his collision with the oncoming truck. He limped to the stand and grabbed the mallet. He slammed it down.

"Guilty."

"I'm not guilty!"

"Order in the court. Order in the court."

The officers grabbed Joy and pulled her away from the stand.

"You'll be going away for a long time."

"Sorry I forgot the apple pie."

They set her on the cart again and wheeled her out of the courtroom. They ended up approaching a prison cell where Fred, Veronica, the man from the Guzzle, and Officer Chambers were waiting for her. All of them deformed shells of who they used to be.

The two officers pushed her cart past the bars.

"Have fun now."

"Maybe I'll bring you that pie a little later."

Joy grabbed a bar in each hand. She watched the officers walk away. *"Please. Don't leave me in here. Wait! Wait! Don't go! Don't leave me in here! I don't belong in here! Come back!"*

The officers never acknowledged her. They disappeared into shadow.

Joy turned to face her cellmates. Each of them had a sinister grin. They were ready for their revenge, and she deserved it. She had brought death upon them; it was her painting that brought the Shadow Man to life. She was guilty.

"What a shame about Joy," Scott said. "But I always knew she was guilty. Pretty girl that's always smiling always has something to hide. Don't you think?"

Bandit barked.

It was a beautiful day outside. Scott read the newspaper in his rocking chair, Bandit next to him on the front porch chewing a bone. Cicadas could be heard at a distance. Occasionally cars passed by on the dirt road. The flowers Margaret planted were growing tall and pretty.

Scott turned the page to the comic strips. "Let's see what Archie and the gang are up to today at Pop's Chocolate Shop."

Margaret stepped outside with a tray of drinks and cookies. She took a seat next to Scott in her own rocking chair then handed him a cold glass of lemonade.

"That really hit the spot."

"It's a scorcher today. Remind me why we ever moved here?"

"For a nice quiet life."

"That's right. Things turned out pretty well, didn't they, Scott?"

"Yes they did. I couldn't ask for anything different. If I could go back in time, as so many people wish they could do, I would never change a thing."

"Me neither." Margaret sipped her own cup of lemonade.

"What are the kids up to?"

"Playing in the yard. Hey, Scott?"

"Yeah?"

"Can you take out the garbage in a bit?"

Scott chugged the rest of his lemonade then stared at her. "Hey, get out of my dream, Margaret."

"Sorry."

Margaret went back inside.

"This is the life, Bandit. This is the life. If this isn't nice, I don't know what is."

Margaret brought the tray of cookies and drinks back into the kitchen, set them down on the counter, then checked on the boys. They were throwing a baseball in their spacious back yard. She watched them from the window for a little while, and the boys were unaware of her.

Then she turned on the faucet and was washing dishes when Scott called to her from the hallway to come check something out. Margaret turned the handle to shut off the water then she dried her hands with a cloth. So much for getting some housework done.

"Come quick."

"I'm coming I'm coming. What is it?"

A door shut.

When she was in the hallway, that strange door Ambrose had vanished behind was in her own home. And now Scott was stuck behind it. She reached for the handle, and as it brushed her hand it faded. It vanished a little at a time until there was only wall behind it.

26

David drove the police car with sirens roaring back to the Ashfall Police Department. He slammed on the break in front of the entrance, jolting his body forward, then ran into the building with the evidence in his hands: the bloodied badges and patches of uniform from Officer Sawyer and Officer Hooper.

"They killed my brother. They killed everybody."

"What on God's green earth?"

An officer who must have been on the brink of retirement looked up from his paperwork and coffee to see David with blood soaking him. The officer approached David cautiously, with one of his hands sneaking down to his belt for his firearm.

"They killed them. They killed them all. The cult of McDougall."

"Walk me through it from the top, kid. Who killed your brother?"

"Your officers are dead." David pushed the badges and remnants of uniforms into the old man's hands. Brenner was written on his badge, and David could see it more clearly now that he was nearer to him.

Officer Brenner dropped the bloodied evidence and put David in a headlock. He pinned him to the wall then shouted out: *"Backup! I need backup quick!"*

Footsteps from within the building. Help was on the way.

"Listen to me, your cops are dead! My brother's dead!"

"What's going on here?" The angry voice of a woman. David couldn't see her because he was pinned to a wall under Brenner's heavy grip. Brenner may have been in his fifties but he hadn't lost any of his strength.

"The cult of maniacs! They killed Jack! Your officers are dead too! Gutted like fish!"

"Pick those badges up from the floor, Kessler."

Presumably she did so. David couldn't see.

"Ripped to shreds! Neither of them had a chance!"

Brenner and Kessler brought David to an interrogation room where they restrained him with handcuffs and pressed record on a tape recorder.

"Why do you have my men's badges?" the fat lady Kessler asked.

"I told you they're dead."

"Why did you kill them?"

David struggled against the painfully tight handcuffs. "I didn't kill them. It was the cult of McDougall. Those maniacs playing God with dead bodies!"

Old man Brenner smacked him across the face. "Do you take us for a couple fools? Their blood's all over you. You were driving their squad car."

"They were helping me arrest my brother's killers!"

"Where are their bodies?"

"In the house."

"What house?"

"That house on the hill!"

Brenner and Kessler exchanged terrified looks.

"The Engstrom place?" Kessler asked.

"I don't know! Me and my brother stopped there for the night and they killed him! There's a group of insane asylum patients inhabiting that place! They've got bodies dissected all over their Assembly Room and they're playing God! Satanic rituals to bring back the dead! They claim they've contacted hell itself! And they're gonna come for me now that I've escaped to tell you! Please listen to me! I beg of you! None of us are safe so long as they're out there!"

"You want us to go up to the Engstrom place?" Kessler said.

"Yes. Right away. Give them what they deserve! Life sentences! Put 'em away behind bars and throw the key far far far away! Make their dreaded house of degeneracy come crumbling down, officers! For the love of God go get them!"

The officers stared at him.

"Well? What are you waiting for?"

"No way are we going up that house," Officer Brenner said. "Two cops disappeared there a few months ago, and now this. I'm not taking any chances."

"Nothing we can do," Officer Kessler said.

27

Scott knocked on David's door.

No answer.

"Hey David, good morning. Margaret made French toast. Bacon's nice and crispy. You up, fella?" Scott knocked again. "David?"

Scott opened the door. David was gone.

Next he went to the Assembly Room to check on the doctor. Doc's body was making progress, regenerating faster than ever before. Noticeable muscle growth. Hair growing in clumps on his scalp. His empty eye socket was twitching. His lips pulled apart as breaths passed through them. The doctor's body was regrowing as fast as could be hoped, but the shape of him wasn't as cohesive as would have been preferred. Instead of an exact copy of Dr. James McDowell, so far he was a parody. Uneven lumps of flesh. Irregular shades of skin color formed at the seams.

Oh well, Scott thought, a new process of regenerating a human body from scratch was sure to have its issues.

Scott put on rubber gloves then set aside the glass lid and inspected the body closer. He turned McDowell onto his back. A little less growth around the spine than the other areas of the body. Scott picked up his measuring tape from the desk and wrapped it around McDowell's forearm, waist, neck, torso, and thighs, writing down measurements in a notebook to properly document the body's progress. Next Scott put his compass to the doctor's skull. The spaces between them had shrunk significantly.

"Hey, honey," Margaret stepped into the room as Scott hooked up the oscilloscope to the body, "bacon is getting cold. Where's David?"

"He must have left. Him and his bags are gone. Look at this, doc's regenerating at the speed of light. His skull bones are nearly finished fusing. I think it's time we finish what Dr. McDowell asked us to do. Today's the day. I can feel it. Can't you?"

They gathered the biggest chairs in the house and set them on the far wall of the living room.

Scott pushed the central table aside so that there was space to lay Dr. McDowell's new body after he wheeled it in on the rusted cart. Scott unhooked a dozen electrode wires previously attached to the walls by the PSI machine and attached them to McDowell's head, arms, and chest.

Meanwhile, Margaret brought in the glass sphere and set it in one corner of the living room. She lit candles then set them around the body.

"Are you ready, doc? We're close."

"What next, Scott?" Margaret wiped sweat from her forehead. "Any of the other equipment?"

Scott struck a match and threw it into the fireplace. "Just get the others."

One of doc's books was on a mantelshelf. Scott opened it up and read until Margaret came with the others. Each of them took a seat.

"Are we really doing this now?" Samantha said. "I just ordered a pizza."

Joy rolled her eyes. "Nobody's gonna deliver to this place."

"It's time to bring him back. The months of research Margaret and I have done have led to this moment, and you all are here to share it with us." Scott looked away from the girls and to the book in his hands. "When the doctor was in Timbuktu, he wrote about a man that had supposedly come back to life with the help of his friends. More than likely, the man was not really dead but in a coma. McDowell didn't show up until after the man had come out of it, and the previously-dead man told him about what it was like in the afterlife. Interviewing the man's friends, it was clear to McDowell that it wasn't a supernatural occurrence at all but a scientific one. What we're doing here is split down the middle."

The girls were quiet.

"This should have been a team effort from day one. Colleen, the doctor brought you here because you wanted answers about your husband. This house took him away from you. Samantha, the doctor picked you because your abilities were so impressive. In your home town you communicated with a boy from beyond the grave. You found his resting place and led authorities to his killer. And Joy, the doctor was intrigued that your abilities vanished. He suspected you could still channel them. Maybe by divine providence you'll be able to help him. Does anyone have any questions?"

"What are you talking about?" Joy said. "I'm not doing anything for you. After this experiment of yours fails and the lease is expired I'm burning this place to the ground. You asked me for more time and I gave it to you. You're lucky I didn't set fire to this place with all of your machines still attached."

"May I remind you that this is what you were brought here for in the first place? You have a gift buried inside of you. The doctor knew that and brought you here."

"I'm not helping you."

"Samantha, will you get things started," Scott said, "at our 'crystal ball?'"

Samantha stood up and obeyed.

"Joy, you too. Come on and help."

"You've got this all wrong. I'm not helping you."

"When you were a child you heard the voices of the dead. James told me all about you."

"That was a lifetime ago. And it's none of your business or anybody's business. You have no right to talk about it."

"I know you don't think you can do it anymore, but the doctor invited you and you accepted. So you can help him," Scott grabbed the gun from his pocket, "or I won't be so kind to only wound you this time."

"It's not gonna work." Joy turned her attention from Scott to Samantha, whose hands were on the sphere. "I really can't help you, Sam. We saw your abilities at work when we were here the first time. I did not and could not do anything then, and the same applies now. When I was a kid, I thought I was talking to my dead aunt. It was a child's imagination. My parents thought there was something wrong with me, so they had a priest come to our house and bless me. After that I never heard voices again."

"Then you have nothing to worry about," Samantha said. "Don't be an idiot, get over here."

Joy listened.

Scott put the gun away. "Colleen, do you have something of Ambrose's with you? Anything in your purse?"

"Yeah I think so."

"Margaret and I owe you an apology, don't we, Margaret?"

"Yes we do," Margaret said.

"We made this all about Dr. McDowell, but whatever powers took him also took your husband. This experiment could help us bring Ambrose back. So what have you got?"

Colleen opened her purse. She dug around then picked something out. She put it into Scott's hands. "His wedding ring."

Margaret grabbed a wooden board and put it in front of the fireplace. On it was a lit candle on either side, and a folded black tie. Scott put the ring next to the tie.

"A little piece of McDowell, and a little piece of Ambrose."

Colleen knelt in front of the altar. "I pray this works."

"What are we supposed to do?" Joy asked. "How does any of this work?"

Scott, still holding Dr. McDowell's book, set it back on a mantelshelf. "The human body is filled with electricity that allows us to think, feel, move. The PSI machine, after my lovely assistant hits the switch on my cue, will pump electricity back into the body. Combined with his resurrected soul that you ladies are pulling through from the other side, James McDowell will once again be James Mc-Dowell as we knew him.

"And yet, this is bigger than only the doctor. The human body already has the ability to regenerate itself when it heals from a wound or an injury. If this experiment allows us to distill this ability, to learn it, to then recreate it and amplify it, and create a new body for Ambrose, we could cure the world of sickness, of disease, of pain. You'll all play a hand in it, and you'll all be remembered for the rest of humanity's existence for your contributions. Now flip the switch."

Margaret did so. Electricity jolted the corpse. Samantha and Joy rubbed the sphere. Abruptly the room was colder.

Everything was still.

Joy stepped away then put her hands on her hips and rolled her eyes. "There. Did it work?"

Scott tapped the corpse with his toe. "I don't think so."

"This house needs to burn, Scott. I'm going to burn it for what it did to me." Joy glanced at Samantha then Colleen. "And if either of you two are smart, you'll help me for what it did to the both of you."

"Joy's right," Samantha said. "This house needs to pay for what it did to Howard. And to Ambrose."

"Nobody's doing nothing until doc's back to normal," Scott said. "Now get back over there, Joy. Margaret, pump him again."

Joy put a hand on the glass sphere. "Wait a second, everybody. I think I hear a voice. I think it's the doctor."

"What's he saying?" Scott asked.

"He's saying... go to hell, Scott." Joy laughed.

The floorboards near Dr. McDowell's body snapped. They fell down below into an unseen pit of darkness where smoke was up-rising gently at first, then all at once.

A sick laughter from the portal in the ground. Everybody was chilled.

The floorboards surrounding the doctor's body fell away, leaving him on his own 'island' of splintery wood panels bordered on every side by hellish flames and blistering heat.

The house was rattled by the roar of continual flames bursting from the opening in the floor. Scott fell dangerously close to one of the chasms and pulled himself away quickly. While on his hands and knees he looked across the open length of flames and when the blaze occasionally parted he saw hell. Tormenting storms of fire descended upon damned souls. Screaming bodies chained to a stone; worms ate their flesh and squirmed through their organs.

Scott staggered carefully away. The thin pieces of wood under his feet were the only things separating him from eternal torture. His guts twisted. He inched toward the PSI machine; Margaret was holding onto it. Scott kept a grip on it as he tiptoed to the other side and wrapped his arms around Margaret.

"Is this what you wanted?" Joy screamed from across the room.

Colleen was dangling. The flames of hell were threatening to pull her in. The floorboards underneath her had cracked, and her body was halfway down, and her palms bled as they squeezed a jagged edge of wood to stay above ground.

"Help me!"

Scott didn't want to leave Margaret but he was the nearest one to Colleen, and the strongest out of everybody in the room, and ran cautiously to Colleen who was continually begging for help. As Scott kneeled, dozens of scarred hands reached for Colleen. Scott clasped his hands under Colleen's armpits and pulled her up. Within moments, the boards she had been hanging onto fell into the pit.

"We're all gonna die in here, we're all gonna die, we're dead, we're dead, we're dying, we're—"

Scott smacked her. *"Shut the hell up."*

"We wouldn't be in this mess if you listened to us," Joy said. *"I told you what we needed to do but you didn't listen."*

"You don't need to burn the house down," Samantha said, *"it's already burning."*

Prolific flames raged and burst from holes in the ground and made the room hotter. The machinery was melting, but the house was still standing, unaffected by the flames. The front door opened and shut rapidly, as did the windows, and suddenly the Engstrom House was shaking.

"Let's all stay calm," Scott said. *"Samantha, Joy, I need you two to listen to me. What we're gonna do—"*

Another rumble of the house.

"What we're gonna do…" Scott was saying again, but by then nobody was listening. Samantha, Joy, and Colleen were running away.

Samantha ran out the back door. She ran past the boarded well-house and into the woods behind the Engstrom place. She followed a path that must have been untraveled for decades. Further down she passed a stream of water. Beyond that, a fallen tree that was rotting. And as deep as she could run into the forest before the adrenaline wore off was a cemetery.

ENGSTROM FAMILY CEMETERY written in big letters on a sign held in place by rusted screws.

Dozens of graves. Most of the stones indecipherable; withered away by time or covered with moss. A few names could still be read, like the group of six graves set apart from all the others on the farthest side of the cemetery.

John Engstrom. Helen Engstrom. Agatha Engstrom. Joyce Engstrom. Timothy Engstrom. Thaddeus Engstrom.

There was a seventh grave dug next to Thaddeus's. No grave marker. It was tiny and shallow, half-full with dirt. Next to that unused grave was an old splintery wooden bench. Samantha took a seat. She caught her breath.

"Mommy..."

She was frozen.

"Mommy..."

The dirt in the empty grave was moving subtly.

"Get me out of here..."

The fingers of a child clawed free from the dirt. Samantha knelt in front of it, reaching her hand down to help the poor trapped girl, when somebody pulled her away.

Howard. The big gash on his neck had healed. No longer did he have the eyes of the demon, but rather he was normal again. He was his old self. He grabbed Samantha's hand and she didn't pull away; he picked her up and helped her onto the bench. She sobbed. He put his arm around her.

"I'm sorry I couldn't help you, Howard. This wasn't how things were supposed to be. You shouldn't be dead."

"How many times have I always told you to stop putting the blame on yourself for what happens to others?"

"I wish I could've helped you."

"Wishing won't get you anywhere, darling. You did all you could do. No sense in beating yourself up over it."

"Howard. You shouldn't be dead."

"The Lord's got a plan for each of us. When it's your time to go it's your time to go. When you start thinking in those terms, there's really no such thing as an accident. Nothing was your fault."

Samantha was quiet for a little while, then said, "What do I do?"

"You go back in there and help your friend. I know you've got it in you."

"I'm scared."

Howard kissed her forehead. "I believe in you."

Samantha gave him a hug. "I love you."

"I love you too, Sam. But I'm afraid I won't ever see you again."

"What are you saying?"

"When you die you have to move on. There's a place for me and it isn't here on earth. I want you to know I'm happy where I am, and I'll be waiting here for you."

"Goodbye," Samantha whispered.

"Goodbye."

Samantha left the Engstrom Family Cemetery and went back to the house...

Joy ran through the front door. Bandit was in the front yard lying in the shade chewing on a femur.

"Come on boy, we're out of here."

RUFF! RUFF!

Bandit followed her through the gate. Even on the other side of the threshold Joy felt the energy of the house. A creeping feeling under her skin. Shivers passed through her despite the cloudless sky and bright sun that was about to begin setting. The quietness surrounding Joy and Bandit was interrupted by the truck's horn.

HONK!

HONK!

HONK!

HOOOOOOOOOOOOOONK!

Amorphous shadows moved in the windows of the truck; at the distance nothing could be distinct. Bandit barked wildly as they descended the hill. Joy wished she had her shotgun; wished Scott had never taken it from her.

HONK!

Joy opened the passenger door and Bandit ferociously hopped up the steps and into the truck. His barks continued. Joy followed him up. Veronica was on Fred's lap in the driver's seat; she was pressed against the horn again.

HOOONK!

"Fred." Veronica smacked him and knocked his hat from his head. She crossed her arms and scrunched her face. *"Cut it out, we've got company. Hello Joy."*

"I knew your name wasn't really Jessica." Fred fixed his hat. Bandit squeezed himself through the truck and licked Fred's face. "I missed you too, pal."

"What the hell is going on?" Joy said.

"Well you wouldn't believe it," Fred said. "Do you mind if I tell the story this time Veronica?"

"You always tell it. Whatever. Go ahead."

"Jess—um, Joy, when you die there's actually a dating program for the recently deceased. Men sit on one side of a set of tables, women across from them at the other side. Everybody has twenty seconds then they switch. Veronica and I were pretty lonely, and we got to talking. One thing led to another and we—"

"That's sick, I don't want to hear this."

"Let me finish. Veronica and I bonded over our hatred of you. But I've forgiven you." Fred hugged Bandit. *"Ah, good ole Bandit. Dogs really are man's best friend."*

"That's nice and all but I need this truck now. Can you two go do your... *business* somewhere else?"

"Heh." Fred put his hand over Veronica's. "Top of the truck, below the truck, mattress in the back. We're running out of places."

"Just give me the truck. Please."

"Nuh-uh." Veronica shoved Joy away. "Not after what you did to me. I had a smoking hot body, a nice apartment, a family, and you took everything away from me. Now I have to spend eternity with hotdog-breath and this smelly truck! How could you stand this thing? I've tried industrial-strength cleaning supplies and couldn't get rid of the stench!"

"Then why are you even dating Fred?"

Veronica rolled her eyes and held up her left hand. A ring much bigger than her previous wedding ring. "We already tied the knot. You know how difficult divorce is in the living world? Well try getting a divorce in the afterlife. It's more difficult to divorce in the afterlife. The line at the Department of Deceased Services is literally a hundred years long! And as soon as you get to the counter they tell you you don't have the right paperwork!"

"You're right," Fred said, "you did have a smokin' hot body. And now it's mine for eternity, baby."

Fred kissed Veronica then lifted her shirt off. "Let's get back to business."

Veronica broke away from the kiss. "One second, one second, relax, Fred," she said. She turned to Joy. "Me and my ex-husband only bought your painting out of pity! Now go to hell! I hope you burn for killing me!"

Joy and Bandit left the truck. They went back up the hill and to the Engstrom House...

Colleen went up the spiraling stairway. With Scott and Margaret's experiment opening up a portal to hell, this was her last chance to open the door. Her last chance to find her husband. Her last chance to make things right.

Even from the third floor she felt the heat of the wicked flames in the living room. Colleen turned corners, coming back to the strange otherworldly doorway Ambrose vanished behind. And it was gone.

Colleen slammed her hands on the empty stretch of wall. *"Come back. Come back."*

She sank to her knees and cried. Uselessly she hit her hands again and again on the space where the hideous door had previously been.

"Please come back."

Tiny steps from down the hall.

Teresa put her arms around Colleen. "He can't come back."

Colleen wiped her tears. "What do you mean by that, Teresa?"

"I'm very sorry."

Silence.

Tears swelled in Colleen's eyes. She was hopelessly lost. The door had been there and she had lost it again. She had ruined all of her chances.

I should have opened it. I shouldn't have been scared.

Would it ever come back? Colleen wouldn't waste the opportunity again if it did. If it were ever back she'd open the door.

Teresa took Colleen by the hand. "Your friends need you downstairs."

Together they went down the stairway and back to the first floor…

The pizza delivery man drove up the hill then parked. The gate was already open. He grabbed the two pizzas from the passenger seat then walked up the path that led to the front door. Halfway there, a hydrilla plunged into his stomach and pushed through his body into his throat.

Lying on the ground next to the dropped pizza boxes, he squirmed on his back and choked on his blood…

28

THE LIVING ROOM FLOOR was restored. The PSI machine was still partially melted, but the floorboards were back in place as if they had never fallen and the flames of hell had never raged. It was impossible to tell any sort of ritual had been happening in the Engstrom House until moments ago.

Colleen stood in the entryway dumbfounded. There was laughter coming from someplace nearby. Then somebody shouting. She followed the noises to the dining room, where Scott popped open a bottle of champaign. Samantha and Margaret were on either side of Dr. McDowell at the table. Joy crossed her arms and sat set apart from them.

"We don't even know that's him. How can you trust a thing he says?"

"Shut up already," Scott said. *"We've heard enough out of you. You having a drink or what?"*

The doctor was saved. His face was rough; the proportions were off, and once again she had the impression that he was a parody of the doctor. Different sized eyes. Swollen cheeks. A crooked nose. Skin that was different shades in different places on his arms. Contorted fingers that were different sizes and had no symmetry.

"Ah, Colleen," the doctor said when he saw her. His voice sounded the same. "Come join us."

Colleen stepped forward. She wasn't expecting the doctor to hug her.

"We couldn't have done it without you, kid. Thank you for sticking by Scott and Margaret here. They tell me you never doubted them for a second."

Margaret wrapped her arms around the doctor. "Finish telling us what it was like."

"Trust me, I've got thousands of stories from the months I spent in the pits of hell. You'll be hearing them for a long time. Let's take a break from that and unwind." Dr. McDowell lifted his glass. "Scottie, my boy, quit hogging all the drinks."

Scott filled the doctor's glass to the brim and it overflowed. Then he poured champaign into glasses for the women, and drank the little remaining champaign from the bottle.

Dr. McDowell lifted his glass for a toast. "This drink's for all of you. My loyal friends. None of you had to stick around and help me, but you all did. Without a great group of people like yourselves, my soul would be in eternal torment."

"I'm burning this house down tonight," Joy said. "So you all have an hour to pack your things."

"No, no, no, hold on a second, don't go burning down the house just yet. In fact, don't do that at all. This property is neither mine nor yours to burn down. However, we haven't accomplished what we came here for." Dr. McDowell nodded toward Colleen. He drank his champaign then said, "There's still the matter of Ambrose. I've been told the door's come back. How about in a few minutes here we set up the equipment and get you the readings by morning. See what we can do."

Warm tears dripped from Colleen's eyes. "It's gone. I checked on it."

Dr. McDowell frowned. "Well, my dear, that's twice now you've seen it. We have a few facts about it now. It's real, for one. It wasn't a hallucination like some rather ignorant speculators in the papers said. We know it comes and goes, but we might not be able to quite measure yet how much time passes between appearances. We know it appears in the same place sometimes, but we can't determine yet if it's a random appearance or what the intervals are. And maybe this door can appear in other parts of the house too. But for now, with the very first inkling of a pattern, we can study it closer, and perhaps I can extend the lease. What day is it anyways?"

"Your lease expires after tomorrow," Scott said.

"The owners will be more than willing to extend it for our research. Trust me. I had to haggle them down from a six month minimum to three months. They'll be thrilled about a prolonged stay."

"Are you sure we shouldn't take you to a hospital?" Margaret said. "Maybe we should have a specialist take a look at you."

Dr. McDowell lifted up his shirt. His flesh had not fully reformed and connected yet. "I don't think there's a specialist that will understand this. I trust you've been keeping a log? What statistics do you have for me on this body?"

"Scott's got them all."

"I can have those for you shortly. Let's just enjoy the drinks." Scott popped open another bottle and poured more for the doctor. "Doc ole pal, it's great to have you back."

"Careful, you know my doctor wants me to cut down on the alcohol."

"Are you kidding me? It's a brand-new liver you've got in you. It's as if you never took a sip in your life. You can drink all you want." Scott refilled Margaret and Samantha's glasses.

"So is this something that will go in a book?" Samantha asked. "I bet you've got enough material from the past three months for a two volume set."

Dr. McDowell shook his head. "No, no. Who would believe it? I don't want to make this about me, anyways. This is about Colleen and Ambrose."

"I can't thank you enough," Colleen said, "for doing this for me. It's unfortunate about the delays, but I've waited this long. I can wait a little longer."

Scott poured Colleen some more champaign. "Drink up."

"No thanks, I don't have a new liver like the doctor does."

"Who cares? You're a young lady. Your liver isn't that bad already, is it?"

"Well no," Colleen said then drank her champaign. "Can we set up the equipment now? I want to call it an early night and be up bright and early for those readings tomorrow."

"Sure thing." Dr. McDowell stood up. He staggered a little bit, and Margaret grabbed his arm to help him keep his balance. "Pardon me. Thank you, Margaret."

"Can't this wait?" Margaret said. "The doctor's obviously in no condition to walk around and get to work."

"Yeah," Colleen said, "just keep piling on the champaign, I'm sure it'll seal up all the holes in his stomach."

"What is your problem?" Margaret said.

"Ladies, calm down." Samantha stepped between them. "Can't we go a day in this house without arguing? Look, we've made a lot of progress today. Insane progress. I'm shocked we've gotten this far. Colleen, be happy. If we can do this for the doctor, we can do this for Ambrose. And you, Margaret, don't you forget that we're here to help Colleen. Don't be so hard on her."

"I'm not hard on her. Don't either of you care about the doctor and the state he's in?"

"Margaret, thank you, but I'm fine enough to help out Colleen. She's been through a lot. Let's go get the equipment, shall we?"

Colleen brought Scott and the doctor up to the third floor after they retrieved the miniature PSI machine. Colleen spread her hands on the wall to instruct them. "Right here. This is where it was, doctor."

Scott and Dr. McDowell attached the electrode wires to the wall.

"We followed your notes dead-on," Scott said. "It didn't feel right to deviate but for technical purposes we had to restructure from of the interior mechanisms in this thing. I told Margaret to attach those notes to the diagnostics we ran on this body and put 'em on your desk."

"You know, I was about a year off from even beginning a prototype. And yet here you are with this thing fully functional. Whatever notes I had written down, you must have taken them and perfected them."

"Well what can I say? I learned from the best."

215

"So you and Margaret, huh?" The doctor said when they were done attaching the wires. "I always had a suspicion you had a thing for her."

"I didn't even wait to purchase a ring. We spent two... three nights in here when I asked her to marry me."

Dr. McDowell hugged Scott. "I couldn't be happier for you two."

Colleen took a couple small steps closer to them. "Thank you both for your help. Goodnight."

"You sure you don't want another drink?" Scott said. "We're gonna be up late celebrating. I'm about to toss some steaks on the grill. Aren't you hungry?"

"No thanks. But thank you so much."

Colleen went to her bedroom. Teresa was sitting on the bed petting Bandit.

"Teresa, honey, are you hungry?"

Teresa nodded.

"Scott is about to make steaks. Why don't you go on downstairs and get something to eat?"

Teresa and Bandit left the room.

Colleen changed out of her clothes. She collapsed on her bed and went to sleep.

Samantha, Joy, Margaret, and the doctor sat in the living room. Logs in the fireplace were burning. Margaret passed around a box of cookies.

"If I'm being honest," Dr. McDowell said, "I *was* hopeless. It wasn't easy. None of it was easy. It was torture every moment. Think about your idea of torture then throw it out, because that would be paradise if you put it up against what I went through. But I can't get into that in much detail now." He nodded his head at the entrance; everybody turned to see Teresa with Bandit. "We've got company. Who's this?"

"Get away from my dog."

"Don't be mean to a child," Margaret said.

"I'm hungry." Teresa pouted.

"This is Teresa." Samantha picked her up. "Colleen found her. Want a cookie, Teresa?"

"Yes please."

Samantha sat with Teresa in her lap. "How long until those steaks will be done you think?"

Margaret shrugged. "Scott takes so long to cook steaks, oh you should see him. He's so methodical as if he's conducting surgery in there. It has to be cooked for a long time on a slow heat or it isn't up to his standards."

"Do we have anything to feed her besides cookies?"

"What ever happened to that pizza you ordered?" Joy said. "Told you no one would deliver here."

"That's right," Samantha said. She moved Teresa off her lap then went to the window. "Hey, there's somebody out there. Oh my God."

Samantha went out the front door. Everybody but Teresa followed her.

The pizza delivery boy was killed by a hydrilla. Next to his body was two pizza boxes.

"Who knows how long he's been here," Samantha said. "And now the pizza's cold."

29

Everybody had gone to bed. Margaret was cleaning up the kitchen, moving plates from the table to the sink, cleaning up a spilled drink, and throwing away garbage. When she was done she took a deep breath and leaned against the counter.

Now what?

The communication device reminiscent of a crystal ball was in the Assembly Room. Margaret pulled up a chair and rubbed her hands on the glass; wisps of purple smoke slithered and intertwined within the sphere.

"What happens now?" Margaret said. "My whole purpose was to bring the doctor back. Now that he's back, do I even have a purpose? This whole thing was what brought me and Scott together. With Dr. McDowell back, are me and Scott going to drift apart? What does my future hold?"

The hypnotic wisps of smoke swirled.

"Will we be happy outside of these walls? Was this house the only reason we were happy? Will I still have purpose when we leave here?"

Something tapped the glass; something she couldn't see through the dense smoke. Suddenly the smoke was darkening; becoming as black as coal. Margaret lifted her hands but the smoke was still turning, and the tapping morphed into a raged slamming of fists. Emerging from the mist of blinding smoke were two melting hands.

The struggling creature moaned.

Margaret was spellbound.

The smoke pulled back and revealed the face of the doctor.

Margaret gasped. Her hands trembled as they lowered to the surface of the glass. She rubbed the ball; his face appeared in agony. Dr. McDowell was sickly. His hands slammed inside the ball again. He longed for a release.

"Escape."

"Oh my God." Margaret stepped away from the sphere. Joy was right. It hadn't been the doctor that they brought back. He was still trapped in hell.

The wisps died down and morphed back to their deep purple color. The connection to McDowell in hell was severed. Margaret needed to tell Scott, needed to warn him, but as soon as she opened the door, the reanimated Dr. McDowell body was before her in the doorway with a devious ear-to-ear smile.

He knew.

"Doctor I—I didn't know you were up. Looking for more of our notes?"

"Yes, my dear. I don't think you attached all the information I needed."

"I can, um, retrieve it all for you in the morning. I'm very exhausted."

"What were you doing here so late anyways, Margaret?"

"Being in this house with Scott for so long has turned me into the workaholic he is." She stepped past him. "I guess I'll see you in the morning, sir. Goodnight."

His eyes flashed black. "Why are you leaving so soon? I've been gone for months. We still have so much to talk about. Why don't we get reacquainted?"

"In—in the morning, duh-doctor."

The doctor pressed his bumpy crooked fingers into her skin as he grabbed her arm. "The night's still young, Margaret. And we've got work to do."

30

"MORNING DOC." SCOTT WALKED into the kitchen. Dr. McDowell was making coffee. "Good to see you're up and running and we didn't even need to assist you."

"Morning, Scott. Sleep well?"

"Yeah I did. Hey, have you seen Margaret? She must've gotten up early because our bed was empty. Must be one of my habits she picked up. Early bird catches the worm and all."

"No, can't say that I have."

Scott found a mug. "Excuse me, doc."

"Allow me." Dr. McDowell filled his cup.

"Thank you very much." Scott drank his coffee. "Doc, you don't know how scared I was when I woke up this morning thinking that yesterday was all a dream. It still doesn't feel real. How about we get you to the Assembly Room and run some tests?"

"We'll have time for that later. Don't we have to help Colleen this morning?"

"It can wait a little. The door's probably not back yet anyhow."

Joy walked into the kitchen. "No rest for the wicked, huh? You two are up early."

"Morning, Joy," Scott said. "Glad to see the house is still standing and nobody's burned it down yet."

"Don't press your luck."

"Hey, you drank more than most of us did last night. I thought you'd be happy. Why can't you be in good spirits for once?"

"Are you kidding me? We still don't even know that this monster is the doctor. The things this house has done to everyone in here, and you think you can pull a soul straight out of hell without any consequences? Scott stop being blind."

"What must I do to prove I'm me?" Dr. McDowell said. "I look a little different, but constructing a new body isn't a tried and true method. This is the first time in history that a human has been... reassembled. Now allow me to prove to you I am the doctor. My birthday is the second of December, I've written four books, and you were brought here because you could hear the voices of the dead. We corresponded for five letters and two phone calls before you were convinced to join me."

"Your phony speeches don't convince me. I've got my eye on you. Now pour me some coffee."

"Cream? Sugar?"

"Both. And plenty of it."

Samantha stretched and yawned as she entered the kitchen. "Guess everyone in this house is an early riser. Good morning. Is there any pizza left?"

"Check the fridge," Scott said.

Samantha did and she found the last remaining slice. "Awesome."

"Coffee?" The doctor offered her.

223

"Sure, thank you," Samantha said. "Did you mean what you said last night, doctor? About hiring me as your editor for eighty dollars a week?"

"Must have been the champaign talking, but we can negotiate."

"Samantha, have you seen Margaret around?"

"No. Why?"

"She wasn't in our bed this morning. She wasn't in the Assembly Room either. Doc hasn't seen her either, and neither has Joy."

Samantha shrugged. "Maybe she went into town."

"I thought of that," Scott said, "but the van's still parked."

The window was cracked open, and Colleen felt a deep chill against a soft blow of wind. She shuddered. Coldness sinking into every side of her body. Her covers were wet.

She opened her eyes. The early morning brightness shined against the deep red blood that Colleen was drenched in. She pulled the covers away; her clothes were also completely soaked in buckets of blood.

Immediately she pulled off her clothes to inspect her body. Was she hurt? What was happening? There were no scars or marks on her body. No injuries. Whose blood was this? Where had it come from? She shivered.

What had she done?

Colleen ran to the in-room bathroom and turned the shower on. She stepped underneath the burning stream of water and rubbed her skin as hard as she could; nothing would take the blood away. Colleen turned the knob as far as it could go; the water had no effect on the blood.

"What the hell is happening?"

Colleen put her head under the stream to wash the clumps of blood from her hair. Scarlet water washed down the drain. Little by little it was coming off of her.

She went through about a quarter of a bottle of shampoo and it was still coming up red. It was as if the russet sludge had been stained in her hair down to the roots. As if the gallons of dark blood had been soaked deep into her skin.

Colleen rubbed her skin with soap and hot water until she was sore. Her trembling hands were weak. She stepped out of the shower and looked herself over in the mirror. She was still red in spots. It was as close as she was going to get to completely being clean. She dried off then went across the room to her bags next to the dresser. She put on a new outfit: the first skirt and first shirt that her hands touched. She didn't even check to be sure that they matched.

Then she checked over the room. No trail of blood. Nothing led from the door to her bed, nor from her bed to anywhere else. The room was spotless, outside of her bedsheets and her old outfit. And she had to get rid of them.

She kept a garbage bag in her suitcase. Colleen brought that out and carefully grabbed her old clothes with the bloodstained towel from the bathroom and put them in. Next the sheets and pillows; all thrown into the memory hole. Then she flipped her mattress upside down. Colleen hid the garbage bag in the cabinet under the sink.

I can't believe this is happening, she thought. *Did I hurt someone? If I did where are they?*

Nerves twisted in her stomach. She tried to play back last night: setting up the machinery with the doctor and Scott. Telling Teresa to go downstairs to the others. Then Colleen went to sleep. And now she was here. Nothing in between.

What was she missing?

"What have I done?" Her tears blurred her vision as she found another rag in the bathroom.

Colleen knelt on the hard floor and scrubbed the blood away. When she was done, she had two bloody rags that were added to the garbage bag, but the bedroom was spotless.

Colleen washed her hands in the sink again, straining to get the remnants of blood off of her skin.

KNOCK! KNOCK! KNOCK!

She jumped.

It was Samantha at her door. "Hey Colleen, is Margaret in there? None of us could find her."

"She's not here."

"Scott's getting a little worried. I'm sure it's no big deal, I'm sure she—"

"Get in here. Quick." Colleen opened the door then shut it behind Samantha. "I don't know what to do."

Samantha grabbed Colleen's hands. "You're shaking."

"I think I did something bad."

"What?"

"Margaret I—I think I hurt Margaret."

"Tell me what happened."

"I don't know what happened."

"Okay. Where is she?"

"I don't know." Colleen led her to the bathroom. Samantha's lips were pulled into a nervous frown. Colleen opened the cabinet and brought out the garbage bag. "You have to believe me. I don't know what happened to Margaret or where she is, I... I woke up covered in blood."

Samantha looked inside.

"I killed her," Colleen whispered. A chill passed through her body. "I killed her. Oh my God I killed her."

Samantha was silent.

"Was she missing last night?" Colleen asked. "After I went to bed?"

"No, nobody was missing last night. Oh God. We have to tell the others about this."

Colleen cried. *"They're gonna kill me."*

"No. Nobody is gonna kill you."

Colleen cried so hard that the words on her lips couldn't form. Samantha hugged her in an attempt to calm her down, then she picked up the garbage bag and tied it up. Samantha put it back in the cabinet under the sink.

"Don't tell anyone. I'm begging you."

"Okay I won't tell. Just calm down. Let's figure this out. Tell it to me again from the top."

Scott and Dr. McDowell waited on the third floor at the miniature PSI machine. Its needle bobbed up and down for a reading. The doctor poked at an open patch of skin on his arm. Scott struck a match and lit a cigarette.

"No sign of Margaret, now no sign of Colleen," Scott said. "Let's forget about this dumb door and go looking for them."

"They had that argument last night. Remember?"

"Yeah, they've been at each other's throat this whole time, doc. Margaret never believed her about the door, but can you blame her? In our time here, everything pointed toward you. Your body coming back in pieces, you talking to us from beyond the grave, but we never saw no sign of no door. Never a peep from Ambrose. I don't like it either, but I kept my mouth shut."

"But you've seen the door, haven't you? Isn't it back? That's what everybody was saying last night."

"That's what Colleen said, doc. But none of us actually took a look at it as far as I know. I sure as hell didn't. I was too preoccupied with getting you back. Seemed more important to me to bring back a man that we knew for sure was on the other side… than someone that might not be there."

"We have no reason to doubt her. These things you're talking about, they're circumstantial. If the door wasn't real, I don't think she'd go around claiming it had returned. If that was a lie, then following her up to the door's location would've made her look even crazier. I don't think she would have done anything to place *more* doubts upon herself. But I'm sure there's an explanation for all this. Let's go check on her, shall we? Do you know which floor she's on?"

"She's on the floor below us."

The men went down a flight of stairs. Scott found Colleen's room and knocked.

Samantha opened the door for Colleen who stood nervously away from the threshold. She sat on her bed fidgeting with a loose fingernail. She wiped away tears before they could completely form, hoping that Scott and the doctor wouldn't notice.

"Is Margaret here?"

"No," Samantha said. "Can you two come back later? We're busy."

"What the hell do you mean can we come back later?" Scott said. "The reason we're up so early is because Colleen wanted us to help her with the door. I put off running tests on doc because he was so insistent we help her. The whole reason any of us came here is to help her. Now she's too busy?"

"I'm sorry," Colleen whispered from her bed.

"Have you seen Margaret, Colleen?"

"No."

Samantha shut the door on Scott and the doctor.

"What's going on around here?"

Dr. McDowell put a hand on Scott's shoulder. "We need to search that room."

"For what?"

"Margaret disappears and Samantha's shutting doors in our face. What are those girls up to in there? Let me ask you this, Scott, did Margaret fight with Samantha at all? Like she fought with Colleen?"

"No, Margaret only had arguments with Colleen. Everyone else got along well with her."

"Maybe I'm overthinking it, Scott, but Margaret's like a daughter to me. I don't want anything to happen to her. She just spent months bringing me back to life. I owe it to her to make sure she's not in danger."

"Doc, I've got a bad feeling about this."

KNOCK! KNOCK! KNOCK!

Colleen slid off her bed and backed away. *"They're gonna kill me. I told you they're gonna kill me."*

"Open up," Scott said from the other side of the door. He tried to twist the doorknob but it was locked. That bought the ladies a little time to figure out what they were going to do.

"They won't kill you, but I need you to be calm." Samantha put her hands on Colleen's shoulders. "Can you do that?"

"Uh-huh." Colleen nodded.

"All right." Samantha crept to the door. "What do you want, Scott?"

"I'm searching the room. Let us in."

"Oh no," Colleen whispered.

Samantha opened the door. Scott and the doctor entered; Scott was smoking a cigarette that was almost finished, and the doctor's hands were casually in his pockets. Colleen thought that Scott would come in with his gun pointed at her like he had pointed his gun so many times during the past three months, like when the spirit first took over the doctor and he was forcing everybody to help, or when Joy came running in with her dog and Scott shot her.

Colleen felt heavy chills as the doctor looked around her dresser. Scott walked around the room toward the window. What did they expect to find? Colleen stayed firmly in place on her bed—she prayed to God nobody wanted to flip the mattress over, and prayed that she hadn't missed a drop of blood when she had been scrubbing the floors.

Something flashed in the doctor's eyes; something otherworldly. He leaned against her dresser. "Are you sure you didn't see Margaret at all?"

"I had no time to see her. I was here in bed."

"If something happened to her, you should tell us right now."

"Why won't you believe me?"

Samantha stood between them. "We just brought you back to life and now you're going around accusing us of murder."

"Sam," Scott said, approaching from the other side of the room, "neither the doctor nor I mentioned anything about murder. But if you've got anything you'd like to tell us, now's the time."

Samantha faced him. "Or what, you'll point that gun at me again? Takes a big man to threaten a defenseless woman. You two sickos implied murder. Well, Colleen's going through hell. Why don't you leave her alone?"

RUFF! RUFF!

Bandit ran into the room with Teresa riding on his back. Her arms were holding onto his neck and she was sliming.

"Easy, boy," Scott said.

Bandit barked viciously at the doctor. Scott walked over to the dog and petted his head. The barks never stopped.

"What's the matter with you, boy?"

Teresa slid off Bandit's back and took off her necklace. She extended it to Scott.

"What the hell?" Scott said.

"Watch your language around those little ears," Samantha said.

Scott held it up for everybody to see. It was a purple heart on a silver chain. It was somewhat familiar but Colleen couldn't place it; couldn't remember where she had seen it before.

"This was Margaret's."

31

SCOTT CHECKED THE VAN. Margaret wasn't there. He checked the basement. No sign of her. He called her name as he went through the long halls of the Engstrom House. Where was she? He checked the Assembly Room, the darkroom, all the rooms where they had conducted research or any room that had any meaning to them throughout their stay.

He went upstairs to Samantha's room on the top floor and knocked on the door. He had spent time searching Colleen's room and hadn't thought about checking Samantha's. Just what did she know? Scott had a suspicion that there was something Samantha and Colleen were keeping from him.

He knocked. No answer.

Scott opened the door. The room was empty.

As he shut the door behind himself he heard Samantha's voice coming from inside the room. "Hey, I'm out here."

He opened the door again, this time noticing the open window. Scott went across Samantha's room and leaned out the window. Samantha was sitting down on the roof, resting her back against the house, and smoking a cigarette.

"Are you the one who stole my smokes?"

"No. I found these here in my room. I guess somebody left them."

"Funny. I can't find mine anywhere. Are those Luckies?"

"Nuh-uh."

"Hand one over. I've been ready to beg, borrow, or steal one all day."

"Sure." Samantha handed him one through the window. "You know I haven't smoked since I was eighteen. A lifetime or longer."

Scott climbed through the window and sat near her on the roof. As he retrieved his book of matches he was mesmerized by the view; the sky was streaked with pink and orange in a curious pattern that spanned as deep as he could see. Down below trees gathered all around the slope of the Engstrom House's hill. The spikes on the gate gleamed under the touch of light from above.

"I needed to have one of these as bad as you did," Samantha said. "God this place is hell. Look I'm sorry about earlier. As long as we're in this house together we should get along."

"I agree." Scott shook his head, never looking away from the spikes.

They were silent for a little while. Samantha struck a match from her own book and lit a second cigarette.

"Any luck finding Margaret?"

"No."

"This house can wear you down. I'm surprised you two lasted in here as long as you have. Maybe she finally had enough and walked away."

"Without telling me?"

"She had no reason to tell you."

"What are you even talking about?"

"Maybe Margaret didn't want you to find her. Maybe she left you. Maybe she thought this was how things needed to be."

Scott finally looked away from the spikes that were sending up winks of light. "She's not that kind of person. I'd know."

"This house does things to people, all right? It changes them. You can't go around… chasing shadows."

Scott looked away from her and back to the fence. "I'm not chasing any shadows."

"I'm sorry… but she left. That's the only explanation."

"No, no, she's an honest girl. She'd have said something to me. Or to *somebody*. Something happened to her and I know it."

"What do you think of me? Do you think I'm an honest girl too?"

He looked her up and down. "I think so. I think you're honest and kind and an all around good person."

"Yeah right. I'm a million miles from home. Do you think my husband even knows where I am? I can only imagine what he thinks I'm up to. Nobody's ever as perfect as they seem. Maybe you didn't… know Margaret as well as you thought you did."

"You're wrong. End of story."

"This house has taken things from all of us. Colleen lost her husband, the doctor lost his body, I lost the man who raised me after my father passed away."

"No, no, this isn't like any of those things. Howard's dead and you know which grave he's rotting in. He didn't disappear. He didn't leave without saying a word. I spent months with Margaret, I know what kind of person she is. She wouldn't do this. She wouldn't leave like this. Everything she could want is right here in this house."

"That's your problem, Scott. You and Margaret and this house. It's an obsession. Maybe Margaret realized how venomous this house is. Maybe she wanted to get out of here. I don't know. I can keep saying 'maybe this' or 'maybe that', but if we keep thinking about all the possibilities we'll go insane."

"I think you know more than you're telling me."

"Come on, Scott, I'm trying to be nice to you. We've been through a lot together and I have a feeling our stay isn't over yet."

"Sure."

"Who ever would have thought we'd still be here after all this time?"

"Not me."

"I thought this would be quick and easy money. Guess there's no such thing."

"Me too. I thought it would be very quick and very easy."

"Things happened so fast it almost felt like a dream. The doctor's possession… oh my God I can't even think about it without wanting to scream. What did you do after it was over? After the house had taken him?"

"After we all split? I stayed in town and ran into Margaret at the bar. We had a few drinks, and like drinking tends to do, you come up with bad ideas. Staying in this house was one of them." Scott counted the spikes on the fence. He lost count after thirteen or fourteen. "She showed me how to develop film. Set up a darkroom to see what was in the pictures we had taken. Right away we started on our mission to find doc."

"I went back home and for the longest I couldn't say two words to my husband about any of this. He still doesn't know the whole story. I couldn't work, couldn't eat. And when things were getting better, who comes knocking on my door but Colleen?"

"Yeah."

"Then Howard…"

"Sorry for your loss."

"Thank you."

Scott counted the spikes again. "Where do you think we go from here?"

"I don't want to think about that. Why don't we just enjoy this moment? A little peace for the first time since this madness started. I like talking to you, Scott, when you're not accusing me of murder or pointing a gun at me."

Scott said nothing.

"Hey Scott?"

Scott turned his attention from the spikes to Samantha. She wobbled to stand up.

"Geez, be careful."

"Don't worry, when I was a kid I snuck onto our roof all the time. I used to have fun but then I grew up because growing up seemed the thing to do. We've both had people hurt us. I was hurt my by husband multiple times. You were hurt by Margaret. Wouldn't you want to get payback?"

"Come on, don't talk about them this way."

"My husband wasn't faithful to me."

Samantha was wearing a light sweater and a scarf because it was a cold day. She undid her scarf and grabbed each end in one hand, sliding it around her body before tossing it aside. Then she unbuttoned her sweater.

Scott waived her away. "Come on. Don't do this. Margaret could come walking up that path any minute and see this."

"You think she's really coming back?"

"Do you know something I don't know?"

"Nuh-uh." Samantha slid off her shirt then brushed her long dark hair back into place.

"You're a married woman and I love Margaret. We shouldn't do this." Scott grabbed her shirt and tossed it back to her. "Put your clothes back on."

Samantha did what he said. "Don't you think I'm pretty?"

"That has nothing to do with it. Did you not listen to a word I said?" Scott put a hand on the house to brace himself as he stood up. "When you love someone you don't do these things. Not even for payback. Whatever's between you and your husband is between you and your husband. Whatever's between me and Margaret's between me and Margaret. If you're so desperate they've got places like that down in the city. You might get paid for it too."

Samantha smacked him hard across the face. *"I'm not some whore."*

"Are you sure about that?"

Samantha headed for the window, but Scott grabbed her by the wrist.

"Get away from me. Let go."

Scott pulled her by the wrist to the corner of the roof then shoved her off the edge. Her hand reached desperately up to Scott but it was too late; the spikes of the fence pierced her body. Samantha was still alive after the impact. Her body twitched against the spikes. Blood dripped from the curled corners of her mouth and she let out a choked gasp.

Scott kneeled on the roof watching life pump out of her torso; fistfuls of scarlet pumping from the gaps in her flesh.

All was silent, then Samantha let out one final harrowing scream.

32

THE WELLHOUSE DOOR NEEDED to be tugged a couple times to open up. It was just as difficult to close. Colleen set the garbage bag of bloody clothes and her bloody bedsheet on the rim of the well then pushed it in; they sank below the darkened waters that were illuminated by an indistinct ray of light.

Colleen tiptoed out of the wellhouse, scanning the back yard to make sure that nobody saw her and what she was doing. Then she went back inside the house. As she stepped through the doorway, a sickening feeling came over her. Something didn't feel right. Her guts twisted and a chill sank through her skin. A creeping premonition that something was wrong; that things were changing.

A faint whisper.

Rasping at strange intervals behind a door.

Colleen followed the persisting noises. In a hallway at the other end of the Engstrom House, she heard the whisper more clearly. Margaret was calling her name.

"Colleen…"

She stiffened.

"Help me…"

The pleas were coming from the other side of the door to the Assembly Room.

"Open the door..."

Guilt pulsed through her. She opened the door and stepped inside; it shut on its own behind her. The room was still filled with the equipment that Margaret and Scott had used to research the doctor's new body and resurrect him.

At the center of the room was the glass case the body had been kept behind. A white sheet was placed around it, obscuring its contents entirely.

"Why did you... kill me..."

The whisper came from within the hidden case.

"Margaret, I'm so sorry. I didn't want to hurt you."

Something shifted behind the sheet under the glass; Colleen stood still a couple feet away from it. The glass lid was opened and pushed away by two mutilated hands. Margaret was almost entirely unrecognizable; her flesh had been stripped away so that there must have been a quarter or less of a person remaining. Her arms were stripped away to bone with thin remnants of veins attached at her palms. Her insides had been dissected and almost completely removed. Sickeningly her head tilted to one side and her lips were turned into an eternal frown. Strips of flesh were pulled from her face and her eyes were threatening to pop from their sockets. Margaret's remaining skin was purpling. Stiffly she sat up in her tomb.

Screams painfully fled Colleen's lips. She ran out of the room and straight into a solid figure. Hands grabbed her gently. She pulled away to see that it was the doctor.

"My dear," he said, "what is troubling you?"

"Nothing."

"I saw you walking outside. What were you doing in the well-house?"

"I didn't want to leave any, um, any stone unturned to find Ambrose."

"You're white as a sheet. Did you see something in my Assembly Room that you didn't like?"

"Uh, no, nothing."

The doctor grabbed Colleen by the wrist and pulled her back to the room. "There's nothing to be afraid of."

When the doctor opened the door, Colleen saw that she was wrong. Margaret wasn't there. Nothing was in the glass case. It was shut, with the white sheet folded in a square on top of it.

"I know this time has been very hard on you. I'll go see if Scott has any pills we could give you."

Colleen visited the wall where the vanishing door had previously been. The PSI machine was hooked up, but she didn't know what good that would do. She didn't understand any of the technology that the doctor and the others were using. She just hoped that it would somehow bring the door back, that it would give the doctor the numbers he needed in order to study the door. She wanted out of here and couldn't stand another minute trapped in these walls waiting for Ambrose to come back to her.

"I wish you'd come back now." Colleen leaned on the wall and cried.

She wished she could go back to that day and stop Ambrose from losing control of the wheel; wished she could prevent the crash that led them to waiting out the storm in the Engstrom House. Wished she could change every single choice that they had made that day. If only they had gone down a different road, made some different turns somewhere, or never passed through Ashfall at all.

Colleen collapsed on her bed. Shortly afterwards there was a knock on the door.

"Samantha?"

"It's Scott. Look, I need to apologize to you about earlier, I was on edge because Margaret is missing. The doctor told me you weren't feeling so well, so I brought you some medicine. I want to help you. Can I come in?"

"I want to be alone right now."

"Colleen I want to help you."

"Come back another time please. I need to be alone, all right?"

"You can't find Ambrose if you're sick." Scott knocked again. "Come on, open up. Let's put whatever I said this morning behind us. I'm willing to move on if you are. Let's work together. What do you say?"

Colleen paused to consider, then said, "Please go away."

"Can I slide these pills under the door? Will you take them? I'll roll them into a napkin."

If he gave them to her, she would toss them down the bathroom sink. So she said, "Go ahead."

"Actually, it seems I forgot to bring a napkin with me. Let me hand you them. Is that all right?"

Nervously Colleen rose from her bed. "Thanks, Scott. I'll take them then I'll get plenty of rest afterwards. Thank you."

Colleen opened the door. Scott was there with Dr. McDowell, who was holding a black briefcase.

"Oh, hi doctor."

"Hello, Mrs. Tillman."

Scott handed Colleen the pills. "Here you are."

"Thanks. I'll be going to bed now. Some rest is just what I need."

Colleen shut the door but Scott stuck his arm through and slid it completely open. The doctor followed him inside.

"What are you doing?" Colleen looked from Scott to the deformed doctor and back to Scott.

"Only a little diagnostic." The doctor set his briefcase down on Colleen's dresser. "The usual checkup."

"I'm okay. I'm only—only a little lightheaded. This won't be necessary, doctor."

"Yeah, doc here was telling me you were a little hysterical after a visit to the Assembly Room. Did you come across anything you'd like to share with us?"

"Nothing. Nothing was in the Assembly Room."

"Calm down," Scott said. "Quit being so jumpy."

Dr. McDowell stepped from the dresser closer toward the bed. "We want to help you. In order to do that, my dear, we need your full cooperation. You're getting a little red in the cheeks. Take a deep breath and have a seat and we can check you over."

"Please leave me alone. I'll take your pills but please—please leave me alone. Don't hurt me."

"I'm not gonna hurt you," Scott said. "Neither's doc. We're only here to help. Clearly you're upset—I understand. None of this has been easy on any of us. The doctor and I are your friends, all right? This is the man who brought us here with the sole intent of helping you. So let us help."

"You can't help me. Neither of you can help me."

"Playing nice won't get us anywhere. What a shame. We wanted to do this the easy way." Dr. McDowell grabbed Colleen's mattress and flipped it over to reveal the bloodstains. "Where did this come from?"

Colleen staggered away from the men and backed into a wall. "I don't know how that got there."

"Stop lying to us, Colleen," Dr. McDowell said. "What did you do to Margaret?"

"I didn't do anything."

"Quit foolin' around, doc," Scott shook his head, "she won't admit it. You can't get a looney to admit when they've done something wrong. Especially something as hideous as murder. I guess part of this is my fault. I should've seen the tensions that were right in front of me. Maybe I could've done something about it before Margaret got hurt. I guess we know now what happened to Colleen's husband."

"Don't beat yourself up over it, kid. Wherever Margaret is, she's watching over you. And I suppose now Margaret will be the first woman to be... reassembled."

"I bet she stayed up all night, waiting until Margaret was alone. Colleen couldn't stand it that Margaret never believed her about the door—but if Colleen was telling the truth, why be so upset that one person didn't believe her? It's because she didn't want everybody else to be convinced. Because she was hiding something. And Margaret was getting too close to those answers."

"Shut up."

"Maybe Margaret would've convinced the rest of us about the truth."

"You know the truth. Ambrose vanished behind that door. This house took him away from me like it took Margaret away from you."

"How do you figure she did it, doc?"

"Well, Scott, I'd say you hit the nail on the head. Colleen was pretty upset about that argument the night I came back, and she was afraid the rest of us would abandon this place if Margaret convinced us otherwise. I'd be willing to give Mrs. Tillman here the benefit of the doubt that it was not premeditated. Perhaps she saw the opportunity and struck."

"Yeah, yeah, but what would Margaret be doing up at Colleen's room so late at night, huh?"

"I didn't kill her. Please believe me."

The doctor cracked his knuckles. "Colleen comes down at night, finds Margaret cleaning up. Tells her she's found something. It's an emergency. Margaret hurries up with her, that's when Colleen... disposes of her."

"Now here's the sixty-four dollar question. Where's the body?"

"She should answer that."

Colleen's legs shook. She slid down the wall and sat on the floor with her face buried into her knees. *"I didn't kill her. I don't know where she is."*

"Where did you put Margaret's body?"

"She's alive. I saw her in the Assembly Room."

"You saw what?"

"She was alive but it wasn't Margaret it was only partly Margaret. She was cut up and pieces of her were missing. The house hurt her, not me."

"She's lying to you, Scott. When I entered the Assembly Room with her, there was no such body. Only the pieces of my flesh and organs that you and Margaret located and set aside in jars."

Scott went across the room and picked Colleen up. He dragged her through her bedroom and ignored her begging screams to be let go. Scott held her in a tight grasp, forcing her to stand up while her slack body tried to collapse under her weakened knees. Colleen was hyperventilating.

The doctor opened the briefcase and pulled out a hypodermic needle filled with green liquid. "Only a sedative. When you awaken maybe we can get to the bottom of this."

"Allow me to do the honors, doc. You hold her straight."

Dr. McDowell held Colleen straight in a heavy grasp.

She pretended to faint. She shut her eyes and let her head dangle to the side.

Dr. McDowell laid her down on the bloodied side of the mattress. Colleen strained to hide her true emotions and keep still.

247

"It's a wonder she had the stomach to kill not only Margaret," Scott brought the needle to her throat, "but to kill Samantha too. Poor woman. She had a family, you know, doc."

Colleen opened her eyes and hit the needle away, then in a split second, as Scott's hands squeezed Colleen's body in an attempt to hold her down, Colleen kicked her foot between his legs; he recoiled in pain and she ran from the room.

"Go after her. I can't leave the house until my body is healed."

He was a few steps behind her.

Colleen's heart was pumping fast. Pain shot in sparks from her bare feet to her ankles and up through her calves. Scott was an arm's length away from her when she went out the front door; she slammed it shut on his hand and maybe that bought her a few seconds of time, but she didn't keep looking over her shoulder to check.

Scott had been right. Samantha was dead. Impaled on the fence and her face scrunched in unbelievable torture. It was unfair she had to die. Colleen was angry—anybody but Samantha. She didn't deserve to die. She was a good person and a mother.

A small cry left Colleen's lips. She didn't have time to mourn her friend.

Colleen rushed past the gate and left it open; she needed to put as much distance between herself and Scott as she could without stopping for needless things and wasting precious seconds.

What the hell am I gonna do?

"*Get back here.*"

The uneven surface of the ground hurt the soft flesh of her feet, but Colleen kept pushing. There was a path she could have taken to descend the hill, but that was what Scott would have expected, so she made a sharp right and passed through spacious trees that grew over the Engstrom House's hill. Her lungs suffered restless stinging as she struggled to keep breathing. At any moment she was sure that her aching knees would snap and her life would be over; Scott would get her and inject her.

Everything was a blur; Colleen had to run so fast that she couldn't think. She moved by instinct. Curling extensions of branches wrapped around her like the fingers of witches and snatched her hair. The trees and everything surrounding Colleen were alive.

Desperately she wanted to stop and breathe and ease the pain that was increasingly pulsing through her tired body. But stopping now was impossible. Scott was nearby yelling her name, and yelling other things that her mind couldn't process because she was so focused on escaping him; outmaneuvering him and somehow getting out of this situation alive.

Never ending running.

Chills swept over her body.

All was silent. She realized she no longer heard Scott—not his running, not his yelling, nothing. She was all alone.

She stopped to catch her breath. She had come completely around the hill to the other side where she saw the nearby farm. Between the farm and the Engstrom House was a lake and a tree that towered over it. Tall grass surrounded it.

A miserable headache was pulsing in both sides of her head. After catching her breathe she stumbled downward toward the lake. Maybe she could hide somewhere in the farm. Someplace where she could lay down.

Then there was Scott's sickening laugh.

Colleen was halfway through the grass toward the lake. Scott was still standing by the outskirt of the trees. The needle was raised in his hands, highlighted by fading sunlight. Colleen turned away and ran as best as her pained body could carry her.

She had the advantage of distance between them, and by the time Scott was near the water, Colleen was already hiding in the grass. She was careful to breathe lightly and stay very still, afraid that any small noise would give her location away.

"Come out come out wherever you are. One little shot won't hurt you, you know. Please be reasonable."

Scott was coming closer.

Colleen tensed.

"Where are you? Where'd you go?"

It was purely chance that he picked the correct direction where Colleen was hiding, although he was completely unaware of where specifically she was hidden.

He was right on top of her. An inch closer and he would have stepped on her hands. The outrageously tall grass shielded her from his peripheral vision and he never saw her.

A step past Colleen.

She had the advantage and she was going to take it.

When Scott was two steps away Colleen stood up and put her arm around his neck. She closed the space between his throat and her forearm. Scott choked. His arms beat against her body forcefully; Colleen braced herself for the pain and reminded herself that it was her or Scott. Either he died or she did. Either she lived to go back into that house and find her husband or she died here at the lake.

His body was going limp in her arms, but she could still feel his attempts at breathing. Colleen pulled her arm tighter around his neck then shoved his body to the ground. She kneeled over him. The hypodermic needle of green liquid had fallen from his hands; she picked it up then injected the liquid into his throat.

His eyes fluttered open and watched her with hatred.

Scott couldn't move.

Colleen was out of breath as she dragged him closer to the edge of the lake and set his upper body into the water. He drifted over the surface of the lake with his arms extended over his head. Colleen waved goodbye.

She lingered with a smile. It made her happy to see him die.

From the depths of the lake, a hydrilla crept like a serpent and wrapped around Scott's right arm. A second hydrilla surfaced and wrapped around his left. A third and final hydrilla coiled around his throat.

They dragged him under.

Bubbles of air popped on the surface of the lake.

33

THERE WERE MANY RED cans of gasoline in Fred's truck. Joy brought down one in each hand after packing away all her belongings into the truck's cabin. No sign of Fred's ghost or Veronica's ghost, thank God—maybe they had finally gotten that divorce.

She walked back up to the house.

Samantha was dead. Her body impaled on the fence in a big tangled mess. Joy dropped the gallons of gasoline.

"*Mother of God.*" Joy approached the body. Samantha's eyes were still open, although all life had left them. "Samantha…. Do you know where Scott put my shotgun?"

Samantha groaned; blood dripped from her mouth. She made an indecipherable noise; the final breath of life.

"I don't know where that is."

Joy walked away from the body. Bandit was where she had left him in the front yard biting into a femur. She whistled to get his attention.

"We've got work to do."

He hopped up, dropping the bone, and followed her through the front door back into the house.

"Good boy."

Joy and Bandit went up the spiraling staircase up to the fifth floor. "Let's drench this place nice and good, Bandit. Make sure every inch of it comes crumbling down."

Joy drained the whole container spilling gasoline around the fifth and fourth floor as well as the lengths of stairway leading to each of those floors. She returned to the living room for the second container where she found the doctor standing with his hands behind his back and a big smile on his face. He was a disgusting creature; partly human and partly *other*. A half-formed corpse brought back from the dead. Joy despised him.

"What do we have here?" Dr. McDowell said.

Joy tossed the empty gasoline can at him; he didn't move or flinch. The can hit his stomach then bounced a couple times on the floor.

"What does it look like I'm doing?" Joy picked up the second gas can. "If we stay any longer in this house we're gonna end up on that fence like Samantha. I don't give a damn anymore if Colleen finds that door or not."

"I wouldn't do this if I were you, my dear."

"I'm not your dear."

Bandit ran up to the doctor and barked at him furiously.

RUFF! RUFF! RUFF!

The doctor brought his hand down and scratched Bandit's neck. "There, there, little fella. Everything's all right," the doctor said. Then his eyes met Joy's. "Dogs really are man's best friend. Especially Saint Bernards, like you've got yourself here. Monks in the mountains used to use them as rescue dogs. They've got an excellent sense of smell, detecting bodies under twenty feet of snow and ice. Saint Bernards would dig people out of avalanches with those gigantic paws of theirs."

Joy said nothing.

"Did you know that Saint Bernards have rather abnormal jaw shape?"

"No, I did not know that."

"It causes them to drool more than any other breed of dog. Especially when they're hungry."

Joy backed away. Terror filled her body.

"When was the last time you fed Bandit? He seems a little excited. Do I hear his stomach growling?"

Joy stepped away again. "No."

Bandit turned around to face Joy. Huge gobs of drool fell from him lips and collected into a puddle. His front shoulders slumped and he was ready to pounce. His tail wagged back and forth. Bandit's eyes flashed red.

"Bandit. No. No."

RUFF! RUFF! RUFF!

"No."

Dr. McDowell snapped his fingers. "Get her."

Joy bolted out of the living room. From there she ran past the spiraling stairway to a hallway on her left that spanned the entire length of the Engstrom House. Bandit was only seconds away from her; Joy furtively glanced over her shoulder and saw him open his jaws wide and let out a loud growl.

Around the corner she found the door to the back yard. It was already open. Joy passed through then slammed it shut; Bandit scratched the other side of the door within moments. Joy backed away, unsure where to go or what to do. She had assumed she had a little time to figure it out, but Bandit's paws struck through the door. It would be torn down in a matter of seconds.

The only place left to hide was the wellhouse.

The door didn't open when Joy first pulled it, and she let out a scream. Hysterically she tugged on the handle until the door swung wide open all of a sudden and almost knocked her over. By then the back door of the Engstrom House was only halfway destroyed, and it was possible that Bandit had not seen where she was.

Immediately upon shutting the door, Joy was overtaken with chills.

The windows in the wellhouse were boarded up. There was an old cabinet between the seats which were all bolted into the floor, but it was sealed with a padlock and she did not have the key. Desperately she looked around for a weapon of some kind, but there was nothing in the void wellhouse.

SNAP!

RUFF! RUFF!

Bandit was free from the temporary diversion of the back door. She heard his steps becoming dangerously closer with each passing second.

Joy backed away from the door and into the small space of wall next to the cabinet.

RUFF! RUFF!

Please God don't let me die. I don't want to die.

Bandit's steps came to the wellhouse door. He circled the perimeter of the grey ugly building. Joy's body shook with nerves. She shut her eyes and pretended not to be there, pretended to be anywhere else, but her mind wouldn't function. It was impossible to think about anything other than the fact that she was about to be dead. The Grim Reaper was on the other side of the wellhouse walls.

God please don't kill me. Please don't let that monster kill me.

SLAM!

Joy screamed at the sudden jolting sound; paws pounding into the wooden boards on the window nearest her. Bandit bit a wooden board apart with his cruel jaws and swallowed it up. Slobber and drool streaked the remaining broken boards and the window's metal bars.

"Bandit, no. Don't do this. It's me. It's Joy."

Bandit devoured the rest of the barrier between them.

After he was done he slid his head and paws between metal slats. He stared at her with his detestable red eyes. Endless drool collected on his lips and fell over the edges. He licked his slobber then let out a soft growl.

"Please don't kill me."

Bandit tried to pull his head out from the slats but was stuck.

For the first time in all of the craziness, Joy caught a break. If Bandit was stuck she could get out of this situation—get back to her truck and drive away.

She stepped to the door cautiously, never turning her back on Bandit. Carefully she raised her hand toward the handle.

RUFF! RUFF!

Bandit's paws wiggled between the slats that his face was stuck between. With unbelievable force he pried his head free and the metal slats came falling down. One of them rolled to Joy's feet; she grabbed it in both hands. It was covered in slobber. Neither end was very sharp.

RUFF! RUFF!

Bandit climbed through the window and was in a standoff with Joy.

"Bandit, I'm sorry." Joy shivered as she moved one tiny step away to put more distance between them in the cramped space.

RUFF! RUFF!

There was nothing she could do to break the spell that was controlling him. Bandit pounced. He jumped on Joy so quickly that she had no time to react; no time to adjust or position the metal slat and figure out a way to fight back with it. Brutal pain erupted in her head and spine and all along her body. Her eyes twitched; a thick warmth was gathering under her skull.

"I love you, Bandit."

RUFF! RUFF!

Bandit's jaws opened immensely wide; slobber connected in strands across his teeth. He clamped them together on Joy's throat and swallowed her flesh without chewing. He licked up her blood then bit into her again.

And suddenly the spell was lifted.

Bandit knew what he had done.

He curled up alongside Joy's corpse and whined.

34

Teresa found Bandit in the wellhouse with Joy's corpse. The dead body did not bother her.

She whistled.

Bandit followed her out of the wellhouse.

She climbed on top of the dog's back. Bandit howled then walked away. They went through the back door of the Engstrom House, through twisting hallways, then left through the front door. The sun was sinking behind thick clouds.

"Slow down a little, Bandit."

They disappeared into the night.

35

The doctor was drinking tea in the living room. Logs burned in the fireplace. Darkness was upon the city of Ashfall and the Engstrom House. Colleen passed through the front door and sat on a couch on the opposite side of the room.

"I should have known better," Dr. McDowell said. "I shouldn't have sent a boy to do a man's job."

Colleen rubbed her eyes. "I came here to find my husband. I'm gonna go open that door now. You're not gonna stop me or I'll kill you too."

"Are you sure it's back, my dear?"

"It never left."

"Uh-huh." Dr. McDowell drank his tea. "You know you're not gonna like what you're gonna find."

Colleen stood up. "What do you mean?"

"There's nothing for you beyond that door."

"What will I find there?" Colleen asked from the entryway into the rest of the house.

"Your destiny."

Colleen went up the stairs to the third floor. From there she retraced her very familiar steps to the damned corner where the irregular metal door had taken Ambrose away from her. It was back. A greenish glow emerged from all sides of it.

She opened the door.

Ambrose's mutilated corpse was being eaten by rats. Set against the wall was the axe that she had used to dismember him all those nights ago.

36

As rain spilled across Ashfall from a raven-black sky, the brooding house on the hill looked especially hideous, but it was good enough for two people with no other place to go. Their car was ruined from its collision with the tree.

Colleen couldn't breathe. Ambrose's hands grabbed hers and studied her. "Are you hurt?"

The words wouldn't form on her lips. She could only nod.

Ambrose came around to the other side of the car, forgetting his jacket that was in the back seat with their luggage, and opened Colleen's door. There were fragments of glass all over her body; she hadn't noticed them until Ambrose brushed it away—the crash was a haze and she was still processing the accident.

"*I'm so sorry.*" Ambrose hugged her. "I lost control."

"Are you okay?" Her lips moved slowly. After he receded from the hug, she turned a little to study him, despite the pain pulsing in her body when she moved.

"Yes. Let's get you inside."

Colleen was in too much pain to try and understand what he meant as he helped her out of her seat, but when she saw the strange house over Ambrose's shoulder, it clicked. Ambrose carried her up the hill. She shut her eyes. When she opened them, she and Ambrose were at the gate.

The gate yawned open, which was strange, because when she first glimpsed the house, she could have sworn that it was shut.

It's pretty, Colleen vaguely thought through warm pain flushing her body. She tried to stand under her own strength when they were past the gate, but she clung tight to Ambrose's arm. Something, Colleen thought, moved in one of the windows, but as she furtively searched, there was nothing there but darkness.

Ambrose turned the knob; it creaked under his touch. Together they stood motionless in the entrance. Colleen shivered as an icy draft of air passed over her drenched body. Immediately, Ambrose grabbed the poker and moved around half-burned logs that were in the fireplace.

"Do you see matches?"

"We need to explain," Colleen said. Her body ached as she spoke. "What?"

"We need to explain to the owners what happened to us."

"Look around. Nobody lives here."

"Ambrose I don't want to trespass. Let's find the owners."

Ambrose stepped with her through the sitting room. *"Anybody home?"* His loud voice spread through the house. *"Anybody?"* Then his eyes met Colleen's. "Nobody lives here."

"Let's make sure."

Exiting the living room, moonlight halted behind them, and instantly they were in pure darkness and total silence. Not even a gleam of lightning's unceasing blaze penetrated the sickly house; not a whisper of the storm reached them here. It was as if they had suddenly been stricken blind and deaf, and Colleen thought that for a moment she had been killed by a stroke of lightning as she had crossed the threshold. They traveled through the unknown. Vague outlines of doors could be seen if Colleen focused hard enough, and for one moment—maybe even less—she thought she had seen the outline of a face, but a closer look revealed nothing, and all she saw was thick blackness spreading through the ugly house. She missed the occasional luminosity of lightning that only reached into the living room. Colleen felt as if she'd fallen through dizzying darkness and end up in another world.

"Anybody home? My name is Ambrose, this is my wife Colleen. Our car is wrecked and we need a place to wait out this storm."

Silence from the decrepit house.

"Okay. I believe you." Colleen pulled on his hand.

Ambrose led her back through the threshold into the living room. Colleen pulled a white sheet from a couch and laid down.

"Are you comfortable?"

"Everything hurts. Especially my head."

Ambrose gave her a kiss then stepped away from her; her hand fell away slowly from his. He looked closely again at the fireplace and surrounding area, running his hands over the mantelshelf then wiping them off on his pants once they were stained with dust. Colleen wished Ambrose could find matches soon because the coldness was getting worse.

"Where I grew up, there were stories about an old dark house," Ambrose said. "Where bad things happened."

"Haven't we been through enough tonight?" Colleen shuddered. "Please, love, don't try and scare me."

"I heard about somebody who disappeared in an old house. Old houses such as this one, they used to have bunkers and places built in to hide. Suppose somebody found their way in, but couldn't find their way out."

"Honey, please, I don't want to hear about such things."

"I wish I were the one who was hurt from the crash instead of you," Ambrose said. "Hey, I'll be right back. I'm gonna take a quick look around. Maybe if I'm lucky I'll come across some matches in the kitchen or something."

"Don't take too long. Please."

Ambrose walked out. "I won't."

Suddenly her body was plagued with a feeling of bugs creeping under every inch of her skin. The laughter of children echoed from deep within the house. Colleen's eyes abruptly swelled with tears at the thought of her own daughter. The laughter ended, and the house was still. The house was so hushed that even the smallest of moments would be heard.

Long minutes ticked by until Colleen heard the footsteps. Ambrose came back holding a box of matches. "They were in the kitchen."

"Ambrose, I think we need to talk." Colleen's skin was crawling with shivers. "There's something I wanted to talk to you about all day. I don't know how exactly to say it…"

"Yes, my love?" Ambrose said as he lit the fireplace. "What is it?"

"Well…" Colleen hesitated for a few moments. "I want us to start a family. I think we should start trying."

"I told you we can. But not right now."

After a few more quiet moments, Colleen said, "Sometimes I still dream of her. Our baby that you made me… get rid of." The sickly words came off her lips and chilled her. Her guts turned at the thought of what he had made her do to their child. "I even thought of a name for her. Amy. But I also like Teresa. Or Vincent if it were a boy. But I always wanted a baby girl."

"Are you sick, giving a name to something that wasn't born? It wasn't our baby, it was… nothing."

"Honey…"

"Look, we're young, we have our whole lives ahead of us. Why have a baby now and ruin it?"

"We shouldn't have done what we did. I wish you never made me…"

"Colleen, not now. Let's not talk about this now. It isn't the time."

She shut her eyes and tried to dream. Ambrose came to her side and held her hand and told her she'd be okay. Behind her closed eyes, she fell into darkness, drifting, dreaming, being carried away to the magical world of sleep.

Colleen's baby called her from its crib. The walls of the crib were raised high so that she could not see her baby, only hear her, and when she approached, she carefully peeked over the edge to find her daughter Amy drenched in mud, a leaf hanging between crooked black lips.

Amy screamed for her mother.

That was all her child could do; scream and try to move its stiff body, failing to shift at all. The poor child was in pain and she couldn't stand it. Colleen rushed to pick up her baby and cradle her, ignoring the mud.

"Hush little baby don't say a word, Mama's gonna buy you a mock-ingbird."

The child was cold all over, as if she had been made of ice instead of flesh. Colleen carried her baby through a long hallway and down creaking stairs until they were at the fireplace in her own home's living room, where she set her baby down after she knelt at the fire-place. One matchstick left in the box. Colleen struck it then dropped it in with the logs of wood. Flames erupted. Scorching warmth over-took the room.

Colleen wiped handfuls of mud from her baby. Flames licked closer. She rubbed her child again before the fire, returning warmth to her baby's body. The cries stopped. Minutes later Colleen felt Amy's pulse again—that beautiful pulse that was infrequent at first, then became a constant vibration. Amy's arm twitched then moved of her own will.

Shadows drew over Colleen's eyes, so that she was awakened with a sense that she was surrounded by souls; souls trapped in darkness, reaching for that one small light desperate to escape. So comfort-able, so warm, so tired in a room full of life, she had not noticed that she was alone. It wasn't until she heard footfalls above her that she reached for Ambrose and knew he was gone.

Colleen sat up. Ambrose was asleep on a couch on the other side of the room.

"Kill him for the child he took from you," a whisper said. *"Let me guide you."*

From the impossibly black threshold leading into the rest of the house, a misshapen hand that was a sick parody of anything that might have once been human reached through. Colleen rose from the couch and held it.

It guided her through the blindness of night through the house and to the back door.

The whispers led her through the forest and to the Engstrom Family graveyard. Past the graveyard, through densely growing trees and thick grass, it brought her to a decaying cabin. Behind the cabin was an open shed. Colleen opened the loose door.

Moonlight highlighted an axe.

Colleen returned to the back door of the strange house. Ambrose was yelling her name, searching for her from somewhere deep inside. She smiled and crept silently back in with a grip tight on the axe. She tiptoed around a corner and watched him.

"Colleen? Honey where are you?" He switched his candle from one hand to the other.

Ambrose went into another hall. Colleen lurked in shadows, trailing him.

When she caught up to him he was at the base of the spiraling staircase. He ascended and followed the sound of fading footsteps that came from upstairs; footsteps that seemed as though they were coming from another reality.

"Colleen?"

She followed closely behind him.

The footsteps were coming from the third floor; Ambrose continued his ascent. His candle's flame tore through darkness like a razor cutting through flesh.

On the third floor the footsteps died.

Ambrose stepped around the third floor searching for her. When he was far enough, she hid in the adjacent hall and shouted for him—begged him to come help her. His heavy footsteps slammed her way; she slid into a nearby room and shut the door.

He passed her hiding place calling her name.

When she was sure he was far enough she left her hiding place and called his name again.

"Ambrose! Oh my God! I need you!"

His footsteps were distant.

She hid next to a cabinet. Ambrose followed her cries for help.

"Where the hell are you?"

Colleen peeked around the cabinet's edge. Ambrose was walking away.

Colleen dragged the head of the axe alongside herself. Ambrose turned around. He ran to her and held her in a white-knuckled grip. His eyes searched her body for any injuries.

"Good God, I thought I'd never find you again. Are you hurt? What's are you doing up here?"

"I'm so sorry."

"For what?

Colleen pulled away from his grasp. She tightened her hands around the axe and raised it high above her head, then brought it down into Ambrose's shoulder; he staggered away dumbfounded as blood spurted in each direction.

A step closer. Colleen raised the axe again and brought it down on his face; he let out a fierce scream.

She didn't stop until he was in a dozen pieces.

Then she realized what she had done. Coldness slithered like a serpent on her delicate skin.

At the corner of a hall was an empty cabinet. Colleen could see a length of an indistinct door behind its edge. She pushed the structure aside to find the purposely hidden wooden door. She pulled it open; using Ambrose's candle as she hid his pieces inside, she saw that the room was completely empty. No windows. No furniture. Nothing at all. What its purpose was, she couldn't figure.

All his pieces were inside the room. She stepped away then she returned to his body and pulled his wedding ring off his finger. Then she shut the door and moved the cabinet back into place, making sure that she adjusted it to cover the door completely. Nobody could ever know what she had done.

37

COLLEEN WRAPPED A FINGER around the phone's cord. She paced back and forth in front of the fireplace. "Did you read what they wrote about me in the papers?"

"Mrs. Tillman, I can't stop the papers from gossiping. This situation isn't unique to you. They can and will publish anything that they want. My job is to convince the courtroom otherwise. Look, you know you're innocent and so do I. Take a breath and calm down."

"All right. But what if—what if... what if they don't believe me?"

"Why wouldn't they? There was no evidence found against you from the investigation of that house. And there's that second team that's heading down there in the next couple days to do more research. If you're innocent you've got nothing to fear."

"I *am* innocent. Have you ever had a calm client?"

"Heh, now that would be a first."

Colleen hung up the phone.

"Don't be afraid," a whisper said. It was coming from the fireplace.

Colleen kneeled in front of the flames.

Deep within the fire, the voice said, *"If you listen to me, everything will be just fine."*

Nighttime came faster than normal. By six PM it was pitch black outside. Colleen didn't know what town she was in; she must have taken a wrong turn. The diner was the only thing she had seen in the endless stretches of land, so she stopped there. She parked her car at the end of the lot behind the building and was surprised to see there were five other cars already parked there.

This was as far as her car could take her. She unscrewed the license plates then used a file from the toolkit in her trunk to scratch off the vehicle identification number. Past the parking lot was a little swamp of murky water. Ducks swam. Bees hummed. For a place in the middle of nowhere, it was full of life.

Colleen threw the plates in. They sank immediately. She walked away, stomach growling, then turned back around and threw her keys in after them.

Even outside the front door of the diner, Colleen could hear music playing through the speakers. Ethel Waters.

A couple men sat on barstools playing cards. A man and woman sat in a booth with a kid who was dozing off and leaning on the woman's arm. One waitress was refilling the men's coffee while the other waitress took empty plates off the counter from a customer who must have just left. Colleen took a seat in the booth furthest away from everybody. It was nice to pretend, even for a few minutes, that things were still normal.

She opened her small purse. Inside was hardly enough to cover a small coffee and donut when the waitress came by and asked her what she'd be having. Colleen drank her coffee and leaned her head on the window.

Oh my God, what am I doing? Colleen thought. *I'm insane.*

She buried her face in her arms. The sobs were trying to burst out of her, but she held them back. The last thing she needed was to draw attention to herself in this diner while she was on the run—but she had completely failed. Somebody sat across from her.

"Hello," he said.

Colleen lifted her head a little bit over her arms. The man must have been about forty. KEYSTONE FREIGHT on the shoulder patch of his uniform—a button-up shirt whose first two notches were un-buttoned. Below that was the name FRED sewn into his shirt. Fred removed his black hat and set it aside on the table.

"Pardon me, m'am, for intruding. Couldn't help but notice you were sitting all alone. Mind if I join you?"

"Go ahead." Colleen grabbed a tissue from the dispenser and wiped her eyes. She was embarrassed that a stranger had seen her cry.

"Did you already order supper?"

Colleen nodded.

"What's good here, ma'am? It's my first time at this establish-ment."

"The coffee's good."

"That's all you had?"

"A glazed donut."

Fred found the menu, opened it, and slid it in front of Colleen. "Please. On me."

"Oh no, I couldn't."

"Look, I can't let a lady sit here crying and do nothing about it. Let me help you out. Order whatever you'd like."

Colleen ordered a burger and fries and a coffee refill. Fred had the same order.

"I can't thank you enough."

"Don't worry about it."

They were silent for a little while. A waitress came by and took their dishes.

"Hey," Fred said, "I'm no idiot. It looks like things are going rough. Believe me, I've been there. And I've seen it a helluva lot too—driving across America, you see just about everything. It'll turn around. Always does."

"Thank you so much. I can't thank you enough."

Fred put down the money for the meal and a couple dollars for a trip then checked his watch. "It's about time now that I get back on the road. It was nice meeting you. Say, I don't think I caught your name."

"Jessica."

"Pretty name. Have a good night, Jessica."

Fred put his hat back on and left. Colleen watched him leave the diner. She couldn't stay here all night—the employees were already giving her strange looks. Nervously Colleen grabbed the two dollar tip and put it in her purse without the waitresses seeing, then she slid out of the booth and smiled at the workers.

"Have a good night," the lady who waited on Colleen and Fred said.

"Thanks, you too."

The headlights of Fred's truck were blinding. Colleen waved and called his name but he hadn't seen her or head her, and pulled out of his parking spot and left. Colleen ran after his truck with her arms frantically waving, shouting his name. The truck was partway onto the street when it stopped and reversed.

Colleen was out of breath climbing up the little steps to the passenger side. She hopped in and shut her door using both hands.

"Somehow I knew I hadn't seen the last of you," Fred said.

"Thank you so much for stopping."

"Where you headed?"

"As far away from here as possible."

"I'm heading south. That good enough for you?"

"Sure. Actually I need to get to a place called Ashfall."

They were off into the night.

"Normally I don't pry, but a lady crying in a diner comes running up to my truck begging to go… anywhere at all. I'm not harboring someone I shouldn't, right? I'm not getting in the middle of something I shouldn't be in the middle of, aren't I?"

"No," Colleen said, taking a few seconds pause to create the many lies she'd need to keep track of. Already she had to keep reminding herself that she had lied about her name. "My husband left me after a nasty fight. That's all."

"You had a fight in the diner?"

"No. The diner's just where I ended up."

"What was your fight about?"

"I didn't love him anymore. There was somebody else."

"Someone else. Is that who you're gonna go see in Ashfall?"

"Uh-huh. So thank you. Without you I don't know how I'd get there."

"No problem."

"How long have you been a truck driver?"

"Coming up on year number nineteen. Might seem like a long time to somebody as young as you are, but it goes fast I tell ya. All those miles fly by. You know, it's nice to have someone with me for a change. This kind of job gets lonely. Sometimes more than anything, you just want somebody to talk to."

"I see."

"Yeah, but the job has so many great things going for it. The chance to see America and spend some time in each place you visit. I have at least one good friend in every state. Hey, Jessica, with all the turmoil you hear about in the news, you might think the world's gone to hell, but it does your heart some good to see the kindness that exists throughout our lovely nation."

"Do you ever get scared being out on the road?"

"Never. I've got a license to carry a shotgun. I keep it up in the cabinets behind us. If anyone were to start some trouble they wouldn't last long."

They were quiet a little while longer. Miles of road passed by. Fred switched lanes to cut off slow drivers. Colleen shut her eyes and leaned against the window but couldn't get comfortable enough to sleep.

"You awake?"

Colleen shifted to face him. "Not so easy to sleep with so much on my mind."

"Still thinking about that fight with your husband?"

"He said some awful things that I can't get out of my head."

Fred pointed his thumb over his shoulder. "Back in the cabin there's a few blankets. Feel free to take one. And don't worry about Bandit, he don't bite."

Colleen wobbled past the front seat and into the cabin where she found a blanket neatly folded at the end of an inflatable mattress. Asleep against the opposite side of the truck was a Saint Bernard. Colleen brought Fred's blanket back to her seat with her and curled up with it. It kept her warm but her mind couldn't wrap around sleep.

"You can talk about it," Fred said. "If you want."

"Is there really goodness left in the world?"

"You've only gotta look around."

Colleen stared deep into the farmland they were passing. "I don't see anything."

"Isn't there anything that gives you any joy?"

"Painting. But I quit that. It... stopped being fun."

"Maybe the change of scenery is what you need to get creative again. Once you get to Ashfall I bet you won't be able to stop painting. What kind of things do you paint?"

"Wildlife."

"What's your favorite animal?"

"Foxes. I like painting their fluffy tails."

Colleen shut her eyes and tried to sleep again. This time sleep found her. It didn't last long.

Not much time must have passed because when she opened her eyes again the area was still dull farmland. The sky was still decrepitly black. She yawned and turned a little bit in her seat, rubbing her eyes.

They were pulling over.

"Morning, sleepyhead."

"How long was I asleep?"

"Twenty minutes at best."

"Why are we stopping?"

"I'm getting tired. Even a trucker needs a break." Fred climbed out of his seat and went toward the cabin. "Maybe you'll be more comfortable back here. With me."

"What?" Colleen said without turning back.

"You might be more comfortable on a mattress."

"I think I'm okay here. Thanks though."

Fred grabbed her by the wrist and pulled her out of her seat. She struggled against him but was too weak to break his grasp. In the back of the cabin, he threw her on his mattress and climbed on top of her.

"Gas, grass, or ass. Nobody rides for free."

A little while later she was asleep on Fred's mattress pinned between him and the wall. Fred was asleep. Colleen was afraid to make any movements but she knew she had to do something, and that was when she remembered what Fred said about the shotgun.

Colleen moved out from under his arm. He turned a little and muttered something that came out slurred and wordless; something that had no meaning because he was still trapped in a haze of sleep. Colleen moved his arm completely off of her and stood up. As she inched herself away from him, his arm fell back into place over the small length of mattress where she had been. He searched for her, but still being asleep he didn't realize she had moved.

Bandit rose. He opened his mouth and drool dripped from his lips.

"Please don't bark," Colleen whispered.

Bandit shut his mouth and sat back down.

Colleen opened the overhead cabinet. The shotgun was there, surrounded by boxes of ammunition and some of Fred's junk. It was a Winchester. Colleen pulled it down and along came several boxes of bullets crashing loudly and spilling throughout the cabin.

Fred's eyes opened.

Colleen panicked and aimed the gun at him. He was running straight for her at the exact moment she pulled the trigger—and nothing happened. Fred laughed and tugged at the shotgun; Colleen held it with a white-knuckled grip.

"To make a gun work, you need bullets."

There was hellish anger in Fred's eyes; he yanked the gun again. Colleen knew that if she didn't keep the Winchester out of his hands, it meant certain death. She pulled on the gun with desperation and when that didn't work, she pushed it directly at Fred and hit the barrel into his chest. She repeated the motion until Fred momentarily let go. He reached for the gun again but Colleen drew it back and swung it across his face; a gash opened and blood spilled.

She swung it again at the back of his head. Fred dropped to the ground. Bandit barked at her to stop, but she wouldn't listen to him. She brought the shotgun down upon Fred's head until he stopped moving.

Colleen tossed the gun aside, sat in the driver's seat, and was off into the night, headed for the Engstrom House.

38

THE HOUSE WAS AS chilling and brooding on its hill as Colleen remembered it. Dark clouds massed over it. Its trees swayed even when there was no wind. The gate yawned open as if it had been anticipating her return; as if it knew all along that she would be back to finish what was started.

The living room was devoid of any people when she walked inside, but their hushed voices were drifting from deep inside the house. Colleen followed the whispers to a room whose door was halfway open; she peeked inside and saw empty chairs across from a fireplace.

A voice whispered to Colleen, *"Come with me."*

She followed it up a nearby stairway. On the second floor it led her to a room filled with dusty instruments. Shelves were set against the far wall and right wall, and against the left wall were boxes of books and sheet music. As Colleen stepped through the room, a paper glided from one of the boxes through the room and landed in a corner cramped between two shelves. She knelt where it landed and found a vent in the floor that looked down into the meeting room.

A man was taking shots of whiskey at the bar in the left side of the meeting room as two laughing women entered. One with dark hair and one with big eyes. They went across the room to the front chairs and sat closest to the fireplace. Dark Hair was drinking tea while Big Eyes was putting a cassette into her tape recorder.

"I never thought we'd find our way back," Big Eyes said. Then, into her recorder, she said, *"My name is Jane Adams. I am recording the first day in the Engstrom House exploration."*

Dark Hair leaned closer to the tape recorder. "Right now we're anticipating the arrival of Dr. James McDowell."

"Yeah," Jane said, "I suppose he wants to make a grand entrance."

"Ladies," the man said, "would you two like a drink?"

"Absolutely," Dark Hair said.

Jane spoke into her recorder, "The Engstrom House is home to Ashfall's most delicious whiskey."

At that moment a woman with long brown hair joined everybody. "God it's so easy to get turned around in a place like this. I don't like being alone in here for one second, I keep thinking that crazy woman's around every corner."

"Thank God she's nowhere near here, Margaret," the man said.

"I told the doctor we should have written up little maps."

"Where is he anyways?"

"Lost without his little map, I assume." Margaret smiled. "You know how the doctor is about punctuality. It isn't like him to be late. I shouldn't have ditched him."

Two more people entered the room a minute later.

"Hello everyone. I'm lucky Joy here found me and pointed me in the right direction. I'm afraid I'm not so familiar with the layout of the house yet—and I should be, considering I was the one who picked this room to be our meeting room." Dr. McDowell put an arm around the blonde woman who accompanied him. "Thank you, my dear."

"You're welcome, doctor." Joy smiled.

A cleanshaven man in his late forties or early fifties with a full head of hair. A pudgy face. Thick glasses. He was wearing a black shirt with a purple tie that he was adjusting. A briefcase in one hand, and a glass of water in the other.

Scott poured the doctor a shot. "Here you go, doc."

"No thanks, Scottie my boy. My physician told me to lay off the drinks. But maybe I'll have a sip when that crazy woman is put behind bars and we have a little celebration."

Colleen felt a chill.

Dr. McDowell went to the front of the meeting room to begin his presentation. "Now that we've all been acquainted," he said, "let's get down to business."

Dr. McDowell was in the third floor hallway taking pictures with Margaret.

"Remember, Miss Lewis, if you find any strange doors, don't open them." Dr. McDowell laughed.

"That won't be a problem, doctor."

Dr. McDowell checked his watch. "I think dinner will be ready soon. Why don't you go on ahead? I'll wrap up this photography business and put the film in the darkroom. Make sure Mrs. Wilson sets aside a rare steak for me."

Margaret gave him her camera. "Sure thing, doctor."

He was crouched taking pictures. It was the perfect opportunity. Quiet steps.

As Colleen plunged the knife into his back he turned around; the camera's flash went off and captured her picture.

He struggled on the ground to move away from her, but Colleen was pinned on top of him with a hand on his throat. She raised the knife high above her head then forced it into the doctor's gut. While the sharp blade plunged inside his body, Colleen twisted it and watched the pain in his eyes.

She pulled the knife out slowly then dragged its point across his body. His face was reddening quick and he was begging and pleading for breath. His fists hopelessly raised then fell. All strength was leaking from his body along with his blood.

Colleen let go.

The first door she opened was a bedroom. There was a dustcover over a vintage dresser; Colleen pulled it off then returned to the doctor. He was still breathing and was trying to mutter something that wouldn't form on his lips.

Colleen wondered if he really saw a light at the end of the tunnel; if his whole life did flash before his eyes, or if the final thing he ever saw was this sheet wrapping over his face. How did it feel to know you were on the brink of death? How did it feel slowly going over that edge and descending into the other side? Was it as painless and easy as falling asleep?

She dragged him into the room where she had hid Ambrose's corpse. She set his body wrapped in the dustcover into a corner. After she left the room she pushed the cabinet back into place and turned corners until she came back to the place where she had stabbed him. His blood streaked the floor but thankfully it did not lead in a trail to where she had hidden his body. The doctor's camera and Margaret's camera were on the ground. She needed to get them and to get rid of the film inside so that way nobody would find her picture, but when she heard nearby footsteps she panicked, and retreated into the nearest room without grabbing the film.

Colleen kneeled and put her ear to the base of the door.

Outside was Margaret's familiar voice. "Doctor? Are you still up here? Everyone's waiting for you. Doctor?"

Her footsteps were coming closer.

"Doctor?"

Silence.

Steps.

"Oh my God."

A piercing scream.

Colleen was frozen. Soon there were other voices in the hallway; all of them blended together in hushed whispers and she couldn't be sure of what they were saying.

Guilt and worry choked her. Would she be caught?

Colleen lingered, afraid to move a muscle.

It was a long time before it was safe for her to leave her hiding place.

39

"ALL RIGHT, BOYS. TELL it to us from the start. Don't spare any details."

Officer Thompson wasn't used to being on the other side of the table, but after the recent events, it was time for him and Officer McKinley to give his testimonies of what had happened. They sat across from the chief of police, the district attorney, and a psychologist.

"Probably the most attention this town's ever got was when that lady said her husband went missing in that old house," Thompson said. "Me personally, I don't like to speculate, so I had no opinion one way or the other what happened to that lady and her husband up at that house. Least of all did I expect she'd come all the way back and... do what she did."

"Just give it to us straight," the chief of police said.

"Sure." McKinley took a big gulp of water. "She killed the doctor. But without a body on our hands, me and McKinley here couldn't do much, could we?"

"Is that what your men are trained to do?" The district attorney asked the chief of police. "Sit around and shrug at a reported murder?"

"No, sir. They are trained to do protect and serve the citizens of this great country."

"Look," McKinley said, "I'm not a fool. I know what you're getting at. Maybe if Thompson and I had caught this woman after the death of that doctor, then nobody else would have died. Well we couldn't have seen the future. And we couldn't have worked with clues we didn't even have, that's for damn sure."

"So what happened?" The district attorney said.

"A woman with a pixie cut comes in here frantic," Thompson said, "screaming about the Engstrom place up by the farm. Someone's dead, she says. So I says to McKinley to step on it, let's go up there and check it out."

"So I did what Thompson said, stepped on the gas and we went on up..."

"The owners of that old place should put a better lock on their gate," Officer McKinley said as he parked at the house.

Everyone was gathered in an upstairs hallway. There was a lot of blood smeared around the floor. Right away McKinley was piecing it together who he thought was guilty and who he thought was innocent, but there wasn't anything to go on—not yet.

"Who was the last to see him alive?"

McKinley and Thompson looked over the group.

"Come on, out with it," Thompson said. "Who was the last person to see him alive? I want to know what each and every single one of you was doing at the moment your friend died."

"Now, now," McKinley said, "we haven't seen a body. Maybe he's not dead. But like Officer Thompson here says, we need to know what each of you were up to at the time of this... incident. Don't be afraid to speak up."

"I saw him last. It—it was me who found him. He told me go down to dinner. So that's what I did. When he wasn't there after a few minutes I checked on him, and I found the blood."

"How did you know where he was? What's your name again?"

"Because we were up here taking pictures. Please believe me."

"Your name."

"Margaret Lewis."

"And the rest of you, what were you doing?"

"All of us were at the dinner table," the only man in the group said. "It couldn't have been any of us."

"And there's absolutely nobody else in the house?" Thompson asked.

"Nobody."

"You understand that the team in that house was investigating a disappearance and potential murder," the district attorney said. "Then the leader of this team vanishes with buckets of blood left behind."

"Again," McKinley said, "we did not know then what we know now. Look, if we had a body laying on the floor, if there was a murder weapon right next to the corpse, and some bogus story like that crazy lady gave a year or more ago, we could have done something right then and there."

"He's right," Thompson said, "I'd have brought them all to the station and put all of 'em behind bars until things were sorted out. We aren't allowed to arrest innocent citizens. So we met them in the middle."

"Meaning?" The district attorney asked.

"We agreed to watch the house. Few hours a day to calm their nerves. What else could we do?"

McKinley and Thompson sat in their patrol car.

"What's your gut telling you, Thompson?"

"I don't know."

"When something like this comes along the little man in my gut ties knots in my stomach."

"So what's your little man telling you, McKinley?"

"There's something here they aren't telling us. It can't be so easy. Cut and dry and wrapped up for us, minus the suspect and minus the corpse. They say they were all together downstairs in the dining room. Check. Dr. McDowell was up alone taking pictures. Check. That assistant of his didn't have a drop of blood on her. Check. So who did it?"

"Like I told you, I don't know."

"That's why it's so funny, Thompson. There's a factor here we're missing. Did they all plan it? All… dozen of them, in on it? Could that be it? No, no, that's too convoluted. Two or three of them, hell even four of them in on it, I could buy it. Maybe. But something's up and I don't like it."

"Well, I've got all their written statements here. I've read 'em over six-seven times. I don't know…" Thompson stopped to think it all over. "Let's say they killed him, whether it's two of them in on it or the whole gang. Perfect place to do it, you can hide a body in there and never find it in a lifetime, I bet. So what do they get out of it? Everyone's still here. Nobody's gained anything, have they?"

"Oh, that's what they want you to think. Criminals work on the sly. It's not always cut and dry as murder for the insurance money. No sir, Thompson. Somebody's up to something in there, and that's why we wait here under the guise of protecting them. Sooner or later, one of them's bound to slip."

"Seen anything like this before?"

"Sure."

"How'd it turn out?"

"In the end, the bad guys always get caught."

"What came of these stakeouts?" The district attorney asked.

"A huge break. And that didn't come until later," Thompson said. "Thank God McKinley had that little man in his gut. After a couple nights I wanted to call it quits."

"As I said at the start, don't spare any details. What happened next?"

Thompson and McKinley exchanged a look.

"We finally got a break," McKinley said, "when a couple brothers came to loot the house."

40

THE DEEP HOURS OF night brought bewitching darkness into the halls of the Engstrom House.

Colleen held a handle close to her chest with both hands.

"Come with me," a whisper said.

Colleen followed it through a blindingly dark hallway. A sudden ray of moonlight passed through a window and illuminated the twisted hand reaching from shadows. Colleen held it. The unseen stranger led her to the center of a hall on the fifth floor.

The dropdown staircase descended on its own.

The stranger's hand was gone.

Colleen quietly went into the attic room. Windows let in a glow of moonlight that gently shined on the vague surfaces of a million lifetimes that had been crammed together in here; the belongings of dead men surrounded her.

A rush of air chilled her.

One of the windows was open.

Below the window was a book that was streaked by the light more than anything else in the attic. Its pages turned with the blowing of the wind. Colleen knelt and read it; its pages showed an archaic diagram of a body on an altar. As she turned the pages, the pieces came back together. The man was made whole again.

Colleen tucked the book under her arm. She brought it back with her to the room Ambrose was hidden inside of.

"We can be together again, honey." She picked up his head and kissed him. "This house will no longer keep us apart."

After Colleen left the room and pushed the cabinet back into place, she heard the cry of a child. A little girl. She followed it through the winding hallways, down the stairs, and to the doorway that brought her into the basement. When she was done there, the cries ended. Her candlelight shined against the metal lock of a treasure chest.

It opened on its own. Inside was a large piece of wood with faded symbols carved into it. It wasn't as precise as the altar that was in the illustrations in the book she had found in the attic, but it would do.

She brought it back upstairs and stacked Ambrose's pieces on top of it.

"You're looking better already."

It had been a few days since the doctor went missing, and Mrs. Wilson was having trouble sleeping. Tonight she was turning in her bed when she heard steps outside her bedroom door.

Somebody walking quickly one way, then the other. Was everyone else up too? What was happening out there? She slid out of her bed quietly and tiptoed to the shut door. She pressed her ear against it and listened.

Quietness.

Then suddenly steps again.

As she turned the knob, somebody screamed. Mrs. Wilson pulled away from the door and stepped backwards, pushing her hands over her mouth to stop her own scream from erupting. The scream had been cut short—an abrupt half a scream.

She opened the door a short length. From the little she could see, the hallway was empty. No signs of anybody. She lingered for two more seconds then opened the door fully and stepped out of her room. The air was full of chills.

"Is anybody there? Is everyone okay?"

Silence.

She stepped down the hall and looked around a corner. Had she imagined it? No, she couldn't have.

Her stomach tightened into nervous knots. She returned to her bedroom. After she shut the door, a rope locked around her throat. Somebody unseen pulled on it until Mrs. Wilson couldn't breathe anymore.

When she woke up, she thought she was dead. She could not move her arms or legs and could not open her mouth. She was tied to a chair. Duct tape over her mouth. Under the glow of little candles that filled an unfamiliar room, she saw an amorphous mountain of body parts stacked on a wooden altar. And nearby was Dr. McDowell.

She knew right away that he was dead.

His corpse was fallen over in a chair, and even though he had been torn open, he was tied by ropes as well.

A groan from the other side of the room.

Mrs. Wilson turned painfully against the aching in her throat and saw that Jane was tied up as well. Her eyes begged for an escape.

Then the door opened.

Jane looked out the window at the police officers in their car. Thank God they were there tonight, she thought, but they had to leave sometime, and she didn't want them to. She felt so much safer whenever the police were around. She wondered what their thoughts were on all this—if they had some suspicion on what could have happened to the doctor. She had no exact suspicion of her own since there was no way it could have been anybody.

What could have happened? The doctor had not shouted, had not screamed, there had been no noises, no exact trail of blood, and nobody could have gotten past the gate and into the house without anyone knowing…

…unless somebody had let them in.

But who had a key? Scott? Margaret? The doctor? And when would this have taken place? Nobody had been acting suspicious, at least not in Jane's opinion. She had seen nobody sneaking away food for a hidden guest. And the more she thought about it, the dumber the theories became.

It had been a quiet couple days around the Engstrom House. She was restless tonight and wanted answers.

Sitting in a bay window overlooking the sudden downpour of rain, she pressed the red button on her tape recorder.

"This is Jane Adams, talking to you in the middle of the night because I can't sleep. It's been… let's see… three days since the doctor disappeared. I guess focus around here has kind of shifted to him. We started out with looking for evidence of one missing man, now we've got to find another. Everyone's a little on edge. Sometimes I can't calm my nerves. The only thing giving me a little relief is the fact that I can see the police right now. Their car's parked out there. I wonder what they think of all this, because I sure don't know what to think.

"I'm scared. I'm scared of what we might uncover as we look for the doctor. And I'm scared of what might get me as long as I stay in this house. There's something wrong here within these walls. I can feel it.

"I wonder if the doctor found out something that he wasn't supposed to. And I don't know what that means, all right? I only wonder… if maybe somebody in here isn't telling the whole truth. If somebody isn't, well, who they say they are…"

Jane stood up from the bay window and walked through the house.

"So now I'm walking through the third floor. There are five floors in the Engstrom House, plus a basement. I don't know what it is about this third floor, but that's where both men that we're searching for have gone missing—Ambrose Tillman and James McDowell.

"Now I'm back to the place where we found the blood. The floor's been cleaned since then. The rooms all across this floor were checked between all of us. That also makes me nervous. If somebody in our group... had hurt the doctor and hid him away, they'd know which room to check. For all I know, the doctor is still behind one of these doors."

Jane dragged her hand across the wall.

"I just want to say this. Nobody ever gets away with anything. It might take a year or a hundred years but the truth always comes out."

Jane was silent for a little while. She opened a door and stepped inside, shining her flashlight. "An old bedroom. I should take pictures of this to go along with my recording. The ancient things I've seen in and around this place are the most fascinating things I've ever..."

She froze when she saw a shadow pass through the doorway; it moved so fast that she almost hadn't noticed it, but from the split second she glimpsed it, it was unmistakable. A person moving through the hallway. Somebody who hadn't wanted to be seen.

"Doctor?"

Her instincts told her to stay in place. She listened for footsteps or noises but there were none; only the eerie silence of the Engstrom House.

Jane turned off her flashlight in an attempt to keep any unwanted attention away from herself.

Her knees shook. Her mouth was dry. Jane wanted to be out of there. She moved her feet one small step and the floorboards creaked. She paused to nervously search the open doorway for any signs of that person; nobody was there.

Relax, she thought.

She left the room and nothing happened. She took a deep breath and took big steps away the place where Dr. McDowell's body had been found and went down to the second floor. She sat at another bay window, held her recorder to her mouth, and realized she had been recording the entire time.

"Definitely... definitely no clues up there."

She laid on her side watching the rainfall. The moon was full and shining bright.

This will all be over soon, she thought. *Things will be okay.*

She shut her eyes and brought herself back to that moment upstairs. Had she really seen somebody? Whoever it was had moved so swiftly as if they were part of the house, part of the *shadows.* A shadow person.

Jane was drifting off to the dreamworld when she remembered her recorder was still on. She'd run out of tape soon enough if she kept it rolling when she wasn't saying anything. She opened her eyes, pressed the button, then caught the shadow moving in the window glass.

The rope came over her throat.

Her scream was cut short.

She struggled against the invader and shoved the surprisingly thin body away. The rope came loose from around her throat; Jane ran away gasping for air. She turned corners, looking over her shoulder, never seeing the shadowy stranger who had attacked her.

Then, suddenly, another subliminal blur moved in the corner of her eye.

Colleen opened the door to the secret room. Her guests were happily awaiting her in their seats. She shut the door behind herself and already the begging was starting; Mrs. Wilson and Jane were making insufferable noises through the duct tape.

"Nuh-uh-uh," Colleen said. "No noises."

She picked up a candle and brought it to Mrs. Wilson's face. "How are you doing? You were out for a while."

Tears fell from Mrs. Wilson's eyes.

"And you, Jane?"

Jane didn't make eye contact. She made no noises. She sulked.

Colleen reached into her pocket and brought out a knife. "Took me forever to sneak this thing. The ritual has a few particular steps that I'll need your assistance for."

Jane wept. She tried to break free of the restrains Colleen had set her in, but they were tied well. Jane did not have a chance at breaking free from them no matter how much she tried.

Colleen knelt in front of Jane and held the candle up to her face. "Now don't be sad. I'd think you'd be happy about this. You get to help me. Aren't you part of the team? Don't you want to bring my husband back to life?"

Jane shook her head.

Colleen set the tip of the knife to Jane's forehead and brought it down across Jane's left eye and to her chin.

Jane was moving against her restraints again, attempting to break loose and her hands were fists. Then the hyperventilating started.

"Okay, I'll give you a little break, but we aren't done here. Under-stand me?"

Jane threw her head back and cried.

Colleen pined the knife off on Mrs. Wilson's shirt. "Your turn, lady."

Mrs. Wilson shook her head side to side. She was begging for freedom with her eyes. Colleen didn't care about any of that. She put the knife to Mrs. Wilson's forehead in the same place as she did on Joy's head, then a hand grabbed her.

One of Mrs. Wilson's hands were free.

"Looks like I didn't do such a good job with that one."

It was easy to subdue her since Mrs. Wilson was still secure to her chair and had no mobility. What she was trying to accomplish with one free hand, Colleen did not know. She grabbed Mrs. Wilson's free hand and forced it down to the armrest.

"I don't think I was supposed to do this until later," Colleen said, "but maybe skipping around with the steps won't do too much dam-age. What do ya think?"

Mrs. Wilson apologized with tears. Colleen didn't care about them. Nor did she care for the shrieks that Jane was trying to make either.

Colleen measured up her knife to the base of Mrs. Wilson's fingers. "This hurts me as much as it hurts you. I can't stand the sight of blood."

Two powerful slams removed Mrs. Wilson's pointer, middle, and ring finger. Her pinky and thumb were hiding under the edges of the armrest as if Colleen would forget about them. Through the squirting blood, Colleen grabbed ahold of the pink and pressed the knife through it slowly—perhaps chopping the others off too fast was generous. Perhaps, Colleen thought, Mrs. Wilson truly needed to suffer.

Mrs. Wilson's thumb wouldn't keep steady. Colleen wondered if the shock of it all numbed Mrs. Wilson's pain. Was she feeling anything at all? Colleen wanted to ask her.

Before the knife could make an incision into the chef's skin, Colleen stepped back. She laughed at the idiot in front of her who thought that she'd escape because one hand was free while her other appendages were tied up.

"Does it hurt?"

Mrs. Wilson did not move; her fearful eyes held Colleen's.

"Does it hurt?"

A slow nod. Then a fast one.

Colleen's lips stretched into a smile. It was an alien feeling to smile again. "That's all I wanted to hear."

She slowed ran the knife across Mrs. Wilson's thumb. Instead of cutting it off completely, Colleen left it to dangle halfway attached to her hand.

Jane's room had spare cassette tapes stacked high on the dresser. Many research books. Many pages of notes. Colleen looked through some of it. Apparently Jane had done quite a bit of research into her and Ambrose—there were notes jotted next to certain years detailing the events of Colleen and Ambrose's lives during those corresponding years.

The clothes in the drawer were Colleen's size. She laid out a new outfit—a pretty pink skirt and a white blouse—then undressed and set her old clothes aside in a messy bloody pile. The room had a bathroom attached to it that was shared with the neighboring bedroom. Colleen turned the water on, and in a moment the bathroom was filled with steam.

She stepped underneath the burning stream of water and rubbed the blood off her skin; she was surprised how easily it washed away. Then she put her head under the stream and washed away the clumps of blood in her hair. Scarlet water washed down the drain.

She stepped out the shower and checked herself out in the mirror. She was spotless. She dried off then went across the bedroom to get her new outfit.

41

"Hey, wake up, kid." McKinley elbowed Thompson. "Wake up."

Officer Thompson rubbed his eyes. "What is it?"

"Shift's about over. We're heading back to the station after I take this leak. Here," McKinley handed him his pair of binoculars, "keep an eye out on that house for a minute."

"Sir yes sir."

McKinley left the van. Thompson's eyes adjusted to the binoculars. The house was fine. The lights were off. No one was awake. Nothing was going on in there that he was aware of.

A moment later, McKinley was back. "I miss anything?"

"No sir. Nobody's getting past that gate anyways."

"Yeah."

They drove away.

Jack ascended the hill and opened the gate.

"I can't believe our luck, David. Gate's open."

"Quiet the hell down or we'll never get to loot the place." David yelled from the base of the hill. "Get goin'."

Jack's fists knocked with desperation to get out of the storm. A second later he tried the knob and found the door was open.

Stepping into the house, he said, "Anybody home? My apologies, but my brother and I need a place to stay for the night. My name's Jack. Can anyone hear me?"

Creeping steps. Someone tiptoeing nearer.

Jack stepped through the living room. "My apologies, I know it's late. Is there anybody in here? I saw some cars parked down in the lot."

"Hi there." A pretty woman with bright eyes stepped into the room. "Who are you?"

"Sorry to intrude, I needed a place to stay. I was caught up in this storm, my brother and I—"

"It sure is coming down. Why don't you… come with me?" The pretty woman took him by the hand. "You're freezing. I'm sure you'll warm up soon. Shouldn't take long in here."

"What luck. I step into this place and I'm greeted by such a beauty."

"You're much too kind."

Jack kissed the back of her hand.

"Why don't I bring you to my room?"

"Probably I should stick around here for a second and let my brother know. He's coming up with our bags."

"Don't worry about him. I'm sure he'll figure something out. You can catch up with him later. I'm sure one of my roommates will give him a tour."

"Lead the way."

The pretty lady led him up a spiraling stairway to the third floor. She opened the door of the very first room they passed. A bedroom. It was devoid of any personal belongings that Jack could see. The pretty lady brought him to the bed and sat down with him.

She kissed him.

"What was your name again?" She asked.

"Jack. Yours?"

"Jessica."

"Jessica. I think I like that."

She push Jack flat on his back on the bed and climbed on top of him. Their hands ran up and down each other's bodies until suddenly she pulled away.

"What's wrong, Jessica?"

"These clothes are just… too in the way."

"Uh huh. I like where this is going."

She stepped away from him and all the way across the room to undress.

"What are you doing all the way over there?"

"In case things get too messy."

"I think you're speaking my language, baby." Jack took off his tie and tossed it on the floor. Then he kicked off his shoes. "Now get over here."

Her clothes were neatly in a pile. She returned to the bed with one hand behind her back. Their bodies wrapped around each other. Jack shut his eyes and traced her body with his hands; he started at her shoulders then brought his hands down to her palms. An icy piece of metal was in her hands.

"What is that for, Jessica?"

She held the knife up to his eyes. "Are you scared, Jack?"

"Well. A little."

"Good. I like that."

"What else do you like?"

She licked the knife. "You decided what I like or don't like."

"You know what I want, Jessica?"

"Whisper it to me."

He pulled her face close to hers and whispered in her ear. She ran a finger along his chest.

"You've got a dirty mind, Jack."

"So I've been told."

"Did you know I'm married?"

Jack shook his head. "I saw that ring on your hand. Doesn't mean much to me."

"You'd think this ritual would want the blood of a virgin. This ritual wanted the blood of a whore."

"What are you talking about?"

Colleen slid the knife across his throat; shock filled his wide brown eyes. Jack's hands desperately reached for the incision but there was nothing he could do to stop the reaper from dragging his soul away.

Colleen moved off of his body. Jack stood up from the bed then dropped to his knees and fell over dead.

"Oops."

David, carrying two suitcases, pushed through the storm and ascended the hill. The gate was open. He set down the suitcase in his right hand and twisted the knob, then walked inside to find an empty living room. Logs burned in the fireplace. The place was dusty and ancient and needed a lot of work done to it. David could only imagine the treasures that must've been hidden within the walls.

He stood in front of the fireplace to get warmed up. "Jack? Where you at, buddy?"

"Oh, were you Jack's brother?" A woman said.

She was standing in the entryway. Pretty young thing. Clear skin. Glowing eyes. Full lips. David looked her up and down.

"Pleasure to make your acquaintance," he said. "You, uh, happened to see my brother Jack you said?"

"Yep. He's upstairs."

"What did he tell you?"

"You two were stranded in the storm. Don't worry, same thing happened to me and my husband before."

"Uh-huh," David said. "Big place you got here."

"Yeah, it's so easy to get turned around. Better leave a trail of breadcrumbs wherever you go."

"Sure."

"Your brother really liked this place. Too bad about his accident."

"What did you say?"

"I said your brother really liked this place. And it's too bad about his accident."

"What are you talking about? What accident?"

"This house... has a way of hurting people. It killed my husband and I'm afraid it hurt your brother. But it's okay, maybe your brother can come back like Ambrose is about to come back. Any day now I'll be done putting his pieces together."

"Are you insane?"

"Why, that's not a nice thing to say to a lady."

David let go of both bags and walked across the creaking floorboards to the lady. "What's going on here? Give me some answers."

"Well, I can tell you, or I can show you. What do you say?" She stuck out her hand.

David took it. "Are you gonna tell me what goddamn happened?"

They went up the stairs silently.

"Who are you?"

"You mean you don't know? About this house?"

"How should I know a goddamn thing about this house?"

"There's some researchers in here trying to find evidence about my husband's disappearance. The leader of the group disappeared in here a few nights ago. Now they're trying to find out what happened to both of them."

David let go of the woman's hand. "I swear to God if you've done something to my brother…. Goddamn, lady, this better be a prank."

"What are you gonna do to me?"

He didn't answer.

She brought him to a doorway behind a cabinet. A smaller doorway that must have been obscured when the cabinet was pushed straight against it. Coming from inside the room was the glimmer of dozens of candles.

The first thing he noticed was the awful smell. Rotten meat. David gagged as he stepped behind the strange woman into the new world of the hidden room. The little flames cut through darkness and streaked the room: a pile of flesh whose head was stitched to a torso. A dead man tied to a seat. A sobbing woman tied to a chair on the left side of the room. A few feet away from her was another crying woman who was missing most of her left hand.

And then there was Jack.

He was missing his face.

Jack was tied up to a chair despite his spirit having left his body. His skin was torn away from the neck up.

"So, it wasn't really an accident. I needed the blood of a whore for my ritual."

"Oh my God." David put his hands on his brother's corpse. "What have they done to you!?!?"

"My condolences," the woman said.

"Jack." David cried. *"Oh my God. Oh my God."*

The woman pulled David away from his brother and put a book in his hands. "Now, if you'll please read from the Book of McDowell, David."

Jack's body twitched. His head fell slack to the side and his dead eyes looked up at David.

"Goodnight," Jack said.

David dropped the Book of McDowell and ran away.

The woman ran after him, but David was too fast for her. By the time he was on the ground floor, she was probably still on the second floor. Passing the gate he took one sickening last look at the house. In an upper window flashed a familiar face for one hurried second. His brother.

Even as David entered the Ashfall Police Department parking lot, he was going well over the speed limit. A speeding ticket was a very minor inconvenience if he were to get one; somebody had to put an end to the madness in that house.

An officer was entering the building with a coffee in each hand. Sawyer on his badge.

"You have to help me! They killed my brother! The McDowell cult!"

"McDowell cult? Out with it."

David paused momentarily to gasp for breath.

"Boy!"

"That house! On the hill! They killed my brother!"

Officers Sawyer and Hooper arrived at the Engstrom House. Sawyer knocked on the door for a while. A few minutes later a lady with brown hair opened the door for them. A bunch of people were gathered in the living room.

"I'm Officer Sawyer, this is Officer Hooper. Do any of you know a name by the name of Jack Simmons?"

Nobody did.

"That's funny," Hooper said, "considering his brother David is down at our station screaming his head off all night that a cult up here killed his brother. Pretty funny too, considering that this house is home to two vanishing men in the past year."

"You all mind if we have a look around?" Sawyer asked.

"Go right ahead," Scott said. "Look wherever you want."

As Hooper followed Sawyer, he passed by a woman with dark hair. He said to her, "Man at our station claims it was a lady with dark hair who showed him around. You sure you don't know a Jack Simmons? Or a David Simmons?"

"Yes I'm sure," she said. "I don't know a Jack or a David and I was asleep in my bedroom until you two showed up."

"Yeah, well, we'll see about that."

When the police officers were gone, Samantha picked up the rotary phone and dialed Howard's number.

"Howard, sorry I know it's late, I—I needed to speak to you urgently."

"My God Samantha, you sound like a nervous wreck. What's going on?"

Samantha paused then said, "How can I explain? Howard, people are going missing in here. I'm afraid we aren't alone."

"Can't you leave?"

"It's my job. I'm being paid for this. I need the money. I can't just walk out. I need this."

"Then stay put. If I can get somebody to watch the shop I can leave this weekend."

42

THE VASTNESS OF JANE'S pain was lost in the haze. Everything blurred through her tired eyes under the suffocating darkness that was only pierced by fading candlelight. Was this hell? Was anything outside of her mind real? Jane lost track of the days she had been in here, and for all she knew a year had passed—for all she knew, everyone else had left the Engstrom House and she was the only one left. The darkness of the rotten room was her only friend.

Her stomach growled. Her mouth was dry. Every movement made her dizzy. Her legs and arms were constantly numb, except for the sharp spikes of pain that occasionally pulsed within her flesh when she moved under her restraints.

I wish I were dead.

Nothing could be worse than the feeling of unreality that swept over her.

Jane tried to remember a previous life, some part of her that existed before becoming trapped in this room, but those memories were impossible to unlock. She saw brief flashes of light; vague images that might have been a better existence before being locked away.

She shut her eyes.

I want to be dead. God if You can hear me, please kill me.

Moments passed; maybe an eternity passed within them.

God can't You answer me? Kill me. Damnit kill me. Kill me.

Jane shut her eyes again and moped miserably. She leaned her head onto her right shoulder. Pain pulsed in a newly formed headache. She imagined herself in another place, in another time, in a world where this house never existed.

When the door opened, she kept her eyes shut. Was it worth it to interact with the crazy lady anymore?

"Jane?" She whispered. "Hey, are you alive?"

A hand shook her.

The tape was pulled back from Jane's lips; Jane gasped for air through her desensitized lips. The motion of breathing through her mouth had become foreign to her. She coughed. She stretched her dry tongue and licked her lips. Suddenly her body begged for water and she shivered.

The crazy lady raised a cup to Jane's mouth. Jane sipped it as if drinking for the first time, reminding her lips and tongue how to move again. It burned touching the dry walls of her throat. It even burned as it settled into her stomach. She drank about half the cup before stopping to breathe. Then she finished the rest.

There was an empty seat. The crazy lady pulled it up two feet away from Jane, then sat down holding a candle between them.

"I'm sorry this is taking forever," the crazy lady said. "But these things take time. You can't rush perfection. Did you see what I got done last night while you slept?"

Jane's eyes darted to the pile of rotting flesh. The body that the crazy lady was constructing was halfway stitched together on the altar. The pieces of what had once been a man were stiff and twisted in strange positions. It made Jane's stomach turn; she thought she'd barf up all the water she had just drank.

She held it in.

"That's," Jane coughed out painfully, her Jaw aching with each movement on the pronunciation of her words, "nice."

"It's just you and me in here. The cook tried to kick me so I cut off her foot. At least that helped me check off a step, I needed to make up for some of the blood that Ambrose lost in his dismemberment."

Jane held in her scream.

"What... do... you...." Jane had to take a break from speaking; pain was worse with each word. After a minute she continued, "Want... with... me..."

"I'm lonely."

Jane said nothing; she didn't know how to respond to that, and had to choose her words carefully since it hurt to speak, and she was dealing with an unstable person that belonged in an insane asylum. There was one nearby, one she had seen on the train ride here. Perhaps somebody would find this room and take the crazy woman there—it couldn't take that long to be found, could it? How long could one person move undetected in this place? How well could she cover up her tracks? Wasn't anybody concerned that Jane was missing? And Mrs. Wilson? Had they all packed up their things and left?

Tears muddied her vision.

The crazy lady wiped them away. "I'm lonely. I wanted someone to talk to."

Jane said nothing.

"Do you want to talk to me?"

"Suh-suh-sure."

"Has anyone ever told you you have such pretty eyes?"

Jane shook her head.

"Well you do. I'm a little jealous."

Jane mouthed the words *Thank you.*

"What's wrong? Cat got your tongue?"

"Need," Jane said. Another pause against the aching in her jaw. "Wuh-water."

"I'll get you some more. Do you want an apple? There's apples in the kitchen. I was just down there."

Jane nodded.

"Be right back."

The crazy lady picked up the cup and left her candle on her arm-rest. She shut the door behind herself, and Jane heard her pushing the cabinet back into its place in front of the door; how could she do that so often without the others hearing? Perhaps there were many floors between the others and this secret room. Jane couldn't remember what floor they were on. She couldn't remember very much through the terror that was coiling her mind and her life.

She had to work quick.

A jolt of awful pain cut through Jane's body as she attempted to move. She jerked her chair in the direction of the crazy lady's. The burning candle mesmerized her. Its blue and red flame shook back and forth. Jane's heart skipped a beat at the thought that the flame might give out. That flame was her ticket out of here.

She moved the chair again. Wicked pain flowed through her soul. She wondered how long it would take the crazy lady to sneak downstairs and come back up here. How much time had passed? Was she on her way back? Jane was paused, then she shifted again. She moved her chair closer again to the candle.

Then she was as close to the other chair as she could be.

Her fingertips stretched between the adjacent armrests for the candle. Her fingertips brushed against it and for one frightening second she thought she dropped the candle.

There was just a little too much space between them.

Jane strained against the ropes and pushed her arm forward; the ropes dug further into her skin. New levels of pain fled under her skin. Jane took a deep breath and relaxed. She shut her eyes and tried to think. She was already thirsty and needed water badly.

Another desperate stretch. Her fingers brushed the side of the candle. Why couldn't the crazy lady have set it down a fraction of an inch closer?

Jane's hand trembled as she heaved her body forward and urged her arm to press against the restraints again. She prayed that something had happened downstairs to the crazy lady; that she was caught and never coming back. She prayed she had more time, because every precious moment of freedom was getting eaten up in the struggle.

Her fingernails dug into the wax. She moved the candle slightly, still afraid it would fall over, and abruptly her shivering fingers clamped around it.

But the job was only partly done.

Jane shuddered as the candle moved through her unsteady hand. She angled it through her thumb and pointer finger, pushing it forward with her pinky, ring, and middle finger so that when she pushed her wrist backwards, the flame would come into direct contact with the rope.

Feeling returned to her skin when the flame of the candle caught the rope; but the heat was a minor pain to bear—she had felt worse, and there'd be worse to come if she did not get completely free from this madhouse.

Her right hand was free. She set the candle down and tried to untie her left hand, but she had neither the strength nor the time, and when it wasn't loosened right away, she burned the rope with the candle. She had seen what happened to Mrs. Wilson when she had gotten one hand free—if the crazy lady caught her... oh God. She didn't want to complete the thought.

As Jane freed herself from the ropes that were skintight around her body, the cabinet was moved outside the door. The crazy lady was back.

Jane didn't know what to do in that moment. She only had a second or two to react and those very short seconds were fleeting. She was dumbfounded when the door open and the crazy lady came back with a cup of water and an apple.

"Sorry I took so long, I thought they'd never leave the... kitchen. What are you doing, Jane?"

Jane stood frozen.

The crazy lady threw the cup at her then the apple; Jane's muscles screamed with burning pain as she suddenly jerked her arms up to cover her face. Her body wasn't used to moving. Every part of her was in perpetual pain.

"I asked you a question, Jane. Where are you going?"

"Nuh-nowhere."

Resting against the far wall was an axe. The crazy lady picked it up and held it over her left shoulder.

Jane stepped backwards. *"Puh-please. Don't."*

The crazy lady brought the axe down with a powerful swing; Jane dropped to the floor to avoid it. Her muscles weren't strong enough for her to stand again; she had to crawl across the sticky floor, and crawled between chairs, passing by the doctor's corpse and his leaking blood.

Another swing of the axe. Jane jolted her body away. The axe was momentarily stuck in the ground; the crazy lady tugged on it, and Jane took the opportunity to grab onto a chair for support. She stood up and staggered through the room, moving toward the door.

There was a sickening laugh, then the furious blow of pain that struck the back of her head. Her vision turned abruptly black, but her mind was still rushing. Dizziness ran through her head and she collapsed.

Beating pain burning through her body.

A faint glimmer of vision returned to Jane's eyes. Above her, the crazy lady smiled. The Axe was raised again over her left shoulder.

43

COLLEEN MOVED THE CABINET back into place to cover up the door. Jane's blood streaked her face and clothing.

She ran down the stairway screaming.

"Somebody help me! Somebody help! Help! Help!"

Footsteps came from several directions. At the base of the spiraling staircase she was met by Scott, Joy, Samantha, and Margaret.

Colleen collapsed. Her eyes shut.

When she woke up she was on a couch in the living room. The others were sitting around the room watching her.

"Who are you people?" She asked, shy and afraid.

"Researchers," Scott said. "I'm Scott, this is Margaret, Samantha, Joy. We were assembled here to research the house because a man disappeared in here recently. Now we're trying to solve a handful of disappearances. Now tell us who you are and whose blood is all over you."

"I… I don't know what happened."

"Who are you?" He asked.

"My name's Jessica. Oh my God. How did I get here?"

Everybody was silent.

"Somebody locked me in a room. I was locked away with a man who said he was a doctor."

"What room?" Scott said. "Where?"

"I can't remember. I don't remember what happened. How did you find me? How did you rescue me?"

"We didn't rescue you. You were screaming on the stairway."

"He helped me. He…" Colleen cried.

Joy came to her side and put an arm around her. "It'll be okay, Jessica."

Margaret pulled Scott aside while Joy and Samantha gave Jessica tissues to wipe away her tears and snot.

"Scott… you can't believe her, can you?"

"Why not?"

"Because…"

"It's the biggest lead we've gotten since doc and the others disappeared."

"I don't believe her."

"What? Why not?"

"I've got a bad feeling about her."

"Why?"

"I don't know why."

"She was screaming on that staircase. You saw her. She's clearly shaken. Her trauma's so severe her mind blocked it out. That isn't uncommon."

"But Scott…"

"Who knows what we can find out from her. Just… relax a little bit. If she can come up with something—anything—that can lead us back to the doctor, we've got to follow that lead."

Margaret crossed her arms. "I don't like this. I can't tell you why, but I just don't."

"What do you think it is?"

"Huh?"

"She shows up screaming out the blue. What could it be?"

"I don't know."

"I've got a gut feeling about her too, Margaret. My gut tells me she's telling the truth. She's scared. Now look, let's get her something to eat, I'll go whip something up. Do you have any clothes that she can borrow? Let's get her out of those rags."

"Her outfit kind of looks familiar… I can't put my finger on it."

"You seen her before?"

"I don't think so."

Scott stood at the bar in the meeting room pouring himself a shot.

"Here's to you, old friend."

"What are you having?"

Jessica was in the doorway.

"Bourbon. Come join me." Scott found another glass and poured her a shot.

She drank it. "Keep 'em coming."

"Didn't think anyone else was still awake."

"What are you doing here?"

"Guess I need some time to myself to get things figured out. My mind's been all over the place. This hasn't been easy on any of us. The doctor and I go way back.... Margaret's his intern, Samantha worked with him on some paper, I don't remember where Joy knows him from."

"The person who kept me locked away... I can only remember them as... being a shadow. But there were candles in the room. And your doctor friend took care of me. He helped me survive. But..." Tears rolled down her cheeks; Scott wiped them away. "I still can't remember."

"We'll figure it out."

"I'm sorry."

Scott drank another shot. They were silent for a little while.

"What do you do?" Jessica asked. "Outside of... this?"

"Back home I work in construction. My girlfriend that I don't even like is living with me in my cramped apartment. A change of scenery can do a guy a lot of good."

"I'm a secretary. I hate it. I always wanted to be a painter."

"Joy's a painter. You should talk to her about it sometime."

"I settled for something because it was easy instead of following my dream because being a painter takes a lot of work. Since I was a little girl I wanted to be a painter. I guess I just *kind of* wanted it. When you get to my age, how do you rethink and replan your entire life?"

"Your age? You look like you're hardly… what? Twenty-seven? You can't be out of your twenties just yet. You know, I bet you won't guess what I studied my first year of college."

"What?"

Scott laughed, pouring another shot. After he drank it, he said, "I went to seminary for a year."

"You? In seminary? You must be joking."

"Nope."

They were silent for a while and drinking shots.

"I wish things were different, Scott."

"Keep wishing. Go ahead and drive yourself crazy."

"What?"

"Get over it. You're a nice girl. You'll figure things out."

"I just wanted to say… I wish we could help the doctor like he helped me. Do you think there's a way we can find him?"

"Well, if you can remember anything that happened to you, that would help us. And we still have this house for another three months."

"Scott I wish I could remember something. I accepted the doctor's invitation because of money. Because I needed money. Was it a mistake to come here?" She cried again.

"No. No mistake."

"Are you sure?"

"What do you want me to say, Jessica?"

"I'm lost. I just don't want to be lost."

Scott kept quiet.

"I feel so alone."

"No. You're not alone."

She looked deep into his eyes. "Scott…"

His hands were on hers. She trembled under his touch. He slid his hands along her arms to her shoulders, then pulled her to his lips and kissed her. She wrapped her arms around Scott's body.

Scott fell asleep first. His bed was warm. His maroon Philco tube radio was going in and out of music and static, and Colleen's mind was hanging on to the glimpses of words loosely. She was on the ledge of sleep when she felt a sudden chill crawl through the room.

Then she heard his voice.

She jolted awake. She checked on Scott. He was still asleep. She sat up and listened closely. Rain spilled outside. Songs played in hushed fragments. Static hummed.

Maybe Colleen had been wrong.

She shut her eyes and laid down, moving Scott's arm over her body, fitting her body to press against his. The merger of soft noises made her sleepy again.

"Colleen, my love."

It couldn't be real.

Colleen lifted Scott's arm and snuck out of his bed. She tiptoed out of the room and followed the voice. She followed it to the cabinet that the door was hidden behind; the cabinet had been moved aside and the door had been completely changed into a strange and unusual metal contraption. Green light glowed behind it.

"Help me, my love."

"You're not real. You're not real. You're dead."

"Open the door."

Colleen grabbed the freezing knob. Chills slithered like prodigious serpents around her body.

"Help me," he said.

Colleen let go of the knob and backed away. *"No. No."*

She sobbed and ran back to Scott's room. She slid under the covers and wrapped herself in his arms again and sobbed quietly. She didn't want to wake him the sobs became louder, and soon his eyes opened.

"What's wrong?"

Colleen said nothing.

"Jessica, what's wrong?"

"I had a nightmare."

"Was it about the doctor?"

Colleen said nothing.

"What happened in your nightmare?"

"Please… just hold me."

44

MARGARET HAD A SECRET meeting with Samantha. They met in the meeting room in front of the fireplace.

"Scott's smitten with her," Margaret said. "He won't understand anything I'm about to tell you, but Samantha I trust you. When we found that woman… Jessica… she was wearing Jane's clothes. That was Jane's outfit from our first night in this house."

"It was?"

"I'm certain it was. I told Scott there was something familiar about her. She was wearing Jane's clothes."

Samantha was silent.

"She said she was locked in a room. With someone who said they were the doctor. I know you can see past it, Sam. Scott's too smitten to understand. I think… I think Jessica knows what happened to the doctor. I think she did something to him."

"Who is she?"

"I don't know."

"Why is she here? Do you remember the doctor inviting a Jessica? Can we go through his notes? See if there's any record? My God Margaret, you're his intern. Can't you find these things?"

"None of those records are here at this mansion and that's if he even kept a log. When he set out to invite everybody, I dropped off his letters at the post office. That was my extent in this."

"You were right, she did seem familiar, but not just her outfit. I think I've seen her somewhere before."

"Where?"

Samantha shut her eyes for a few seconds. "I think I might know her."

"But from where?"

"Shut up a second, I'm trying to think."

"We need to do something about her."

"Do something about her? Like kick her out? How can we do that? Nobody besides me cares about your gut feeling."

Margaret paused to think. "It's just me you and Joy and Scott left. Our group is shrinking by the day. Is it any coincidence that this woman none of us have ever seen before arrives just after the doctor, Jane, and Mrs. Wilson disappear? What are we waiting for? To disappear with them?"

"Well if we're this certain about things we need to contact the police. They still wait outside the house each night."

"You're right. They wouldn't do anything with a baseless accusation."

"Don't get me wrong," Samantha said, "I understand what you're saying. I understand you perfectly. Where did she come from? Why did none of us see her before?"

After Margaret and Samantha parted ways, Margaret saw Jessica turning a corner in one of the Engstrom House's long hallways. Margaret followed her with quiet steps. She snuck down the hallway after Jessica and kept a far distance.

Jessica went around a corner.

Margaret counted Jessica's steps to make sure there was enough distance then followed her.

Jessica went up a stairway; Margaret had an idea she knew which floor Jessica was headed. She went up a different stairway to avoid encountering her. Margaret was chilled with every little step she took.

At the third floor she found that she was all alone.

Jessica wasn't anywhere around her.

Margaret crept through the third floor silently, looking for any sign of Jessica. In a minute or two she came upon a cabinet that had been moved away to expose a small door. A horrible stench wafted from the entryway. Within the dense darkness of the hidden room was a glow of candles. Curiously Margaret went inside.

One glimpse of mutilated bodies streaked with candlelight struck pure terror into Margaret's heart. Everybody that had gone missing was in the secret room tied to chairs. There was a body whose face had been ripped off that she could not identify.

Margaret's heart was racing. And its speed increased when the door shut.

"Hello Margaret."

Margaret shuddered.

"Jessica oh my God what have you done!"

"Don't worry, Margaret, they didn't feel a thing." Jessica stepped closer. "And neither will you."

"Why are you doing this?"

"It's simple. Don't you see?" She pointed to the lumps of flesh collected on an altar. It was a half constructed man sewn together dementedly. "My husband needs your help to come back to life. I need you to be part of this ritual."

"*He's dead. You can't bring him back.*"

"But the doctor thinks I can bring him back. Isn't that right, doc?"

"*You're sick in the head. Let me out of here and I can get you the help you need. It doesn't have to be like this.*"

"*Margaret, trust me on this, okay? I know the ritual better than you do. I've studied the book. I can save his soul.*"

"*You can't save a dead man's soul.*"

"*Margaret…*" Jessica stepped forward again.

"*You're crazy. Stay away from me.*"

"*Margaret, I just want your help. The doctor was willing to help, and Mrs. Wilson, and Jane, and even Jack helped.*"

"*Who the hell is Jack?*"

"*You'll have plenty of time to get acquainted with him. You'll be spending a long while in this room.*"

"*Oh God Jessica please let me out of here.*"

"*I can't do that.*"

Jessica kept coming closer. Margaret backed away into the wall. There wasn't much space to maneuver with the dead bodies and chairs. Suddenly it was all hitting Margaret at once—the hideousness reality of this room. It might be her resting place. She might be seconds away from the end of her life. She didn't want to die, and not here—to die and never be found in this hidden room. This couldn't be how things ended. This couldn't be the end of her life.

Margaret threw the first punch and hit Jessica in the nose; blood squirted down and Jessica was temporarily distracted by the pain. Margaret grabbed Jessica's head and slammed it into the wall. Then her grip on Jessica's face tightened and she was about to smash her head again when Jessica's fingernails dug into Margaret's flesh.

"Ah!"

Jessica twisted Margaret's left arm and bit into her wrist; blood exploded in every direction.

Margaret tried to pull her arm away but Jessica's teeth were locked into her wrist; Jessica's mouth closed tighter and ripped through Margaret's flesh. With her free arm, Margaret punched Jessica in the gut; Jessica opened her mouth and gasped.

"Go to hell." Margaret kicked her.

Jessica moved backwards against the wall, never taking her eyes off Margaret. Margaret held her injured wrist; pain pulsed with each passing second. Margaret needed to get to a hospital urgently; blood wouldn't stop emerging from her wrist. How was she going to get out of this room? How was she going to get past Jessica?

Margaret scanned the room quickly for a weapon. The only one she could find was in Jessica's hands; an axe raised over her shoulder and reflecting winks of candlelight. Margaret was frozen. Jessica smiled and inched closer.

"Just like I promised, you won't feel a thing."

"Jessica no. Oh my God no. Don't do this. We can help you."

Jessica brought the axe down on Margaret's face.

Margaret's head was split open down the middle. The body twitched.

Colleen wiped the splash of Margaret's blood from her face. Then she sat in front of the altar and turned a page in the book. She was on the right track. The pieces were coming together. She had almost everything that she needed.

She kissed Ambrose. "Look at all the progress we're making, darling."

A few minutes later she stuck her head out of the doorway. The hall was empty, of course. She went down the stairway to the second hall then to Jane's room. She laid out an outfit of Jane's then she went into the shower. Warm water washed all the blood away.

Joy was passing through the ground floor when she saw Samantha trying to pick a lock.

"What are you doing?"

"Have you seen Margaret?"

"No. What are you doing? Isn't that the doctor's research room?"

"Damnit where is she? I need the key. I can't find Margaret."

"I don't know. I haven't seen her all day."

"We need to get in there. I think there's something in there that can help us."

"Help us with what? What are you talking about?"

Samantha looked over her shoulder to make sure nobody was with them, then she leaned in close to whisper, "Margaret and I think Jessica hurt the doctor. I think there's proof in this room."

"How do you know?" Joy whispered too.

"You have to see it."

Samantha went back to picking the lock. She struggled with it, but it opened.

On a cluttered desk were mountains of books, notebooks, notecards, and loose papers. A diagram of the house. Scattered pens without their caps. A mountain of loose change. A brainteaser of two long twisted nails stuck together. As soon as the girls were inside the room, Samantha shut the door then went through the doctor's paperwork in a hurry.

"What are you looking for?"

"A newspaper."

"I don't see any. What's in the newspaper?"

"If I were the doctor, where would I…" Samantha stepped around the room. A briefcase on the floor near a shelf caught her eye.

She put the briefcase on the desk and opened it.

Inside was a newspaper folded a few pages into an article where Jessica's face was below the title **WIFE CLAIMS HUSBAND VANISHED IN 'HAUNTED HOUSE.'**

"Her name's not Jessica," Samantha said, "it's Colleen."

"I'll call the police. You go get Scott and Margaret."

Joy picked up the phone in the doctor's research room and was dialing the police when sprawling heat plunged into her skin. It didn't immediately register that the severed arm clinging to the receiver was her own, and that she could no longer control it because it was no longer attached to her body.

She was smothered with shock and her screams were painfully caught in her throat—she choked trying to force them out. Blood disturbingly squirted from her wound. Joy staggered away from the phone as unreality washed over her; it felt like a dream to see Colleen smiling despite the splattered blood across her face and holding an axe over her left shoulder.

Grotesquely Colleen moved forward.

"Hello, Joy."

Joy couldn't speak; she could only scream.

"Now you'll be a part of this house forever."

Joy stepped away screaming; Colleen came forward, tightening the axe in her demented grip.

"And ever."

Another scream.

"And ever."

45

Samantha knocked on Scott's bedroom door. He opened it.

"Scott I need to talk to you." She pushed past him. "I need you to listen to me. We're all in danger."

Scott said nothing.

"Her name isn't Jessica. It's Colleen. That's why I thought I knew her—I recognized her from the picture in the papers. She's the one behind it all—she killed Jane and stole her clothes. She probably hurt the doctor. We need to get out of this house *now* before she gets us. Where's Margaret?"

"Are you insane, woman?"

"Scott, I saw the newspaper. Scott. We need to get out of here, and I'm leaving with or without you."

"What, you're going to go to the police?"

"Joy is already calling them. I bet they'll surround the house any second."

"Maybe it's not too late to stop her." Scott took a step past Samantha.

"Stop her? Scott why on earth would you do that?"

Scott smacked her; Samantha looked at him with disgust and rubbed her stinging cheek.

"I'm happy here. Jessica and I are happy together. I'm not going to let you idiots ruin this."

"Her name isn't even Jessica. She lied to you, Scott. Scott don't do this, I know you're upset but we have to do what's right."

Scott smacked her a second time. "You're not going to get in the way of us."

Samantha shuddered as she twisted the doorknob and stepped out of the room. *"You're as crazy as she is."*

Scott watched her with sardonic eyes.

Terror jolted through Samantha's heart; she ran from his bedroom. Scott chased her through the hallway and was too fast for her to outrun; looking over her shoulder she knew she wouldn't last long unless she did something. Since the cabinets in the twisting hallways of the Engstrom House were too heavy to push into his way, the only thing she could possibly do was lock herself into a room and try to escape through the adjacent room if they happened to be one of the ones that shared a bathroom.

A tight turn around a corner. Her heart was beating madly and her lungs were straining for her to breathe. She opened a door on her right and slammed it shut, locked it, then stepped forward and collapsed on the floor to catch her breath.

Within five seconds Scott was trying to break the door down by ramming it with his shoulder.

"Open the door. I just want to talk to you."

Samantha crawled a couple feet away then quietly stood up and saw that there was a door linking this room and the adjacent room with a bathroom; and the light between them was turning on and creeping beneath the doorway. Samantha twisted the knob and opened the door. Stepping inside she saw the corpse of a female police officer with Kessler written on her badge. The woman was slumped against the door that Samantha needed to go through, and her guts were pulled from gashes on her body and twisted around her throat.

"Ahhhhhhh!"

Samantha stepped backwards away from the body and bumped into a solid figure whose hands gripped her so tightly that she thought her skin would burst under its sharp touch. Scott turned her around so that she was facing him; in her shock she hadn't heard the door break open.

"Let me go, I swear to God I won't say anything. Nobody will know."

Scott shook his head. "I can't do that."

"I swear to God I won't tell anybody please let me go I want to go home."

Scott grabbed Samantha's face with his left hand, keeping hold on her arm with his right hand, then slammed the back of her head into the bathroom mirror. Immeasurable fragments of glass were lodged into Samantha's skin; unimaginable pain unlike anything she had ever felt before reverberated through her head. Suddenly her vision was blurring into darkness and she couldn't keep them focused. Scott's grip squeezed her head, and he slammed her again into the mirror. Then he turned her around so that she was facing what remained of the glass, and her fading vision caught one look at her misery and pain.

Another slam into the glass.

"Scott…"

Remaining on the bottom of the mirror was a jagged row of glass like the fangs of a monster. Scott held Samantha in both of his hands, then brought her throat down on the spikes.

46

THE DISTRICT ATTORNEY DRANK his water. "Tell me about Officer Kessler. If you two were watching over the house, how did Kessler get in without anyone knowing?"

"We weren't there all the time, you understand," McKinley said. "There are other matters in this town for us to attend to besides sitting in our car watching over the old Engstrom place."

"You understand how bad it looks that there's no record of Officer Kessler being assigned any matter involving the house? She walked in under your noses. She was killed. So why was she there? Can either of you answer that for me?"

Late at night there was a knock on the door. Colleen peeked outside. A fat lady in a police officer uniform was knocking.

Colleen opened the front door just a crack. "Yes?"

The fat lady raised her gun and pushed past Colleen. "Ashfall PD. Let me in."

Colleen put her hands up and moved out of the lady's way. "Take it easy."

Fat Lady looked around the living room suspiciously, taking in the details of the room. "My husband is in the patrol car in case you're not cooperative."

"Geez, don't point that at me every time I speak."

Fat Lady lowered the gun. "Sorry. It's my first time going something like this. I'm usually the phone lady, but all of our officers were busy tonight…. I was asked to do a little checkup on the house. A certain disappearance of the head of your investigation team has been a particular interest down at the station. So… tell me what you know."

Scott stepped into the room. "What's going on in here?"

Fat Lady stepped toward him. *"Oh hello."*

"I wasn't expecting a guest this late or I'd have cleaned up a little. I would've had one of my teammates here put a teakettle on the stove so I could offer you something to drink besides water. How are you doing tonight, officer?"

"I'm with the Ashfall PD. I'm doing a routine checkup on the missing doctor, they sent me since our other officers were busy. And don't think I'm fooled by a pretty face, mister."

"You're welcome to have a look around. Just try not to wake anyone. And I'd appreciate it if that gun stayed in its holster, ma'am."

They went through the halls of the Engstrom House. A random door opened, and Officer Kessler reached for her holster, then she drew her hand back when Joy opened the door and peeked into the hall.

"Has anyone seen Samantha? Oh hi officer."

"Officer Kessler is here to check up on us," Colleen said. "I guess the men couldn't watch the house tonight."

"I think Samantha's gone to bed," Scott said. "What's up?"

"She forgot her purse in my room. I'll give it to her in the morning."

"Good night."

"Good night." Joy shut her door.

Again they went through darkened halls, and Colleen pushed her hands over light switches causing the fading lightbulbs to flicker then give them vision. Officer Kessler looked over the ancient house with curiosity.

"Seen enough?" Scott asked.

"I think so," Officer Kessler said. "I think I'll call it a night. Sorry again about the gun—I'm new to this and all."

"No problem."

"It's all right," Colleen said.

Going through a murky hallway whose old bulbs did not work, Colleen and Scott's eyes met briefly in a fading glimmer of light and they smiled.

"You know," Scott put his hand on Officer Kessler's shoulder, "this was the room where the doctor stayed. Maybe you'd want to take a look. Maybe you could find something that the other officers couldn't."

"Which room?" Officer Kessler stopped walking.

"This one here." Scott opened the door on their left. "Maybe we can find something."

Officer Kessler stepped inside after Scott did, then Colleen followed behind the fat officer. Scott turned on the light. Officer Kessler looked around the barren dusty room. A slight realization crept over her face.

Colleen snuck up behind Officer Kessler and forced a rope around her neck. Scott immediately grabbed the gun from the holster and set it aside on a dresser. The fat lady wasn't so easy to take down, and moved backwards slamming Colleen into the wall.

Scott grabbed the rope from Colleen's hands then forced the officer to her knees. She laid down as her body begged her for breaths. She clawed at the rope, tearing up her skin as she tried to free herself from strangulation.

Then Scott dragged the body to the bathroom.

He undid the rope and the officer choked. Scott and Colleen stood in the doorway watching their plaything cry and choke for breath.

After a few minutes of the officer pleading with them through bleary eyes, she said, *"Please don't kill me. I have a family."*

"What do you think, Scott?"

Scott brought out his pocket knife. "I thought we'd maybe play around with her a little."

Colleen pulled Scott in for a big kiss. "I love you, Scott. I love you so much."

"I love you too, Jessica."

Officer Kessler buried herself in the corner of the room begging. She covered her eyes with her hands.

"No. No. No. No. No. No. No. No."

Fat Officer Kessler was dead. When they were finished mutilating her and were freckled with blood, Scott and Colleen embraced each other for another kiss. Then they turned off the lights and crept out of the room.

"Do you think anyone heard her screams?" Colleen asked.

"No way. Now let's go back to my room, baby. After what we did in there I want you more than ever. We make a great team, you and I."

"Scott, I feel like I'm forgetting something."

"About what?"

"I think Officer Kessler said something important."

Scott paused. "Nothing sticks out to me."

"Waitasecond. You weren't there when she said it."

"Said what?"

"Said her husband was in the patrol car."

"Well," Scott raised his knife, "we'll just have to take care of that."

Scott and Colleen went down the hill to the parked police car. There was a man asleep in the passenger seat. The window was rolled down and Scott reached in to shake him. The man's eyes fluttered open with concern.

"Are you Mr. Kessler?"

"Yes I am. What's going on here?"

"It's your wife. There's been a terrible accident, just terrible."

"Who are you? Is that blood? Are you hurt?"

Scott raised his pocket knife in his fist then slammed it into Mr. Kessler's eye. Mr. Kessler screamed as his shaking hand reached for the weapon and pulled it out of the socket; a long strand of blood connected from his eyelid to the sharp edge of the blade.

The knife fell from his hand.

Mr. Kessler fell over dead.

The keys were still in the ignition. Scott drove the car out of the parking lot at the base of the hill, then brought them around to the other side of the adjacent farm, where he was able to bring the car to the lake that was set between both properties.

"How did you know this was back here?"

"Don't worry about it, sweetie. See, you had nothing to worry about."

"Yeah. I was really scared, Scott."

Scott stepped out of the patrol car and held the door open for Colleen.

"Thank you," she said.

Scott kissed the back of her hand. "Help me move him."

Mr. Kessler was equally as fat as his wife. Together the couple moved him from the passenger seat into the driver's seat, using all their strength to move his heavy body. Scott shifted the car into drive then hopped out of it in a split second.

The police car splashed into the body of water.

It disappeared below the rippling sable surface that was patterned with hundreds of glowing stars.

47

HOWARD STOPPED AT A payphone booth. He put a coin through the slot and dialed the number Samantha had given him. The phone rang. Nobody answered. Then Howard tried it a second time, dreading the quickly passing seconds that went without answer.

Then somebody on the other end picked up.

"Hello?" Howard said.

Nothing from the other end.

"Samantha? That you, girl? Can you hear me?"

Silence.

"Samantha? Hello? Samantha?" Howard paused. "Do I have the right number?"

Whoever was on the other end hung up.

Howard went back into his car and drove down the road.

After Scott killed Samantha, Colleen walked into the room. She looked over the mutilated body.

"Nice work, Scott."

"She wanted to keep us away from each other. But I told her we won't ever be apart, you and me, Jessica. You're the love of my life." Scott pulled her shirt off. "Oh Jessica…"

Colleen took her shirt back from his hands. "Honey… I need you to help me with a little project first. Then we can have all the fun that you want."

"Anything for you, darling. Just say the word."

She grabbed his hand. "Come with me."

She brought him through the second floor hallways around to the main spiraling staircase. Before they could ascend, there was a furious banging on the front door. Together they went to check it out.

"Who could that be?" Colleen said.

"I wasn't expecting anybody," Scott said. Then as they passed the entryway into the living room, he gave her a kiss on the cheek. "Stay here."

Scott was halfway to the door when it was kicked open by a big fat man. In his hands was a shotgun. The fat man stomped through the living room and pressed the gun against Scott's temple.

"Don't hurt him."

"Shut up unless you're spoken to, lady. Where's Samantha?"

"Who?" Scott said.

The fat man smacked him across the face with the barrel of the shotgun. "Next time you answer me like a fool I'll put a bullet through your head. Where's Samantha?"

Colleen stepped forward. *"She left."*

The man never took his eyes off Scott. "You're a bad liar, miss. One more lie and I'm putting a bullet through him then a bullet through you."

"Please be reasonable," Colleen stepped closer again, "can't you put that gun down and talk to us? I promise you Samantha left. Can't we talk about this?"

"You're pushing it, lady. If Samantha left she would have called me. Last I heard from her was a few days ago and she was panicked. Now you tell me she's missing. Well, if she left she would have contacted me. Would've told me she was on her way back home. I've watched over her since she was a girl and her father passed."

"I know you're confused, but please, sir, I knew Samantha better than anyone else in here. I can tell you where she was going, just take the gun away from Scott's head. I'm begging you, please don't shoot him. I love him."

The man stepped away from Scott, keeping his distance and lowering his gun. "Get talking. And make it quick."

"Me and Scott are all that's left, sir. The others left. They set out last night, they couldn't take it in this house anymore."

"Bullshit," the man said.

"Jessica," Scott said, "you aren't gonna fool him. Tell him the truth."

"You do the talking." The man raised his gun again at Scott.

"Only if you aim that gun somewhere besides my head. Please. I want to help you. Samantha had a little... accident."

"Where is she?"

Scott discretely slipped his hand into his back pocket and pulled out Officer Kessler's gun. "In hell."

The man pulled the trigger on his shotgun at the same time as Scott; since the man did not aim and pulled the trigger in a hurry, his bullet went past Scott by a foot or more. In that split second, it was apparent in the man's eyes that he knew he was a dead man.

Scott's bullet ripped through the man's head between his eyes and splattered his brains on the wall. His eyes twitched and blood seeped between his lips. With his last breath of life he fumbled with the shotgun; it lifted slightly then fell from his hands. The man fell over with the immense weight of his body and slumped over on the floor.

Colleen took Scott by the hand. "Now let's finish what we started."

Together they went up the spiraling stairway.

"Scott, baby, you're still holding that gun." Colleen grabbed it from him with a kiss. "We won't need this anymore. Let's put it away."

"So what did you need my help with? After this are we celebrating? Oh Jessica, there's no better feeling than having this whole big home just to ourselves. Maybe we'll buy the thing. Maybe we'll stay here for good. You and me, here forever. God bless doc, wherever he is, for putting this group together or I'd have never met you. I can't imagine my life without you."

She brought him to the hidden room behind the cabinet. Ambrose's body was fully connected back together, sewed into place. He was sitting on a chair surrounded by mountains of glowing and flickering candles.

"What is this?" Scott looked Ambrose up and down. "I thought you had given up?"

"I couldn't give up. He was my husband. He *is* my husband. I'm sorry, Scott, but I need to bring him back. And you're the final piece that I need to complete the ritual. It's all written in the book."

"I won't be part of this."

"Scott, I thought you loved me. If you love me you'll help me do this."

"I won't help you replace me. I thought you loved me, not this... *ghost.*"

"Scott..."

Scott smacked her. He stepped across the room to Ambrose and pushed him over.

"Don't hurt him."

"He's dead, you idiot. And I'm not helping you get him back. You betrayed me, Jessica."

Colleen aimed Officer Kessler's gun at him. Her hands shook as she did. "I'll... I'll pull the trigger."

"Then do it. Kill me."

She stood frozen.

Scott stepped closer. "What are you waiting for?"

"I... I..."

Another step closer. "Kill me."

"I can't do it."

Scott ripped the gun from her hands. "Everything I've done for you, and you don't even love me. Why did I do any of this for you if you don't even love me? Why did you pretend to love me? Was it so you could get what you wanted? I shouldn't have done anything for you—you didn't even love me."

"I'm sorry Scott."

Scott pushed her to the ground. He crawled over her and brought his fists down on her face.

"Scott stop it! Stop it! Scott!"

Footsteps in the hallway. Two people quickly approaching.

Officer McKinley and Officer Thompson stepped into the room with their guns ready.

"Police. Freeze."

"How did you fellows know where to find them?" The district attorney asked. "How did you know to go snooping around the house at all?"

"For the love of God," McKinley said, "first you blamed us for doing too little, now we're getting the blame for doing too much?"

"No. No sir. No blame."

"The door was kicked down. As we pulled up to the house that day we heard gunshots. What else are two officers supposed to do?"

"Well," the psychiatrist said, "I got the whole story… but not from Colleen. I got it from… Jessica. Colleen Tillman no longer exists. She only half-existed to begin with. Now, the other half has taken over. Probably for all time."

"Look," the district attorney said, "if you're trying to lay a lot of psychiatric groundwork for some sort of plea…"

"A psychiatrist doesn't lay the groundwork for anything. My job's only to explain it. To understand it, we have to look back a couple years. Colleen was already dangerously disturbed, had been ever since she had her abortion and killed her baby.

"'Jessica' seems to think something in the old Engstrom place got into her head. Something in that house pushed her over the thin line... and she killed everybody in a bizarre ritual to resurrect her husband that she had killed.

"In the process, Colleen's brain tried to become someone else. That's what I meant when I said I got the story from Jessica. She thinks Colleen has been taken away... because of her crimes. Jessica insists she did nothing, that Colleen committed all the murders."

48

Catherine Blackwell went down the stairway into the basement of the Ashfall Public Library, where they kept an extensive collection of old newspapers, some of which were so old that they fell apart under her touch. All the boxes in the library's basement were musty and needed to be replaced.

She had the dates Bruno had scribbled for her written down on a piece of notebook paper, and looked through the filed boxes accordingly until she had a little collection of vintage newspapers. There was a small table in the corner of the room where she sat and read under the light of a single bulb.

The headlines:

WHO WERE THE ENGSTROM FAMILY?

WIFE CLAIMS HUSBAND VANISHED IN 'HAUNTED HOUSE.'

DR. JAMES MCDOWELL'S CORPSE FOUND IN THE 'ENGSTROM HOUSE!'

THE DEVIL MADE HER DO IT! NEW INFORMATION ON THE VICIOUS 'ENGSTROM HOUSE' MURDERS!

Catherine cut out the headlines and put them into her purse.

When she went back upstairs she found an employee. "Do you have any books by an author named James McDowell?"

"Let me check for you."

AUTHOR'S NOTES

SEQUELS ARE NEVER EASY, especially when you scrap the first three drafts and start from scratch with a similar premise as before, and you think of the countless hours and effort you put into the previous drafts, but nothing is ever finished until it's finished, and you have to follow the ideas even if it means scrapping a lot of hard work. You want a finished book that's also good, not just a finished book. I've been foolish before and accepted a "final draft" as final just because I was afraid to make changes, although those changes would have elevated the book. While I've never been lazy about writing every day, I've often been lazy at making significant changes and throwing whole chapters—or in this case, whole books—out the window. But this can be necessary to turn in some of your best work.

I don't like to often reuse characters. I liked the Engstrom House a lot and wanted to use that as a setting to tell another story with new characters. I needed an idea, so I borrowed a little bit of an idea from Ambrose Bierce's *The Spook House,* a public domain short story about these guys that enter a haunted house during a storm, one gets locked into a room, and the other accidentally shuts it. Then, upon returning to the house, there is no such door that the other guy had been trapped in.

You might be wondering the differences between the scrapped drafts. Well, for one, the original three drafts were boring. I could not nail down the story, because I kept approaching it from the wrong angle and made the whole book focus on Colleen. But a story is made up of many things, and it's easy to write a bad story when you focus on one particular thing. Colleen was not interesting enough to be the focus of 99% of the novel, so I decided to open it up.

After talking to my friend and editor Roy Guntherson, he suggested that things go wrong immediately and that the doctor gets possessed. Some of the novel could focus on saving the doctor. Turn things on its head. Great idea, Roy.

So I followed that idea and slowly realized how difficult it was to write each subsequent chapter. The house was much more vicious than book one, and this book is supposed to be a prequel to book one! So I kept trying to figure out why the house would be so powerful here, but weaker in the future. Nothing was making sense to me but I kept going. I was writing, and the book was speaking back to me. It kept telling me there was more here under the surface to be discovered, so I kept writing, questioning what I was writing, digging deeper, rewriting things, until I got through fifty thousand words and realized I had no ending in sight, and fifty thousand words is the length of a novel. Most people work to get their novels to fifty thousand words so that they can do the bare minimum and put out many novels very quickly. And here I was with fifty thousand words, I'm deep into this thing, I've scrapped these inferior drafts to make something better, and here I am without knowing the ending. The questions kept coming up of what do I do about the ending? How can I weaken the house so it isn't so vicious—and a plot hole—when we look back at book one?

Well, the ideas came when I thought of some favorite movies of mine: Mulholland Drive, The Woman in the Window, The Cabinet of Dr. Caligari, Lost Highway. And I realized that the story did not have to be completely linear, and did not have to be within our exact reality, or the same reality as book one. The book could have completely taken place in a character's head for all we know. Or perhaps the whole book is reality. I don't want to spell everything out for the reader, because I want some things to be up to your interpretation of what was real and what was not, but I realized…

…maybe everyone was right. Maybe Colleen did kill Ambrose. That's why the door is hard to find or impossible to find—because deep down, she did not want to find it. So her mind created a world where the investigators come to the house to find her husband, and of course everyone is warm and friendly and believes she's innocent—something Colleen's mind made up because… of course the world revolves around her—but the hunters can't find her husband because of a distraction. The doctor's possession. Which means the door can't be found, and Colleen does not have to face the reality of what she has done to her husband.

I saw each character as part of Colleen.

Margaret in a way was Colleen's mind, her self-conscious, who was the only one to believe Colleen was guilty. She was the part of Colleen who knew the truth.

Joy was cold and mean because she was the part of Colleen who wanted to be strong. Colleen gave in to Fred's advances, and Joy was the version of a woman that Colleen WISHED she could be, because Joy was able to kill Fred, to get away from him, to be more than just a sex object for this strange man on the road.

Samantha's character, in the beginning, in Colleen's mind, was shown as someone else who was hurt by the house, convincing Colleen that this could have happened to ANYONE, and was another way of Colleen telling herself she was not crazy, she did not kill her husband, the house got Ambrose as it got Howard.

Scott was the part of Colleen's mind that was determined to be in the house and search for something, and like Colleen's love was in the house, so was Scott's love—when he fell in love with Margaret.

Those characters were all "real" people, of course, but Colleen's mind projected onto them and twisted what she saw of them into something else, into a strange unreality where things were a certain way—where things were the only way she could cope with what happened. Everyone loved her, related to her, and wanted to help her, went out of their way for her, bended over backwards for her. I had to set that up in a convincing way then turn it on its head so the reader would see the truth.

But I also left blurred lines in this book, setting it up so that even after the "truth" of certain events were shown, it would still leave you guessing what was real and what was not real, and the fun is in picking it apart.

Like most of my books, both published and unpublished, the characters are yearning for something. Longing for something they can't have, longing for something they want, desperate for something that's out of reach. Sometimes the theme is right in front of you and you don't see it until later. I have had books where I didn't know the theme or meaning until years later. And I think for this book, the theme is that longing for something that's not yours—especially something in the past. Something that you might have had before, but it's your fault that the thing is no longer yours and it's gone.

That's something I've experienced quite a bit in my own life—always wishing for the past. And I think I've seen that in every person I've ever met. But if you keep doing that, then life will completely pass you by, and you missed your chance at living. In 2015 I wished it was 2014. In 2016 I wished it was 2015. In 2017 I wished it was 2016. In 2018 I wished it was 2017. In 2019 I wished it was 2018. In 2020 I wished it was 2019. In 2021 I wished it were 2020. In 2022 I wished it were 2021.

I guess when things get worse, we always wish for a past time, even if the past times were bad, just because they're *a little less worse* than things are now. I guess this book was me expressing myself about my longing for past times, times that'll only exist in the past, times that are over with and can never be gotten back.

I hope you all enjoyed this book.